Over the course of the next hour or so, as Tom made Randall's acquaintance, he realized that Randall wasn't the good old boy he imagined. He was thoughtful, measured, and well-spoken. They never left the museum and Eveline, dutiful as ever, thought to bring out coffee and tea. Tom listened as Randall recounted his original plan, submitting the application that would put it into action, and subsequent disappointment. It was all pretty straightforward, Tom thinking that there were infinite variations of the circumstances leading up to the injustice, but they all boiled down to the same thing: A citizen's constitutional right to free speech and free association denied. Sometimes, as in this case, it was an agency of the very government that instituted this right doing the clamping down, the reining in, and sometimes it was private enterprise. Either way, it was wrong and it was his job to go to bat for the wronged person or group. And, he told Randall, he swung a pretty mean bat.

Tom Consolino sensed that his would-be client was somewhat dubious about his lawyerly motives, having driven down from St. Louis and meeting with him like this, in his own place, making it very convenient for Randall to sign on and get the case going. He tried to reassure him that his motives were honorable. "I'm doing this for my own reasons," he told him plainly, "not yours. I don't make donations to your group. I don't agree with your viewpoints, but this is an important First Amendment case."

"You could join," Randall encouraged. "We don't bite, you know."

Tom Consolino sighed. "Mr. Fortner, I am not in your camp. Frankly, the Ku Klux Klan is anathema to me. Bad news, and besides, you wouldn't even have me as a member."

Randall pursed his lips in consternation. "Don't be silly, we've got lots of lawyers."

NO BIG THING

ALSO BY WM STAGE

Ghost Signs: Brick Wall Signs In America

Mound City Chronicles

Litchfield: A Strange and Twisted Saga of Murder in the Midwest

Have A Weird Day: Reflections & Ruminations on the St. Louis Experience

Pictures Of People Portraits 1982 – 1993

The Practical Guide To Process Serving

Fool For Life – A Memoir

The Painted Ad: A Postcard Book of Vintage Brick Wall Signs with Margaret Stage

Not Waving, Drowning [Stories]

The Fading Ads of St. Louis

Creatures On Display – A Novel

NO BIG THING

Wm. Stage

Floppinfish Publishing Company Ltd.

St. Louis, Missouri

NO BIG THING Copyright ©2017 by Wm. Stage. All Rights Reserved. No part of this book may be used or reproduced in any manner whatsoever without written permission except in the case of brief quotations embodied in critical articles and reviews. For information address Floppinfish Publishing Company Post Office Box 4932 Saint Louis, Missouri 63108.

This book is a work of fiction. References to real people, events, establishments, organizations, or locales are intended only to provide a sense of authenticity, and are used fictitiously. All other characters, and all incidents and dialogue, are drawn from the author's imagination and are not to be construed as real.

Library of Congress Control Number: 2017906076
Stage, Wm. [1951-]
—fiction, contemporary

1. United States—the Midwest—rural life—Ku Klux Klan—First Amendment / free speech litigation

ISBN 978-0-692-87027-3

Cover Photoshop: Robert Ferd Frank 2017
Cover and Interior design:
Michael Kilfoy www.studiox.us

www.wmstage.com
Printed in the United States of America
Set in Adobe Jenson Pro
First Edition

for Pete Bastian
who stood for something decent
down in Kay-ro

PREFACE

THIS STORY, like all my stories of late, is taken from actual events in the busy world around St. Louis. In this case, it began with an ordinary request to the state highway department to be admitted to their Adopt-A-Highway program. The request came from a special interest group who hoped to be treated the same as any other applicant, that is, to be accepted into the program, honor the established bargain of keeping that portion of road free of litter and junk and in return get a sign placed in public view proclaiming them good citizens. The special interest group was the Ku Klux Klan, and their request was summarily dismissed. It was the only time the bureaucrats in the Adopt-A-Highway program had turned down an applicant.

As the saga of this First Amendment battle unfolded over the years, I followed it with interest. What would happen next? Would the State be forced to put up a highway sign promoting a despised organization? Would Klansmen in pointy white sheets be seen collecting roadside trash? Would there be protests leading to riots? The ongoing situation was fodder for endless conversations on radio and television talk shows, and aired in the print media like wash on a clothesline. The Klan's Jewish lawyer—a rich irony, eh?—defended his clients in Circuit Court and again in the Court of Appeals and would have defended them in the U.S. Supreme Court, except the justices declined to hear the case. Though the State argued vigorously at every level, the Klan prevailed and got their coveted sign. But in the end the State had the last laugh. Read the story and you'll see.

Years later, driving along the interstate, seeing for the nth time that very ordinary patch where the Klan would make their stand, it occurred to me that while the original story was intriguing all by itself, the facts of that narrative could be played with, embellished, to create a work of historical fiction. I imagined a family living not so far from St. Louis, a family respected in their community, a family experiencing typical problems in their workaday lives. What if the patriarch of this family had been involved in white supremacist activities in the distant past and was coasting on romantic notions of that time? What if he initiated the application to join the program and enlisted his grandson, recently discharged from the army, to do the clean up? What if litter patrol on the outskirts of St. Louis was an even more dangerous mission than those the grandson had experienced in the deserts of Kuwait and Iraq? What if that patriarch was gradually slipping into dementia and perhaps unmindful of the conniving forces—neighbors, reporters, state bureaucrats, even the hierarchy of the Klan itself—hoping to take advantage of the snowball he had set in motion. It would be one more irony if I could show the Klan as the target of discrimination, which shouldn't be too difficult as it really did happen. I could throw in a colorful cast of supporting characters—an ambitious meth dealer, a fledgling social anthropologist, a Baptist minister, a Deadhead with wanderlust, an obsessive thief, an idealistic lawyer.

The story is also about loyalty, estrangement, and changing one's attitude over time.

The idea seemed enticing, use the KKK sign debacle as a launching pad for a novel. As a veteran journalist / columnist with several books to my name, I knew what exacting work creating fiction could be. I had to ask myself if I was willing to make the serious commitment to writing about this thing. Six months to a year of getting up very early, going to bed even before the kids, wife not getting kissed goodnight, dog not getting walked in the morning, no time to shower and shave before starting the day. I asked myself with utmost diligence and the answer was yes, because it was a good story to begin with and I knew I could have some fun with it.

So I went ahead and wrote it. I didn't make it long, I tried not to labor points. What I did, essentially, was to re-package a story that had unfolded some 20 years before, and to put fresh names and faces on the original characters. With the exception of the civil rights lawyer, I don't know the identities of any of the parties from the original drama—not the Klansman / plaintiff in the lawsuit, not the Mo-

DOT administrator who dismissed the application, not the lawyer who argued the case for the State. It doesn't matter because they are now constructs of my imagination. The lawyer who represented the Klan in that original litigation is Bob Herman, still practicing in St. Louis. Bob was kind enough to speak to me at length about the case, the obstacles encountered and strategies employed. Our talk was very helpful in the writing of this work. I, in turn, disappointed Bob by changing his ethnicity from Jewish to Italian. All I can say is, I had my reasons.

I read tons of crime fiction, a diet of murder and mayhem by the likes of Ken Bruen, Dennis Lehane, James Crumley, and the great Elmore Leonard. Yet, this work is not of that genre. It contains no real violence, only characters who are decidedly malicious but stop short of violent acts. The same with cursing; unlike my last novel which was peppered with salty language, you won't find one F-word in here. Again, I had my reasons. One, it's my experience that rural folk are more mild—courteous, perhaps—in their language than their urban counterparts. They use many a colorful phrase, but don't throw around obscenities like confetti. That, and as I was writing this I had thoughts that the book, when finished, might be accessible to young adult readership. That hope is still there.

Then, there was the concern about delving into the social structure of the KKK. The author, a guy who has met not one Klansman, presuming to know how they act, interact, view the world, or feel about certain issues. Well, it is a work of fiction so I had to mentally place myself in their shoes and do a little walking around in them. It seems they are not that much different than you or me; we all have our agendas, hidden or not; we all carry a certain amount of negative baggage; we all flash our very personal, if not biased, attitudes. But in fact there are only a few minor characters in this work who are portrayed as actual Klan members; the rest are average people caught up in the saga of *Fortner et al v. The Missouri Highways and Transportation Commission.*

During the writing of *No Big Thing,* two events of note occurred, and they are coincidental to this work. One, the Confederate Memorial in our own Forest Park is under siege. It started a few years back when then-mayor Francis Slay suggested the 40 ton monument, erected in 1914, should be removed from public view. Recently, Slay's successor promised that it would be removed, just as other statues and memorials commemorating the "lost cause" of the Confederacy have been taken down in New Orleans and Louisville, calling them symbols of oppression and slavery. The monument in Forest Park has stood for more than a century without much attention or controversy, most St. Louisans having never really looked at it or studied it. But now that the new mayor has threatened its existence, there have been angry confrontations and altercations at the site. It has been repeatedly defaced. Protestors have been arrested. Action-reaction— bitter feelings surfacing after all this time. Just now a barricade has been placed around the monument and dismantling is imminent. As my ancestor, David L. Stage, who soldiered for the Union, might say, the Civil War is alive and kicking in St. Louis.

Two, the body of the Imperial Wizard of the Traditionalist American Knights of the Ku Klux Klan was found in a creek down in St. Francois County, not so far from the fictional town of Pine Grove. Very few had ever heard of Frank Ancona before he was murdered; now the world knows that the Klan is out there, doing their thing in the Missouri hinterlands. Having said that, the Klan does not have a large presence in and around St. Louis, although you do see Confederate flags and bumper stickers with some regularity. As my protagonist Birch Fortner points out, the actual Klan today is small in number, yet there are many times more honorary members, and by that he means there are vast numbers, especially in rural areas, who by and large think along the same lines as a Klansman might when it comes to hot button issues such as affirmative action, living on the dole, gun control, gay marriage, the yearning for "law and order," concern over unfettered immigration, and so on. This faction may constitute what has been called The Silent Majority, and "majority" or not, they are definitely a presence in our society.

In holding up the KKK and certain extreme viewpoints that it represents, I hoped to produce a thought-provoking work, one that overpowers the initial reluctance, as I imagine it, of picking a book when the back cover blurb states it is about the dreaded KKK. I think of Pete Dexter's extraordinary novel, *Paris Trout*, winner of the National Book Award. What if no one cared to read that book because the main character and titular namesake was an extremely nasty human being and a dyed-in-the-wool racist? So, fingers crossed here, hoping the phrase Ku Klux Klan is not so great a stigma to the book buyer that my book will be automatically consigned to the remainder bin. In fact, the Klan is the ideal vehicle for discourse on racial and / or cultural intolerance.

— St. Louis June, 2017

THE CHARACTERS

RANDALL FIELDING FORTNER, 68, runs a grain elevator, selling feed, seed and ag supplies, has the modest Old South and Southern Heritage Museum behind store. Once a member of the feared White Hats in the Cairo, Illinois civil unrest of the early 70s. Now, gradually showing signs of senility.

PATRICIA SUMNER FORTNER, 45, one of two daughters by Randall's first wife. Having left home as a young woman, Patricia lives one county over, has disowned Randall for his "racist" views.

SAMUEL BIRCH FORTNER, 21, son of Patricia, Randall's estranged daughter. An army vet, he took part in Operation Desert Storm, Kuwait and Iraq.

EVELINE FORTNER, 56, Randall's second wife, very supportive of him. They have no children together.

CY WAINSCOTT, 46, Randall's son-in-law, farmer-rancher, lives nearby, supportive of Randall's views.

REBECCA WAINSCOTT, 42, Randall's younger daughter, married to Cy.

JAMIE WAINSCOTT, 19, son of Cy and Rebecca. Randall's grandson, Birch's cousin.

BILLIE GOLDIE, 29, meth dealer, former partner-in-crime with Birch.

DALTON HANKINS, 51, has auto repair shop in town, pushes white power, has mail order business selling self-authored pamphlets, bumper stickers, etc. Wants to resurrect the Klan.

CASSIE TELLER, 19, Birch's girlfriend since high school, who has taken a different path while Birch was in the service. She runs a T-shirt shop with her best friend, Amanda.

MARK "JINX" JENKINS, 21, Birch's boyhood pal and drinking buddy.

REV. MARSTEN PINKARD, 55, Pastor, Pine Grove Baptist Church, friend and ally of Randall Fortner.

SHEILA COWAN, 42, MoDOT administrator, heads up Adopt-A-Highway program.

TOM CONSOLINO, 46, ACLU attorney with a civil rights background, who takes on Randall's case against the State Highways & Transportation Department.

TYRA SINGLETARY, 22, ambitious and conniving graduate student, she is out to "study" the Fortners like her hero Margaret Mead studied Polynesian peoples.

NO BIG THING

August, 1992

"Dang it, Bowswer, you let go that money. C'mon, boy, give it here." Birch tugged at the ten dollar bill clenched in the mutt's jaws, wet with slobber. Tugged gently, not wanting to tear it any further. He could maybe wait the dog out, pretty sure that if he didn't act like he really wanted the ten spot then the coonhound would just release it and go on to something else. Besides, there were other bills for the taking in the immediate vicinity, and if he didn't get a move on the other barflies would get everything. He looked across the gravel parking lot at Jinx, rushing around, stooping here and there to pick up greenbacks like a kid at an Easter egg hunt. Just minutes before a drunken, hairy biker named Sweeney had staggered out of Spud n' Velma's, mounted a Harley Fat Boy, closed the kickstand, hit the ignition, savored momentarily the sonorous combustion of the twin cams' *potato-potato-potato* chorus, then sped off doing a fairly impressive wheelie just for the hell of it. What Sweeney failed to notice was that the wad of bills he had stuck in the side pocket of his denim vest had worked its way up to the point where it was about to be free of its owner, and the inertia from the wheelie did just that. Bills coming loose, separating and fluttering in the afternoon air like manna from heaven.

"Money, free money!" came a shout from the doorway and the tavern emptied. Birch, about to sink the three ball, dropped his cue and he and Jinx ran out to see for themselves. Now he was just a hound's tooth away from having enough to buy drinks and burgers on into the evening. He knew Bowser would eat practically anything and, if he swallowed this bill, it wouldn't be pretty having to look for it a day or two later coming out the back end. It was now or never.

"Bowser, look—squirrel!" The dog snapped his head at the pretend squirrel, his jaws going slack enough for Birch to snatch the bill from his maw. Birch reached down and gave the animal an affectionate scratch behind the ear. "There ain't no squirrel," he told him. "Sorry to trick you, I'll make it up to you."

The errant money gathered and put away in pockets and chained wallets, they went back into the bar, guys laughing, wisecracking, slapping each other on the back in congratulations of something for nothing. Birch and Jinx resumed their game. Birch sunk the three ball with a straight, clean shot and then banked the five into a side pocket. That left the eight on the far side of the table, half-obscured by Jinx's twelve. Jinx still had all his balls on the table.

"Eight ball, corner pocket."

"No friggin way," countered Jinx, shaking his head like a teacher confronting a wrong answer.

"We'll see then, won't we?" Birch tucked a hank of brown hair behind one ear, hunkered down to where he was eye-level with the cue ball, moved the stick back and forth a few times, a study in concentration. The white ball ticked the black eight at the exact right locus and sent the eight through a field of striped balls, narrowly clearing the nine and rolling straight into the corner pocket.

"That's how it's done." Birch grinning.

Jinx pounded his fist on the table. Mock anger. "Can't believe you skunked me, twice in one day!"

"I got my mojo working, that's all."

"It was a beautiful shot, I'll say that."

Birch nodded, accepting the praise. "Last time I ran the table, back in February, we were at Fort Dix, waiting on our discharge papers, sitting around the mess hall, nothing to do, just waiting for Sam to get his act together. There was a day room down the hall with a pool table, some of us went over. I played this guy from Denver. We flipped for break. I won, sunk two on the break, kept on going—bim, bam, boom—one after the other and before you could say Minnesota Fats I had nothing left on the table. Eight ball went down easy. That soldier's jaw 'bout dropped to the floor."

"Your last hurrah in the army, go out with a flourish."

"You got that right."

"You don't hear much about Fort Dix. It's in New Jersey, right? How'd you get from the East Coast to this podunk town?"

Birch lifted his Busch longneck, took a long hit, Adam's apple bobbing. "Took a Greyhound, almost twenty-four hours with all the stops. But it was a nice journey, no hurry, gave me time to think about where I'd been and what I was gonna do next."

"Yeah? That was six months ago, and what I see you doing is shooting pool, riding around in your pickup, you and Bowser, and mooning around Cassie with your tongue hanging out."

"Not a bad life, uh? Now if someone would just pay me for doing that." He gave that bemused half-smile that Jinx had known since they were chums in grammar school. "Well, all right. Since you're so interested in my welfare, I've enrolled at the community college and I start in a few weeks. Gonna take just a few courses, English comp and history, stuff I've always liked."

"Good for you, man. Anyone around here, if they go beyond high school, it's always some trade school. Plumbing, welding, appliance repair."

"But not auto repair," said Birch, setting it up.

"Oh hell no," laughed Jinx. "Any joker from Pine Grove can fix a car. They say about rich people, 'He was born with a silver spoon in his mouth.' Here, we're born with a socket wrench in our mouth."

"Kinda makes it hard to spit the words out."

They retired their cue sticks and moved to the bar where guys were still carrying on about their windfall, already on their second

No Big Thing

round thanks to the besotted biker. One raised his glass, proclaimed, "Here's to Mike Sweeney, one generous son of a bitch even if he don't know it!"

They all drank lustily and called for another round. Birch felt a tap on his shoulder. Pivoting on the barstool to see a gangly kid towering over him, peering down through Ray-Ban knock-offs. Goofy grin. His cousin, Jamie Wainscott.

"What's up, Doofus?" Jamie faking a blow to Birch's ribcage.

"You, treetop, you're what's up. Sit your butt down and have a beer, yeah?" Birch called for Dee, the bartender. Dee glanced down to the end of the bar at Spud, the old-as-dirt character who owned the joint and lived upstairs with his dog, now that Velma was gone. Spud gave a slight nod, and Dee came back with a Busch longneck. Spud knew that Jamie was 19 and that he could lose his liquor license if the agent happened to walk in and demand a show of ID, but Spud also knew the odds of that happening were practically zilch and besides, he liked flouting the laws; it was the last vestige of a rebellious youth.

They talked a while in the way that young men talk while drinking, catching up on all sorts of stuff—some new album they really liked, who was seeing who on the sly, some trip they were thinking about taking, who was in the slammer and so on. At length, Jamie got this look, suddenly serious, and said directly to Birch, "The old man wants a family meeting this evening, six o' clock sharp."

—2—

PINE GROVE, MISSOURI, 55 miles southwest of St. Louis, was founded in 1855 by a one-eyed slave trader named Tom Griffin who later served honorably under General P.G.T. Beauregard in the War of Northern Aggression. In the 1990 census, workers counted a population of 307, the racial mix overwhelmingly lopsided with non-whites represented by just five Native Americans and 11 black persons. Pine Grove could barely be called a small town. It was just a pinpoint on the map, but it did have a barber shop which was also a ladies hair salon two days a week, a service station and repair shop, a consignment shop, a shuttered motel overgrown with weeds and brush, a volunteer fire department, a convenience store with a small kitchen and a video rental section, and two churches: one Baptist, the other Pentecostal. Pine Grove's claim to fame was the Palm Sunday tornado. This occurred in April, 1967, when an F-2 tornado came through pretty much unannounced on a Sunday morning and yanked the gabled roof off the Baptist church with the congregation inside at prayer; besides Eunice Talbot fainting and Old Man Barton hyperventilating while trying to open his vial of nitroglycerine pills, no one was harmed. They talk about that to this day. Some kind of miracle.

The nearest place that could actually be called a town was Acadia, seven miles distant as the vulture flies. When the denizens of Pine Grove needed decent groceries or stamps, wanted a kitchen that served something other than gizzards and fries, or, for whatever reason, desired the tranquility of a library, they went to Acadia. If they wanted feed or seed or farm implements, ropes, hoses, mole traps, tack, live bait or any article from the Carhartt line of clothing, they'd head for the Pine Grove Grain Elevator & Mercantile operated by Randall Fortner and family. And even though the store was a half-mile beyond the main intersection of the town, it was pretty much the hub of Pine Grove. Farmers, too, lined up in late summer, trailers hitched to their rigs, knowing Randall would give them fair market for their corn or soybeans. Pine Grove was located in southwestern Jefferson County, named for the third President of the United States. Randall Fortner liked to think the county was named for that other president, Jefferson Davis.

The Fortner residence, a nineteenth-century farmhouse with lightning rods on its gables, was located on Bond Road, a gravel-topped offshoot off Highway M, which ran through Pine Grove

No Big Thing

under the name of Main Street. Its 27 acres was mostly woodland and meadow and scrub, uncleared, for the family never did go in for farming. Randall, however, liked a nice presentation and the front yard of the place was bordered by a rough hewn cedar log fence with wagon wheels stationed at the entrance to the drive. What you'd call rustic. Birch parked his pickup, got out and strode along a flagstone-paved walkway to the house where he'd grown up. The porch swing was occupied by a young girl with brown, wavy hair and a rather serious expression. Birch mounted the steps, went over and gave his cousin Elsie a big hello, asked how she was doing. "Doing just fine," she replied, "gonna be in the fourth grade this time, already met my teacher and I like her." Birch said that was swell, how it's a fine thing to like school otherwise you'd be miserable all day.

"They're inside," she said, "Grampa, Eveline, dad, Jamie, Reverend Pinkard. We're waiting on mom and some others." Birch said he'd best be going then. As he turned for the door, she blurted, "I got a hit today. I'm with the Pine Grove Half-Pints. Girls softball."

Birch stopped in mid-stride, said, "Knocked the cover off the ball, did you."

"Nah, it was just a blooper, barely made it to the pitcher but it got me to first base."

"*Just?* Like Nolan Ryan is *just* a pitcher? You've got talent all right. Keep 'er going, you never know where it'll take you."

He stepped into the foyer and out of habit snapped a salute to the portrait of General Robert E. Lee hanging on the wall. A quality replica of a painting done by John A. Elder, it was the first thing one saw in entering the home; it was a family tradition to pay respect to the old warrior.

They were gathered around the big dining table, the ones that Elsie had mentioned. There was Cy Wainscott, Birch's uncle who had a ranch down the road, bending Jamie's ear over something or another. Bustling around the table, Eveline, Randall's second and much younger wife, laying out a modest spread—sliced cantaloupe, succotash, chicken dumplins, tater tots, fresh-baked bread. The Reverend Marsten Pinkard, fanning himself with a postal flier he had found, already consuming the food with his eyes. Each place at the table had a plate, a bowl, utensils, and a drinking glass, all neatly placed on matching place mats. There was a lazy Susan in the center with salt and pepper and various condiments and homemade sauces. Randall, at the head of the table, stood to welcome Birch and bade him take a seat beside him. Eveline started to fill Birch's glass with lemonade, but when Birch saw that Jamie had a beer, he asked for one too. They commenced to talking among themselves, trading views on this and that, snippets of local gossip, just waiting for Randall to end the suspense as to why they were there.

They were joined eventually by two others. Dalton Hankins who owned the town's only service station, and, although he was not family, was invited by Randall for having the "right political leanings." Then there was Rebecca, Randall's younger daughter, married to Cy Wainscott, and the mother of Jamie and Elsie. Apologizing for her tardiness, Rebecca set a large Tupperware container on the dining table; German-style potato salad, paprika sprinkled on it. At length Randall cleared his throat and called the meeting. He thanked everyone for coming and said he'd get right to the heart of the matter, and that it would be all right if they ate their supper while he was holding forth. He added that this was a two-way thing and he'd like to hear reaction to the idea he was about to relate, but to let him finish first.

Randall left his chair at the table, moved a few steps back toward the wall, and stood before a full-sized Confederate flag that hung from the ceiling over a sideboard. The old man, tall and groomed, looked quite presentable, if not distinguished in pleated khakis, white dress shirt open at the collar, and seersucker sport jacket. Birch had the feeling he was in a press conference.

Randall looked around the table. "Where's Lance?"

"Lance is in Potosi, Dad," said Rebecca, "He's still got eight more years. You know that."

No Big Thing

Randall looked at her, frowning in consternation. "Huh," he muttered, seeming to clear his thoughts. "Anyway," he resumed, "an idea came to me last month. The Klan, once a mighty and influential fraternity, has fallen in stature. Membership is down and that's a shame. Why, in this room I'll wager that Dalton and myself are the only two card-carrying members, Grand Knights until the day we die."

"How you gonna build membership when you don't have meetings?" asked Dalton Hankins in a sour tone. "Heck, we ain't even had a meeting in what, five-six years?"

"Who is it plans the gatherings anyway?" wondered Cy Wainscott.

"Why that'd be Jim Ed Burnett down in Cape. But look, I'm not here to recruit or start bothering Jim Ed. I just want to get to the idea that come to me." He took a moment to look at each of them, and when he was sure he had their full attention, he went on. "So, I suggest that membership is down mostly because the Klan is misunderstood. Our image has been tarnished, and I admit, sometimes rightly so—"

"What you're saying is Robert Redford won't be playing one of us in a movie," said Jamie.

Randall chortled. "Tommy Lee Jones maybe. But as I was saying, the negative image, we can change that. What's the general public's view of us?"

"They think we're down on blacks," offered Cy. "They think we go around at night in white robes terrorizing people."

"Bingo," said Randall, stabbing a finger for effect. "Negative publicity follows the Klan like a big black thundercloud. Except this is a different time with different attitudes. Think about it, there ain't a one of us would want a slave today. Shoot, nigras too brazen these days, throw a boycott or a sit-down strike on you, you ask 'em to put in a full day's work. Forget them, we got Mexicans."

Randall, who always thought of "nigger" as vulgar, had taken to calling blacks nigras ever since he heard Governor Strom Thurmond use the phrase. Randall was stationed at Fort Jackson, South Carolina in 1947 when Thurmond was running for president as a Dixiecrat. In one campaign stop in Columbia, Thurmond told supporters that "there's not enough troops in the army to force the Southern people to break down segregation and admit the nigra race into our theaters, into our swimming pools, into our homes, and into our churches." Randall, standing front and center of the podium, decided that Strom was his man.

"So, I stress that we need to improve our image, and one way we can do that is to join this state-sponsored program where we adopt a stretch of interstate highway and keep it clean. For that we get a nice sign telling thousands of motorists every day that the Klan is on the job." He reached behind him, took a sheet of paper, a typed form, from the sideboard, holding it up significantly like it was a proof of something. "This here's the application for the Adopt-A-Highway program, sent to me upon request by the Missoura Department of Transportation."

"All right!" quipped Jamie, "South's gonna rise again."

There was a collective chuckle at this, a line from a Charlie Daniels song, a popular redneck anthem. Mirth from everyone except Dalton Hankins, who took this quite seriously and felt that Jamie was mocking the situation.

"Yeah, well," said Randall, "I've filled it out and it's going in the mail tomorrow. We'll see what happens."

"I can guess what happens," said Rev. Pinkard, about to make a spoonful of succotash disappear. "Some pencil-pusher in Jeff City sees that the Ku Klux Klan wants to pick up trash on the state highway, he takes his favorite rubber stamp, the one that says 'denied' and he stamps it all over your carefully filled-out application."

Randall looked away thoughtfully, pursed his lips, waited a few beats, then, "If that does happen it'll be a real kick in the teeth. Downright un-American. We've got as much right to join this program as any other group, including the Quilting Bee Society or the

No Big Thing

Jeff County Daffodil Club. That's right, they let these other groups participate, they got to let us as well. Far as I can tell, there's no criteria, no rule that allows them to exclude one certain group just because they don't like what they stand for."

"I saw one the other day for the Helping Hands 4 H Club," offered Dalton Hankins. "Ain't that much a difference between four Hs and three Ks."

"And besides," said Rebecca, "it isn't like we're up to the same old tricks, trying to oppress minorities. That's the old Klan. The new Klan is about civil rights for white folks and respect for Southern heritage and culture."

"Well put," nodded Rev. Pinkard. "Also, a refuge, I might add, for decent Americans fed up with the craziness on the evening news."

Randall seconded that. "We've got to educate the public who we really are, a benevolent organization not that much different from the Elks or the Masons or the Oddfellows."

"Well, sure," retorted Dalton Hankins, "that's part of it, but y'all know the whole underlying idea is to stop the ni—"

Eveline broke in, politely but firmly. "I'll thank you not to employ vulgarisms at our table, Mister Hankins. Would you care for more succotash?"

"Sure, you got any Country Bob's?"

"I'm afraid not," said Eveline. "Maull's, we have Maull's."

"Dalton puts Country Bob's on everything," put in Randall, the trace of a smile. "Eggs, grits, gizzards, you name it."

"Well, yeah," Dalton, flustered, "that's why it's called Country Bob's All Purpose Sauce."

"My granddad was an Oddfellow," interjected Cy. "They're really a secretive bunch, talk in code, keep to themselves."

"Practice black arts, so I heard," added Rev. Pinkard.

"Talk about a dying fraternal organization," said Dalton, "them and the Rosicrucians."

Randall returned to the table. Eveline had dished his plate up for him. "We're getting a little off track here. We should discuss the practicality of this undertaking once the application is approved."

Birch quit slouching and sat up a bit more straight. "You mean like where's this highway and who's gonna go there and do the donkey work?"

Randall fixed Birch with a meaningful gaze. "Well, now that you mention it."

"Dang, I knew it!"

"Now, hold your horses, son. It don't mean you're doing all the work yourself. Jamie can help out, when he's not needed at the farm. I can see the protest rising up and I understand, but you're the best choice for several reasons: Unlike some of us here at this table, you're young and energetic, and since you don't currently have a job, you've got time to spare. The rest of us don't."

Birch shook his head in the negative, but he knew it was a thing already decided. He was raised on hard work and respect for his elders. Besides, he owed Randall big time. When Birch graduated from high school he was busted for drunk and disorderly in a public park in Acadia; it was his 11th misdemeanor in three years, and he was already in dutch for felonious assault that a family lawyer had gotten knocked down to *intent* to beat the crap out of the other guy with a prosecutorial stipulation of probation for two years. One more mark on his record and it was the Southeastern Missouri Correctional Center. If life was a game of chess, he was in check. The military seemed like a good solution, whisk him out of this dead-end life, but the navy, air force, and marines had all the volunteers they wanted. The army recruiter was considering him; if only his record could be partially expunged, cut down to maybe three convictions, or at least covered up somehow.

He spoke to Randall about this dilemma: him not quite 18, restless as all get out, and stuck in a quagmire. The old man phoned George McCracken, the state senator and former Grand Knight,

No Big Thing

who wrote a glowing letter of recommendation, assuring the U.S. Army that Samuel Birch Fortner would make a fine soldier. Just like that he had a wardrobe of olive drab outfits, and it was bye-bye to Pine Grove for three years. Now the old man was calling up the debt. How could he refuse?

"We can get you one of those sticks with a spike on the end so you won't have to stoop over so much," said Eveline.

"They also have a kind of mechanical arm," declared Rebecca, "you squeeze the handle and a pair of tongs come together, grip cans and bottles and such."

Birch looked at his aunt who had always reminded him of a duck. He tried to imagine himself on the side of a busy highway picking up litter with tongs at the end of a pole, looking to all of Christendom like a total dork. But something was missing.

"A Walkman would be nice," he said, tentatively.

"Sure, sure" said Randall, nodding enthusiastically,"whatever you need. I'll even give you a little something, walkin' around money."

"How much, Grampa? Can I help, too?"

Randall shone a smile in her direction. "No, dear, I'm afraid that just won't work. This is a busy highway, not a place for little girls." Elsie put out her lower lip in disappointment.

"That's right," said Randall, waving a fork speared with tater tots. "It is a busy highway, busier than anywheres around here. The place we're looking at is a stretch just south of St. Louis, below the I-270 interchange, down near the Meramec Bottom Road exit. It's about, oh, five hundred yards long, it's grassy and banked. There's a guard rail all along so you won't be able to park on the highway itself. You'll have to walk in. But here's the good part: MoDOT says that stretch gets 24,000 vehicles a day."

"That is a passel of cars," agreed Birch. "I can guess that not all of them will be happy to see a fellow out there if he's what the sign says he is."

"You don't worry about that," said Randall, "any aggression

from outsiders will be dealt with." Randall abruptly dived into his chicken and dumplins, glad that no one thought to press him about that last statement as he had no idea how to make that happen.

Then they put their energies into putting away the food at hand, all of them going for seconds. There was a peach pie for dessert. Dinner finished, the table cleared and dishes in the sink, they retired to the living room to smoke and drink and watch the Cardinals game in progress. Dalton Hankins passed out his latest pamphlet, a light-blue tri-fold titled "Miscegenation: An Abomination to All Mankind." This piqued the interest of Rev. Pinkard, who roundly complimented him on a well-written piece, praising his use of colorful words and phrases such as "trollop," and "misbegotten mullatoes," and assured the author of yet another "informative tract" that there is "nothing morally or ethically wrong with wanting our race to remain white."

When the game ended, Cards victorious over the Reds, the sun was going down orange into the trees. Cicadas droning something awful. Walking to his truck, Birch cast a long backwards shadow on the driveway. He sensed that his life was about to change, and he didn't see how it was going to be for the better. In fact, a little voice in his head kept calling him "tool."

—3—

LATE AUGUST in Missouri is as hot and humid as any place in the country. Mississippi, Alabama, Georgia–places you think of as being unmercifully hot–got nothing on Eastern Missouri when it comes to sun beating down like a humongous heat lamp. Plus, you're in a valley, the great, wide Mississippi Valley, with a big old river running through it, and that river generates humidity and the valley holds it until a storm comes along and blows it away. At least that's the way Birch saw it; thinking about climate and geography and such helped him pass the time.

No Big Thing

It was such a day when Birch and Bowser went to visit Cassie over in Acadia. While many similar-sized towns in the region had a town square with something in the middle to form a hub, Acadia was laid out in linear fashion along the rails of the Union Pacific Railroad. There were shops and stores all along this strip, and Awsum Tees was one of them, sandwiched in between a head shop and a shoe repair. The idea for a custom T-shirt shop belonged to Cassie and her best friend Amanda, conjured while following the Grateful Dead for six months while Birch was in the army. Everywhere the Dead would play, especially open air venues, encampments would spring up a day or two in advance of the concert, colorful kiosks selling anything and everything Deadheads could desire. And despite their mendicant appearance, a lot of them had money. Cassie and Amanda bought loads of Dead gear, taking note how the T-shirt business always did a brisk trade. Back home and thinking it over, they approached their families. Cassie's mom loaned them the start-up money, and now eighteen months later they were successful entrepreneurs.

When Birch walked through the door Cassie was ringing up a sale, some kid buying an over-sized T with a depiction of a skateboard and the slogan SK8 DON'T HATE. It was a Cassie original, Birch knew. As soon as the kid left, petting Bowser on the way out, Cassie came around the counter, grabbed Birch by the waist and planted a kiss on him, a prolonged kiss tinged with the fragrance of patchouli oil, prompting a bulge in his jeans. Cassie drew her hand to the affected area. "Bread's not the only thing that rises. Looks like I still got it, huh?"

"Oh, you got it all right, and then some. I think I told you that back in tenth grade."

"We do have a history, don't we?" She laughed playfully, and broke off, turning to a rack of T-shirts on display. "Look, I want to show you some new styles we came up with."

"Aw c'mon, Cass, you started my engine and now I'm revved up. Let's go in the back room and take a test drive."

She ignored that, and instead held up a T-shirt, black with white lettering: YOUR KARMA RAN OVER MY DOGMA. There was a cartoon drawing of a dead dog, belly-up, tongue hanging out, little Xs in his eyes. Big grin on her oval face, brown eyes twinkling. "Isn't this just the funniest? Cracks me up. It's graffiti, I saw it in a bathroom somewhere."

"It's funny, yeah, makes you think. I forgot, what's karma?"

She adjusted the mass of hair piled atop her head, dreadlocks coiled into a clump and fastened with colorful pins, clips, and bands. Birch still getting used to seeing her like this, the long chestnut mane she once sported turned into a Medusa hairdo. She said, "It's a belief from some Eastern religion, meaning basically, what goes around comes around."

He was still thinking of how to get her in the back. "Oh, okay, now I get it … I think."

"There's no end to what you can put on a T-shirt," she said, "messages and slogans everywhere for the taking. Besides the ones you make up in your head, I mean, and new ideas are coming every day. You can do message only or message with image, or just image. The possibilities are infinite."

He really liked her like this, showing enthusiasm, proud of what she was doing. Spreading sunshine most of the time, a real asset to the human race.

"Course it's not all creative," she went on, "you get orders for various groups, sports teams, civic organizations, and that's nice because it's usually a run of 20 or more, same style, hundred percent organic cotton." She went to a counter, picked up a box, opened it. "Like this," taking out a clean white T, unfolding it, a green four-leaf clover on the front with an "H" in each leaf. The back saying MERAMEC RIVER RAMBLERS.

Birch smiled knowingly. "Brings back memories. I was a Four H kid, the Deepdale Happy Harvesters. We made a lot of birdhouses, fed a lot of chickens and pigs."

No Big Thing

Cassie went to the sink in the corner, brought a bowl of water for Bowser, who immediately began to slurp. "That takes care of him, so what's up with you?"

He wondered if she'd heard about the family's attempt to adopt the highway up in St. Louis and the reason behind it. If so, it would have come to her through the grapevine by way of Jamie and his big mouth. He planned on telling her, but only if and when the thing was actually approved and he was skeptical of that. In the past, she had voiced disdain over Randall's supposed involvement with the Klan, calling it "un-good." Now that sentiment would likely be even more pronounced, Cassie having become really liberal in the last few years judging by the bumper stickers on her Subaru.

"Well, you know, I'm signed up at the community college, start right after Labor Day. Otherwise just living my life and pretty much enjoying it."

She took his hand with both of hers. "Oh Birch, I'm happy for you. Happy and envious. I wish I'd gone on after high school. College makes a person so … um, well-rounded, don't you think?"

"Yeah, no rough edges on me." He moved in on her, this expectant look on his face. "Hey, you up for an adventure? They have these wine country tours over in Illinois, down around Murphysboro. You drive from one winery to the next, getting more and more looped as you go. They have bed and breakfasts, too. How 'bout we take a couple days and do that, a fun little getaway?"

"Oh man, that sounds fantastic. I'd go in a second except I'm working the shop by myself while Amanda's away."

"What? Where's Amanda?"

Cassie gave him a kind of mischievous smile and raised her eyebrows Groucho-style. "She went Mandingo."

"That's in the Caribbean, right? I thought you went to those places in winter, not summer."

"No, no, she's not on vacation. Well, she is in a way. She's on an extended visit with her new black boyfriend in Memphis."

Amanda with her blonde hair, green eyes and freckles, about as golden as a California swimsuit model, with a black guy? Birch didn't know what to make of that. He started to say something when a customer walked in.

Playfully, Cassie pushed him away. "We'll talk about it later," she said.

When Randall saw Billy Goldie come in the grain elevator, he first mistook him for an overgrown chimp what with his side-to-side gait, stooped shoulders, and long arms hanging down. A real knuckle-dragger. It was a steamy Tuesday afternoon, not much business, even so Randall didn't like the looks of this customer. He watched him head for the hardware-home repair section—scaled down big time, this was no Home Depot—saw him picking out items, examining them, returning some, keeping others. Randall moved in, went to the far end of the aisle, acted like he was organizing stuff, making his presence known. The guy was talking to himself, Randall could hear only murmurs that seemed to convey disappointment or irritation. He glanced at Randall a few times, shuffled around, looking here and there. Finally, he turned and called out, "Hey, pops! You got any camp stove fuel?"

Randall walked over, told him they used to carry it but discontinued it because of a lack of campers in the area. "Well, I don't want it for camping neither," he drawled. "How 'bout Benzene, you carry that? Or anhydrous ammonia?"

"Ammonium nitrate we got," replied Randall, "big call for that. Anhydrous too volatile."

"Well, hell, I'll take some of that and about 12 foot of this tubing. Oh, and matches. You got matchbooks? I'll take a couple boxes of matchbooks."

"Sure enough," said Randall. "That be all?"

No Big Thing

"You still got salted goobers? Last time I was here you had 'em. I'll take a nice bag."

The man grinned big, possibly at the thought of popping peanuts in his piehole, and Randall saw that his teeth, those he had left, were a dental trainwreck. "Just curious," ventured Randall, friendly-like, "what sort of crop you working, you need fertilizer? Almost everything harvested by now."

Randall watched this galoot dig into his front pocket and come out with a tin of Copenhagen Long Cut. He put a pinch in his mouth. "Hell, I ain't no farmer, pops. This stuff's for a science 'spare-mint. My kid's in the science fair at school, gonna build him a rocket runs on low-cost fuel."

Randall put that away. He looked the man up and down, pretty obvious about it. Besides the bad teeth, he saw a sandy-haired roughneck, probably under 30, unshaven, a smug look on his ugly mug. "You know," said Randall, "I've seen you before."

Billy's jaw rhythmically working like a cow chewing cud. Out came, "Yeah?"

"Yeah, you used to run with my grandson, you and those other hoods, got him in all sorts of trouble. I saw you in the cell with him in the Hillsboro jail when I come to bail him out. Breaking and Entering. That was four-five years ago. I remember you because at the time I thought, What's this up-to-no-good grown man doing hanging around with a teenager unless he's using him for some nefarious activity? And that's what it was, busting into a church looking to raid the poor box or hold up the preacher or God knows what else."

Billy Goldie curled his lip and gave a wicked chuckle. "You're right, pops, we were partners in crime. But Birch was a willing student, no one forced him to do anything. And he was lucky to have you, I'll say that, 'cause I'll be damned if anyone in my family thought to come bail me out."

"We take care of our own," Randall confirmed, "and now no thanks to you he's made good."

Billy Goldie cocked his head, pretended to be impressed. "Joined the army, took orders like a good soldier, went to Iraq, maybe killed him a few sand niggers, came back in one piece. Good for him."

"That's right, good for him, he improved his lot in life. And what have you been doing, huh? Cooking meth in some trailer out in the woods? There's a fine pastime, getting young people addicted to drugs, lives wasted."

Billy was astounded at the allegation, for he *was* cooking meth in a trailer out in the woods. Lucky guess, he reckoned.

"You don't know squat about me, old man," sneering now, "but I know something about you." He paused, nodding like a bobble-head. "I know you're tryin' to get into the trash pickup business, highway clean-up in the name of the Ku Klux Klan. Well, I'm all for that, spreading the good word any way we can. But damn, why you gotta be so ornery? Down on me like that? We could be allies in this thing if it does happen."

Randall was only mildly surprised that Billy knew about his plan; word gets around in a small town. "I don't need your support in any way, shape, or form," he told Billy, "and I'll thank you to leave my store." He walked back to the end of the aisle and stood there, arms folded, seeing what Billy would do.

What Billy did, he spat a brown sluice onto the floor, gave Randall the finger, and walked off.

There goes trouble, thought Randall.

—5—

Sheila Cowan was in her office on the phone when her assistant Stefan Piontek knocked at the open door. She motioned him to enter and take a seat, and with an index finger held up indicated she'd be with him in a minute. It was a nice office on the fourth floor of the government building with a panoramic view of the state capitol and tree-lined streets to the east, the Missouri River to the north.

No Big Thing

As Chief Financial and Administrative Officer of the Missouri Highways and Transportation Commission, Sheila Cowan was a very busy woman, always smoothing out wrinkles, stamping out fires before they spread, clamping down on insubordination, laying down the law, a/k/a protocol. She believed in diplomacy but only up to a point, the point where her decision was final.

Stefan could tell that Sheila was nearing the end of her conversation with what sounded like an engineer on the other end. "Mitch, that the price of steel has increased over the last year is unfortunate," she was saying, "it really is, but we can't control these things. To increase the distance between guardrail sections is out of the question, even if it is only four feet. You'll have to do your best with what you have and if that means we fall short, then so be it. We'll just allocate more funds and get it done late, yes, but within proper specs. Agreed? Great, now back to work."

She looked to Stefan, took a hit of mocha latte—her second that morning, Stefan knew, because twice he had trotted over to the Java Hut—and said, "Wants to jerry-rig the highway, not on my watch. Okay, sport, what's on your mind?"

In response Stefan stood and placed a MoDOT form in front of her, an application for the Adopt-A-Highway program. "This, this outrageous request." His voice quavering, Sheila saw he was distraught. "Look at the group." With the eraser end of a pencil he pointed to the box labeled NAME OF GROUP, INDIVIDUAL, OR ORGANIZATION. No need for that; it was easy to find for Stefan had taken a yellow highlighter to the answer: THE MISSOURI REALM OF THE KU KLUX KLAN.

"Perfect, just perfect," said Sheila, unfazed. "I knew this was coming. If it wasn't the Klan it'd be some other detestable group, the Bestiality Society or—"

"Toad Lickers," interjected Stefan. "I heard this piece on NPR how they lick a certain toad to get high. Can you imagine?"

"I think I'll stick with vodka tonic, but what I can imagine is putting the kibosh on this ridiculous notion. Think of all the problems this would cause if we consented and Klan members did show up to do their duty, especially if they were wearing their robes. Fights breaking out, mayhem on the highway, motorists rubbernecking, causing accidents. Not to mention the embarrassment it would bring this agency to have to erect a sign referencing a hate group. No way is this going through."

"I never thought it would go through," concurred Stefan, less flustered now that his boss wasn't apoplectic. "And even if it did that sign would be gone within a day."

"Overnight," smiled Sheila.

"They'd have to be crazy to wear their robes."

Snorting dismissively, "Anybody who'd belong to a group like that probably isn't compos mentis anyway. I wouldn't put anything past them, but none of that is going to happen. Who's the requester?"

"A Randall Fortner of Pine Grove, Missouri."

"Well, you return the application to Mister Fortner and mark it denied. No explanation necessary. Meanwhile we'll alert legal in case he wants to make a stink about it. They'll come up with the right wording to justify the decision. So that's that." She took a noisy sip of mocha latte. "Anything else?"

Stefan rose from his chair. "Just that it's a real pleasure working for you, so decisive, so—"

"Magisterial."

"That's it exactly," said Stefan and scurried out the door.

—6—

Tom Consolino would have never heard about Randall's rejection letter had it not been for Dalton Hankins writing a letter to the editor of the *Jefferson County Gazette* in which he backgrounded the

No Big Thing

request to participate in the Adopt-A-Highway program and Mo-DOT's unfair response. Hankins, who had dropped out of school in mid-10th grade to work in a rendering plant, concluded his piece by saying, "It's a sad day for all American citizens when a government agency is able to deny a certain faction their God-given right just because it doesn't like what that faction stands for." Dalton was of the firm belief one did not need a high school diploma to be able to express one's thoughts well on paper.

A stringer from the Associated Press saw the letter and made it into a news short, which ran in the Regional News section of several periodicals with wide circulation. Tom Consolino, along with thousands of others, read about it in the *St. Louis Post-Dispatch*.

Tom was a staff lawyer with a well-known civil rights organization looking for a good case to galvanize his career.

Since it was unethical to directly solicit clients, Tom decided to go the roundabout route. The article mentioned Fortner owned a store in Pine Grove, so he called information and got both phone number and address. Then he penned a letter by hand to Randall Fortner urging him to get in touch with a certain lawyer in St. Louis who would be willing to offer counsel. This man was Tom Consolino, and he was with the American Civil Liberties Union, a body whose mission it was to support the civil liberties of wronged citizens such as yourself, regardless of their ideological stance. In fact, stated the anonymous correspondent, the ACLU prides itself in defending individuals with unpopular viewpoints. In closing, he wrote, Please give Mr. Consolino a call as he will likely take on your case and do it *pro bono*, that is, at no cost to you. Signed, A Friend.

There was no business card, too obvious; he hand wrote his work address, work number and home number. Then he waited to see what would happen.

The Letter from the State Highways and Transportation Commission was a personal slap in the face to Randall. No explanation, no "Please Try Again at a Later Date," no "We are very sorry, but ..." Some unfeeling bureaucrat had just returned his application with a check in the box marked DECLINED. With a simple stroke of a ball point pen his hope of advancing a knowledge and appreciation of Southern Heritage was out the window. With considerable mental effort, he put himself in this faceless bureaucrat's place, sitting in a cubicle in Jefferson City, coffee stains on his shirt, eyes watering from reading too many forms, yearning for Friday. Grudgingly, he supposed it looked as though he wanted "to spread hate," as he'd heard it put, by invoking the name of the Klan, the mere mention of which had once put fear in the hearts of a many a black, Jew, or Catholic. But that was in the past. They weren't like that anymore. No one wore their robes out in public and the last time he'd seen a cross burn was 25 years ago in Cairo, Illinois, and that recollection growing dim. Dastardly deeds were a thing of the past. Well sure, some guys like Dalton Hankins talked a good game, but to act on it? Nosirree, the sinister element had departed the ranks of the Klan the same as it had left other secret societies, the Order of the Veiled Prophet for instance, and what remained was a benevolent organization, a helping hand to widows and orphans and farmers down on their luck. A champion of civil rights for white folks. The KKK had cleaned up its act. That's how he saw it. Why couldn't those blockheads in Jefferson City see that too?

Maybe instead of trying to claim the highway for the Ku Klux Klan he should have applied under the name White Citizens Council, which was a political faction in Cairo, where he'd lived before marrying Susan Preston Walker and coming to Pine Grove to work in her daddy's grain elevator. Everyone in Cairo knew that the White Citizens Council was another name for the KKK and its members had all five "at large" seats on the city council. The mayor of Cairo belonged to this party as well. Randall didn't know what had become of the White Citizens Council, probably disbanded by now, but if he'd had the sense to use that as a euphemism for the KKK, well, maybe that wouldn't have scared them off in Jeff City.

No Big Thing

Hindsight was always twenty-twenty.

Then the anonymous letter came a few weeks later, Randall still feeling on the outs. It told him there was someone out there who might help; take up his case is what it said. It was then that Randall thought that he would like to have his case taken up. In fact, he'd been putting off going to see Clement Waller, the family lawyer over in Acadia. Now he had motivation.

He dropped in unannounced and was lucky that Clement was free to chat. Clement, an affable, beefy man younger than Randall, ushered him into his office, piles of paper everywhere, diplomas and citations on the walls, an ashtray full of cigarette butts. First thing Clement did was shake hands and offer Randall a Dominican cigar.

"Don't smoke," said Randall, "remember?"

"How about a bourbon then? I've got some Old Crow here."

Randall glanced at his watch: one-fifteen. "A little too early for me, Clem. Thanks anyway."

"You won't mind if I indulge? It's five o' clock somewhere." From a drawer in his substantial desk, he took out a smudged glass and filled it. He set the bottle, label facing outward, on the desk between them, the crow beckoning. "Just in case you change your mind," he winked. "Now, what's on your mind?"

Randall ran down the situation while Clement listened patiently even though he was aware of most of it as was everyone in the county who read the newspaper. His tone was matter of fact, no noticeable rancor, the delivery measured to show that he was a reasonable man and was prepared to accept the outcome however disappointing. He had no evidence that any one person was out to prejudice him, but still it seemed unfair. All this leading up to the one Big Question: Did he have a cause of action?

Clement Waller chewed on this a moment before answering. "Well, it is an interesting pickle to contemplate, I'll say that. What you have done is to open a can of worms for First Amendment free speech issues. We might be able to make a case that you and your organization have been discriminated against based on your beliefs which you have a right to express or display under the constitution. And you might—very small might, *minuscule*—eventually prevail in this battle, although it will be an epic battle with untold hours billed at great cost to you, the petitioner."

"Yeah, that's what I figured."

The lawyer gave a sympathetic nod, and tipped his shot glass. "And for what outcome?" he pursued. "The opportunity to clean the highway? Oh, I know it's the principle of the thing, but let's be pragmatic here for a minute. You won't win and trying to win will probably leave you spent and bitter over the entire process which will drag on for years. The way I see it, the state bureaucracy, hell, *any* bureaucracy, is like a giant assassin robot controlled by a mad scientist. It's so formidable that nothing can actually faze it, it just rumbles along doing what it does and any puny person who gets in its way will be stepped on and the robot won't care one way or another. A lawsuit directed at this robot would have the effect of a bullet glancing off its steel-plated armor."

"What if I had a bazooka?"

Clement chuckled. "Sure, a bazooka might make a dent, but a frigging rocket launcher with a nuclear warhead would be even better. You have something like that in your arsenal?"

Randall brought out the letter, handed it over. "Yes, yes, well and good," said Clement, having scanned it, "and this is what you call serendipity. Someone sympathetic to your cause wishes to lead you in the proper direction. Or, perhaps, is this person thinking only of his best interests and looking to use you as a pawn? It may not matter so far as you're concerned, you only want to see justice done."

Clement paused, studied the man before him, an attentive look on his long, craggy face. "Now, having said that, I can tell you that this is not a bad idea. The ACLU is all about defending free speech, it was created for such a situation as this. They've been around a long time and have gone to bat for American communists, the rights

No Big Thing

of blacks to attend schools, rights of women to vote, and so on."

"They defend coloreds and they'd still defend us?"

"That's right, because they're neutral—supposed to be. Your beliefs no matter how ugly or reprehensible make no difference to them. In theory, anyway. What really flips their switch is suppression of free speech and your thing is just that. The ACLU lawyer doesn't care if it's Joe Blow down the street threatening to kill you if you don't stop preaching Klan or if it's the State of Missoura trying to put a muzzle on you, he'll go after each one with the same vigor." Clement paused to let that sink in.

"You sure you don't want a little snort? No?" Refilling his glass, "Randall, my friend, you came to me for advice, not daring to assume that I would take on this monster litigation. I mean, there's no way. I don't have the time, resources, or inclination. My best advice, if you really want to pursue this, is to give this lawyer a call and get the ball rolling."

—7—

THEY WERE FOOLING AROUND in the back of his pickup, a sleeping bag spread out on the bed, empties all around, trains coupling in the distance, he not sure where it was going since Cassie had mentioned it was that time of the month. The Curse, she called it. Birch said he didn't mind at all as a medicine man once told him that menstrual blood nourishes the penis and makes it grow. She gave him a kiss and said she liked him the most when he was being playful, downright silly. Who's being silly? I'm hard as Chinese algebra. She smiled her secret smile meant only for him. Let's see what we can do about that.

It was getting on sundown on a Saturday in early October, the day still warm. He had parked on a gravel road which dead-ended at the entrance to an old Primitive Baptist cemetery. It was one of their spots, isolated and picturesque, the poor man's motel room. Better than a room because a motel wouldn't allow pets and Bowser was here with them, off chasing squirrels. They had stopped at the Colonel's and gotten a bucket, which they were now digging into. Birch switched on the ignition so they could have music. "I'm Too Sexy" was playing on KSHE, which gave them both a laugh.

He looked at her, munching on a drumstick, shirt unbuttoned, dreadlocks unbound, cascading down her shoulders and back like matted ropes of hemp, and he thought for the twentieth time that day how lucky he was to have her, from her toenails painted with peace signs to the detour on the bridge of her nose, a souvenir from a thrown baseball bat during a sandlot game long ago.

"You wanna hear something funny"

"I can laugh with the best of 'em, go ahead."

"When I was in boot camp there were these guys from Nashville who were just funny as all get out, always clowning around, and they had their own names for stuff, like they called, um, you know, pussy—they, they called that cock." Pausing for her reaction, "So you can imagine how weird that was, to a guy who knows it by the right name even if it is slang, to hear, 'Hey, let's go into Louisville and get us some cock.' And you know they're not gay, so you're left scratching your head."

She laughed lightly, "Wonder how that got started? Maybe they're so plugged-in to their own self-gratification they can't get past their own genitalia in describing sexual activity."

Birch just stared at her. "Wow. That went right over my head."

"I do have a brain," she asserted. "I like to use it. Anyway, it's just an idea. It's either that or in Nashville the designation for vagina— pussy not being one of *my* words, mind you—somehow got switched with a name for penis, creating confusion for outsiders. It'd be like if your parents told you a fork is a spoon and until someone told you different you'd be calling that utensil by the wrong name. But, you know, maybe the more interesting question is why do we have so many names for sex organs."

No Big Thing

"I don't know, but there's a slew of 'em. Maybe it's 'cause we're embarrassed to call those things by their true names so we make up funny words."

"Money's got lots of names, too," she put in, "and money's not embarrassing."

" 'cept if you need some and don't have it." He was relieved that they were off on this tangent as the conversation could have turned to her asking if he ever went into town with those guys to get some cock. And he would have answered no, he liked to stay away from those painted women in the Cardinal Hotel when the others lined up in the hallway, twenty dollar bills in their sweaty palms. Which was the truth. But he didn't think she would believe him, women being naturally suspicious, so he was glad it didn't even come up. At the Greyhound Station, just before he headed off for three years, they had sworn their love for each other, vowed to be true, and that was that for Birch.

"Dick, prick, boner," counting on her fingers.

"Snatch, twat, bearded clam," he added.

"Bearded clam? Really? Okay, pee shooter, snake, schlong ..."

"C'mon, *schlong*? Never heard that."

"It's Yiddish. You don't hear it much around here."

"Then where'd you hear it?"

"On the Deadhead trail. Following the Dead you wind up in all sorts of interesting places, meet all kinds of interesting people. It's a trip and a half, it really is."

"You and Amanda did it for real, right? Living like hobos, you once said. How'd you make do?"

"Well, we had sleeping bags, camping gear, some money, and a positive attitude. Amanda's mom was kind enough to wire some dough a few times to keep us going. And kind is the key word, because among Deadheads kindness is everything. It's right there in the song 'Uncle John's Band,' if you listen."

"Yeah?"

"Absolutely. Listen," crooning "*Woe, hoh, what I to know-oh-oh, is are you kind?* So you see, Deadheads tend to help each other out. Kindness makes more kindness. As we say, 'No worries, man.'"

Not for the first time Birch mused how that three years had changed them each in their own way. She was just a teeny-bopper when he left, and he, he was a punk kid. He'd gone out into the world, far from Podunk Grove, thriving in the company of men, growing more confident of his abilities, becoming more open-minded, less fly-off-the-handle. She, taking her own winding road, evolving into a very free-wheeling person with open ideas about drugs and sex and boundaries, having lived like a gypsy months on end, associating with unwashed, disheveled people who were probably no better than shifty beggars. He imagined her on one of these Deadhead bivouacs, passing joints and bottles around a campfire, she doing some tribal dance, guys around, leering, itching to get her into their pup tent, if they hadn't already.

Well, he tried to be open-minded, but sometimes it just didn't work.

Now Cassie was eager to get off the subject, seeing the look in Birch's eyes. In fact, what he envisioned wasn't far from the actuality of her experience. To wit, she and Amanda down on funds, outside Redrocks in Colorado where the Dead would play later that day. A couple Mountain Girls they were, soliciting, calling to anyone in earshot, "A cream cheese and cucumber bagel for a Miracle Ticket!" An older white guy in a dashiki, turban, and pot belly, gives them both a Miracle Ticket and takes the yummy bagel. But that's not all he wants. Later that night, after the concert and everyone feeling mellow, Rainbow—his name— invites Cassie into the drum circle. Passing the hash pipe, they drum themselves into a state of nirvana, and he makes the suggestion. She wrestles with her conscience for a while, then chooses to sleep with him that night and a few nights after that until all remaining diehards disband and go their own ways. That episode doesn't end well; later, much later in an early morning ER, she is diagnosed with gonorrhea which by then has

No Big Thing

advanced to pelvic inflammatory disease and now it is iffy if she will ever conceive.

Back to the naming game. "Beaver, nookie ..."

"Dingus, tool, bone," she countered.

"Don't forget manhood."

"Oh, pul-*leez*!"

"Okay. Cooter, strange, and another one, begins with a 'c', that I won't even say in front of you."

She saw him turning red. "Thanks, I guess. But strange? That's a new one."

"It's what the black guys in my unit would say: 'DeMarco got him some strange last night.' I think Richard Pryor started it."

This was the segue she was looking for, to broach another topic on her mind. "That reminds me," she said, "I've been meaning to ask you about this thing with the highway department. Your family wants to collect litter for the KKK? It was in the paper, everyone's talking about it, and you never mentioned it to me. What's up with that?"

He snorted, shook his head. "Yeah, it's gotten blown all out of proportion. I didn't say anything about it because I didn't think it was ever going to happen and I was right. State doesn't want to be associated with the Klan. But the thing is, we're not really the Klan. Randall used to be with some white rights group down where he used to live, and I think he got it in his head that he was a Grand Wizard or something. It was his idea and he asked me to pitch in. I said okay, but only because he's my Grampa and I love him."

"That's sweet, Birch. Self-sacrifice is a noble thing."

"Don't lay it on too thick," he cautioned. "I'm *glad* that MoDOT turned down Randall. Now I don't have to think of myself as the trash man, janitor of the roadside, a chump with a litter bag. I mean, c'mon, anyone who's done time in a war zone, actually seen live action, been fired on, well, that sorta thing is beneath him. You know? But I owe Randall and I'd have done it only for that."

"I don't know," she wavered, getting that dubious look, "I'm hearing a proud man tell himself he's better than a janitor. What if I said I was better than a burger flipper at McDonald's? Wouldn't you think that was egotistical, hoity-toity?"

"I'd think you aspire to greater purpose." He paused. "It's weird, though. I thought you'd be down on that whole thing, Klan and Deadheads seeming like oil and water."

She shrugged. "I'd be down on it if it was anyone but you involved. Just the name of the group leaves a sour taste in my mouth. Maybe it's the ying-yang of it, opposites attracting, I don't know."

She pulled a number from her shirt pocket, fired it up and offered him a hit.

He waved it away. "Nah, you know I don't do that stuff. Stunts my growth."

She went to town, sucking it in, holding it, slowly exhaling. After a bit, "The point is, Mister War Zone, you don't *have to do* the shit work, good for you. But if you did, if it ever came to that, you shouldn't be *above* it. You should be down *with* it. Humility, man. You ever read Gandhi? I did, I read his biography, and he was out there. In a good way. Know what he said? 'One must be as humble as dust to be able to discover the truth.' Don't you want to discover the truth?"

Truth about what? He didn't know what to say.

"Anyway," she said, leaning into him, blowing smoke in his ear, "I think humility is sexy."

—8—

THERE WAS AN OUTBUILDING behind the grain elevator. It was a solid wooden structure, built to last in the 1930s, and originally intended as a workshop or storage shed, obvious from all the shelving. One day Randall had gotten the idea to turn it into a gallery, a repository of artifacts, antiquities, and sundry items relating to his

No Big Thing

passion. The collections of the Old South and Southern Heritage Museum, amassed over a decade, were modest in scope yet intriguing. Among its treasures, old-time farm implements, a yellowed and brittle manifest of slaves to be auctioned in antebellum Little Rock, a section of religious articles including a prayer book that once belonged to Alexander H. Stephens, vice-president under Jefferson Davis. Civil War memorabilia took up the lion's share of the space, that being the reason for starting the little museum since the Fortners along with several townspeople had forebears who had fought in that conflict on both sides and had scads of weaponry and paraphernalia, heirlooms gathering dust in their closets and on their mantles. Swords, scabbards, cast iron cooking pots, cannonballs, parts of uniforms, insignias. And what can one do with great-great grandfather's musket? Bring it out once a year at Thanksgiving to show the kinfolk? Become a Civil War reenactor? Better yet, why not donate it to a museum which will care for it and proudly display it.

To round out the collections there was one wall devoted to Native American relics such as buffalo hides, pottery, beaded leather pouches, and arrowheads galore that local farmers had turned up while plowing. Admission to the museum was free.

On this particular day an old man named Spencer Gage had dropped by with a donation. A retired pipefitter, Spencer lived alone in the neighboring town of Ringer's Mill, and grew pumpkins for the fall market. The two had spoken at the church Wurstmarkt last Sunday and Spencer told Randall that he had something for him, something he would appreciate. Well, sir, then bring it on by. It was mid-morning when Spencer arrived. Eveline, minding the store, told Spencer that Randall was puttering around in the museum and to go on back.

Spencer wasted no time in showing off his hoard. From a manila envelope he produced a stack of wrinkled currency, banknotes issued by The Confederate States of America. There were different denominations, but lots of hundreds and they originated from various cities—Augusta; Richmond; Columbia, South Carolina. Randall was extremely pleased, saying what a generous gift this was and how he would keep it under glass as it was likely quite valuable. Spencer saying what the heck, he was glad to do it, and besides, he had no heirs and anyone he might think to bequeath it to in his will would probably just turn around and sell it.

Randall got out the magnifying glass and they were studying the writing on the bills. Spencer pointed out that although the face value of the note was not to be paid until Two Years after the Ratification of a Treaty of Peace between the Confederate States and The United States of America, the notes did pay interest while the war was ongoing. There were hand-stamped validations on the obverse noting, for example, "Interest Paid to 1st January, 1863, at Augusta."

"Reckon these didn't get cashed or we wouldn't be looking at 'em now," said Spencer.

"This really is a piece of history," Randall gushed, "I'll be sure to note that it was kindly donated by Spencer Gage."

"Aw shoot, that isn't necessary," waving his hand in chagrin. "I don't need no publicity, just say an anonymous benefactor."

Just then Eveline appeared at the door. "Randall," she announced somewhat formally, "you got another visitor." She stepped aside and Randall saw an eager-looking middle-aged man, olive-complected, black frame glasses, with dark wavy hair, smiling at him.

Whenever Tom Consolino left St. Louis it was cause for reverie. Alone in the car, coffee within reach, windows up or down—it didn't so much matter—scenery going past like he was driving into a movie, he was given to reminisce. And if he headed southward, as he was today, that reminiscence often turned to Cairo, Illinois, the southernmost city in Illinois, two-and-a-half hours from St. Louis

No Big Thing

at the confluence of the Ohio and Mississippi. A place that Tom used to say was stuck in time, the 1930s, say. A place where civil rights was once considered to be a joke at best. A place where he took his first assignment as a young lawyer.

Pine Grove was an hour from St. Louis, a straight shot down I-55 then southwesterly on US 67 towards Valles Mines and finally onto a series of two-lane back roads unfolding into the hinterland. Tom had never ventured into these parts before and a road map was folded on the seat beside him, the village of Pine Grove a mere blip on the map amid a blank light-green background. Not much else around it.

A half hour before, he had crossed over I-270, the highway that loops around St. Louis and takes you to Memphis or Chicago depending on where your nose is pointed, and there, between the cloverleaf and Meramec Bottom Road, he saw the area that the Klan hoped to adopt and maintain. It wasn't much to look at, just a ho-hum stretch of highway, grassy here, scrubby there, some limestone outcroppings, no refuse in sight. This was to be the site of the great legal battle. He tried to imagine a state highway sign claiming this for the Klan, but his imagination failed him.

As he sailed along into pastoral settings, the memories bubbled up. Upon graduation from Saint Louis University Law School, Tom was given a fellowship to the Reginald Heber Smith Community Lawyer Fellowship, a high-minded activist troop administered by Howard University in Washington D.C. New recruits were expected to attend an opening convention or learning meeting and so Tom and another free spirit jumped in the MG and drove to the capitol arriving on August 8, 1974. It so happened that Nixon resigned the next day and in Tom's mind, now twenty years later, he saw himself with a gang of other idealistic young lawyers that historic day, spontaneously heading over to 1600 Pennsylvania Avenue, massing in the street and shouting "Jail To The Chief" at the White House lawn as Tricky Dick gave his farewell. Ah, those were the days, deriding a beleaguered president, piling it on when the man was already washed up.

Historically, Howard was a black university, and the Reggie folks urged their fledgling lawyers to be radical and pro-civil rights when they went to work in their assigned legal aid offices around the country. He was going to Cairo, Illinois, and, all he knew about that, you pronounced it "Kay-ro," and Huck and Jim had once floated by on a raft.

At a cocktail party in Georgetown, he ran into Thurgood Marshall. To a neophyte civil rights champion, Marshall was a god—not only the first black Supreme Court Justice and still on the bench, but the former head of the Howard group which had run civil rights cases around the nation including *Brown v. Board of Education*, which essentially abolished state-sponsored segregation. Tom saw the portly Justice moving around the room, greeting the incoming class, joking with them, seeming genuine and down-to-earth. Then he was coming toward Tom and his entourage, but took a sudden detour, Tom and the others following his movement, whispering, "That's Thurgood Marshall over there in the buffet line! A legend, a great legal mind, scarfing down Swedish meatballs."

Later, Thurgood sidled up to Tom and extended his hand. He had spotted Tom's name tag which had CAIRO on it and he explained that he had done cases in Cairo and that it was a Sundown Town and how he would always leave on the afternoon train after court adjourned. Tom said he'd heard the term Sundown Town, though he never imagined he'd be living in one. Thurgood said there were hundreds if not thousands of Sundown Towns and Cairo was among the most notorious, a town fraught with discriminatory laws. "Why, they had a political party, an offshoot of the Klan, that ran the city and, believe me, son, they weren't above intimidation and outright violence in their tacit goal of 'keeping the niggers down'." Thurgood put his arm around Tom's shoulder and warned him not to live outside town in the country like he'd planned. He was right.

The Justice had represented a Cairo resident, Hattie Cox, in the early 50s, and he asked Tom to look up Hattie and to tell her that

No Big Thing

Truegood said Best Wishes. That was his name between he and Hattie. Hattie later told Tom that she had cooked many fine meals for Truegood when he was in town to argue her case, and he had always cleaned his plate.

Tom was in Cairo for two years assigned to the Land of Lincoln Legal Assistance Foundation. It had been known as the Lawyers Committee for Civil Rights Under Law, which, a few years before, had a case heard and won in the U.S. Supreme Court about voting rights. The city had a long history of racial tension dating back to at least 1909 when a black man and accused murderer named William James was sprung from jail by a mob of Cairo's white citizens to be lynched from the nearest telegraph pole. Then, in a nod to medieval barbarism, James's head was placed on a stake for all to see. Sixty-five years later, when Tom arrived the situation was still grim. Seven years earlier, in 1967, the suspicious "suicide" of a black man in the city jail—initially stopped for a defective taillight and jailed for verbal abuse—led to riots and in response the sheriff deputized a "citizens protection group." The White Hats, as they were called, numbered in the hundreds and fought openly with the Cairo United Front, an alliance of up-in-arms blacks. Violence ruled the day and several businesses were torched. Firemen responding to one of the fires were shot at by a sniper. By the time Tom Consolino arrived, population had greatly declined and businesses were giving up on Cairo due to the almost routine occurrence of violence, arson, and general lawlessness.

Of course all these stories came to Tom after he arrived, recounted over beers after work by George Hinson, the office investigator. George had been a United Front soldier during the riots and didn't mind regaling Tom with first hand, hair-raising accounts of street battles as long as Tom was buying.

He pulled into a gas station in the village of Poches Vides, a big hand-lettered sign at the entrance saying TRY OUR STINKBAIT, CATFISH LOVE EM! Gassing up, he consulted his memory of French class and surmised that Poches Vides translated to Empty Pockets or Whole Lot of Nothing, but from the looks of the roadside businesses he'd just driven past he thought that "Used Tires" might be a better meaning. He checked his map and it looked like Pine Grove was about 12 miles distant, through hill and dale. He placed the fuel hose back on its cradle, got back in his Dodge. Randall Fortner, in Tom's mind probably "a good old boy," awaited him.

—10—

The Visitor extended his hand, Randall took it, and said, "You're early."

"Oh," said Tom, "I thought we said eleven."

"We did, but I'm still on the old time. Probably should've told you, but I can't be expected to change my watch, all my clocks including the one in my head, just because the government decides to mess with the time."

"The time change was two weeks ago."

"It's gonna take a while to adjust, and I might never adjust, just keep on with the old time until it comes back around in six months."

At once Tom saw that he was dealing with an obstinate, if not eccentric man.

Spencer Gage excused himself, saying he didn't want to leave his dog in the car too long. On the way out, he stopped at the donations jar and made a show of stuffing a couple bills through the slot on the lid of the jar.

Over the course of the next hour or so, as Tom made Randall's acquaintance, he realized that Randall wasn't the good old boy he imagined. He was thoughtful, measured, and well-spoken. They never left the museum and Eveline, dutiful as ever, thought to bring out coffee and tea. Tom listened as Randall recounted his original plan, submitting the application that would put it into action, and subsequent disappointment. It was all pretty straightforward, Tom thinking that there were infinite variations of the circumstances

No Big Thing

leading up to the injustice, but they all boiled down to the same thing: A citizen's constitutional right to free speech and free association denied. Sometimes, as in this case, it was an agency of the very government that instituted this right doing the clamping down, the reining in, and sometimes it was private enterprise. Either way, it was wrong and it was his job to go to bat for the wronged person or group. And, he told Randall, he swung a pretty mean bat.

Tom Consolino sensed that his would-be client was somewhat dubious about his lawyerly motives, having driven down from St. Louis and meeting with him like this, in his own place, making it very convenient for Randall to sign on and get the case going. He tried to reassure him that his motives were honorable. "I'm doing this for my own reasons," he told him plainly, "not yours. I don't make donations to your group. I don't agree with your viewpoints, but this is an important First Amendment case."

"You could join," Randall encouraged. "We don't bite, you know."

Tom Consolino sighed. "Mr. Fortner, I am not in your camp. Frankly, the Ku Klux Klan is anathema to me. Bad news, and besides, you wouldn't even have me as a member."

Randall pursed his lips in consternation. "Don't be silly, we've got lots of lawyers."

At one point, Tom giving his background in this sort of thing, mentioned Cairo, how he'd been there in the mid-70s, a lawyer for the local legal aid society, doing a fair amount of civil rights work for oppressed blacks. He brought up the White Citizens Council which controlled the City Commission and passed any discriminatory law or ordinance they damn well pleased. How 45 percent of the population was black and had been shut out of the political process.

"That's fine and dandy," said Randall, "you help the nigras all you want, but we are Caucasians and proud of being so. Around here we got Germans, French, and some Slavs—whites who don't know the meaning of welfare or food stamps. We *built* our lives, haven't had nothing handed to us. And so far as government programs to which, I say *to which we are entitled*, we aren't asking for nothing that hasn't been given to other groups. Why, there's road over in Rolla been adopted by Atheists Anonymous. They get in the program, but we can't?"

"I saw one on the way here, Cowboys For Christ. You think that doesn't put off any passerby who's not Christian? Are Muslims going to feel comfortable with that? And there's my point: The decision-making process is not equitable, and we're going to bust that wide open."

"I'd like to see that," mused Randall, "them two get together. Probably end up in a brawl."

"Oh, and what's that?"

"The Atheists Anonymous and the Cowboys For Christ, put 'em together and see who's left standing."

"Yeah," said Tom, "that would be something to see. Then he looked squarely at Randall, told him plainly, "Listen, you're going to be approached by the press over this matter and you've got to watch what you say, how you comport yourself. You seem like a very capable man who can handle himself quite well, but these reporters are shrewd, they'll take your words and print them out of context, often just to push a certain agenda they may have."

"Well, I don't know ..."

"Take that word you just said. 'Nigra,' as I heard it. That sounds very close, too close, to a certain pejorative used to demean blacks, the one we've all heard and the one that is considered taboo in our society at large."

"I've been using it my whole life, it's accepted."

"Maybe in your world it is, but even so I strongly advise you to go with something else. Colored is out of date, black is all right, African-American is even better."

"You want me to start calling a huckster a salesman, too?"

"It's just that the word doesn't play well in 1992," careful not to

No Big Thing

take an argumentative tone, "it will likely set people off. Give you an example. Back in Cairo, there was a class action suit brought by a man who had been denied a job with the Municipal Utilities Commission. He was a qualified electrician, yet he wasn't even considered for the position. The City of Cairo handled all the water, sewer, and electrical utilities provided to its residents through this city-run commission, and yet, there was not a person of color to be seen anywhere in that work force. This man claimed that he was a victim of racial discrimination and asked the court to address it. Well, to use an old saying, it was a tough row to hoe, and the case went from the lower court on up to the Seventh Circuit Court of Appeals, which happens to be in Chicago. I was there for the arguments, not participating but observing as a young lawyer."

"I can see it," said Randall."

"What happened was, the case was called, and since the appellant, the one who is appealing the previous ruling, has first crack, that meant that the City Attorney for Cairo, Chet Ramsey, had the opening argument. He stood before the judges, introduced himself, and began to speak in his Southern Illinois twang about the history of the proceedings. About one minute into the opening arguments, one of the judges interrupted him. 'Mr. Ramsey, we on this panel have reviewed the case carefully and we have some questions, one of which will perhaps resolve the issue forthwith. You say in Footnote 34 something to the effect that the reason behind the decision of the City Utilities Commission to deny employment to Negroes is that "they" are all fearful of electricity. Can you elaborate on that or am I mistaken in taking Footnote 34 for having true relevancy in this case?' With that question floating, Ramsey took about one second and responded, 'Nigras *are* 'fraid of 'lectricity, your honor.' That was all they needed to hear. The judges promptly ended the oral argument and ruled for the 'nigra' plaintiff who had been denied being allowed to even apply for a job."

Randall chewed on this a moment. "What's fair for one is fair for all, I'll go with that. But you're not saying he lost the case because he used that word before those Northern judges, are you?"

"It sure didn't help," said Tom.

—11—

THEY WERE STANDING at a counter, the top of a large glass case which held Civil War armament and munition. Randall shifted position, took a sip of tea, and said, "I was there at that time."

Tom just stared at him, puzzled by the non sequitur, wondering if Randall was daft.

"I was in Cairo the same time you were, got there in sixty-seven, just in time for all the commotion."

"What commotion was that?"

"Riots, the town burning, stores looted, folks seriously hurt."

"Yeah, I heard about it," said Tom. "Our lead investigator was in the fray, he told me some stories, sounded like all hell broke loose."

"Was this fellow white or black?"

"Black."

"Then he was with the United Front. I was a White Hat, properly deputized to put down this uprising, protect the town citizens. It started with that prisoner in the jail. Found him hanging in his cell, and the nigras ... uh, blacks automatically assumed it had to be murder. Well, the jailer and police chief say it's suicide, that's good enough for me. Happens all the time, don't it? Next thing you know the streets are filled with angry blacks, shouting and chanting and busting windows. They get bolder at night, bigger numbers, probably hopped up on booze and dope, breaking into stores and stealing merchandise. Now how's that gonna bring back this dead boy? And the citizens are scared outta their wits, saying please do something."

Tom was all ears, waiting for Randall to say how he summarily dispatched a few rioters.

"White Hats were united, too. We fought them in the streets, in the alleys, behind houses, fought them with knives and truncheons, one man had a cross-bow. It was no different than being in a battle in a war. You feared for your life and you did what had to be done."

"As I recall, the National Guard was eventually called and order was restored."

"You're dang right the National Guard was called, but not before we had 'em on the run. Probably ran 'em all the way to the mudflats of the confluence, and afraid to come back to this day. We fought and we won and the matter was settled. There is great satisfaction in that."

"It's interesting to hear it from a different perspective," said Tom, diplomatically. "George, our investigator, always maintained that the White Hats were thugs and bullies fueled by hatred for blacks. But what do I know, I wasn't there."

"Yeah, right, a goodly portion of the town is common thugs. Does that make sense to you? We were protecting our own, and that's that."

Tom decided that *was* that, and went on to a more seminal topic. He then asked Randall did he really want to take this on. Was he willing to become lead plaintiff in a federal lawsuit *Fortner et al v. State Of Missouri*, which would likely drag on for years and generate all sorts of publicity which could be detrimental to his family life, his business, in this quiet, little town.

By then Randall had decided that this lawyer was all right, and that he would allow him to represent him and his interests and damn the consequences. But he did not give his answer outright. Instead, he opened the sliding doors in the big glass case, and took out a long rifle. "This here," he informed, "is an Enfield Pattern Rifle carried in the Civil War by my great-great grandpa, Ike, wounded in the Battle of Pilot Knob, just fifty miles from here. It's an English rifle. At the beginning of the war, the Rebels captured some federal armories, but there still wasn't enough to go around so the South bought more'n 300,000 of these rifles from the British. This probably wasn't new when it was issued. It could've been used in the Crimean War or any other of the global conflicts the Brits had going back then. Colonialism—so many uprisings to put down, right?"

Tom nodded politely, wondering where was his answer.

"Don't know if you're a history buff," said Randall. "I am and it just amazes me that this rifle could've plugged a Turk across the ocean then come back over that ocean and plugged a Yank on American soil. But not at Pilot Knob, the South got their ass handed to 'em on a platter. It was one of the worst defeats of the war. One of the most humiliating, anyway. Here, hold this."

Tom took the proffered weapon with great caution. He didn't like firearms at all, especially those that might've taken human lives. "It's heavy," stating the obvious. "And they carried this all day, every day, marching around the countryside?"

"That's right, and wearing wool uniforms, too. Almost ten pounds there, fifty-five inches in length, and that's without the bayonet. Listen, you wanna hear a story of valor, one that should never be forgotten?"

How could he say no?

"You don't have to hold that any longer. Here, I'll take it back. Well, see, it was September, eighteen and sixty-four, the South needed a victory, a major victory, to embarrass Washington, maybe crush Lincoln's chances of reelection. Maybe with a new president the two sides could settle their differences and get on with life. So there's this fellow by the name of Sterling Price, he's a Major General, and that summer he goes to Arkansas and Oklahoma, raises 12,000 troops, infantry, cavalry, along with so many horses and cannon. Now, 12,000 is no mean number of men. It is an army unto itself and Sterling Price called it the Army of Missouri, and set out to claim Missouri, his home state, for the Confederacy.

"The Fortners lived down around Springfield at that time and as Price's army passed through, Ike Fortner joined up. He was just eighteen, and itching to fight. So this army is making their way

No Big Thing

toward St. Louis where they hoped to take her and capture the armory, which'd be a real feather in Price's war bonnet, you can be sure of that. But on the way there they come upon Fort Davidson in Pilot Knob, with a Union garrison of 1,500 soldiers. A tempting target, wouldn't you say? So General Price, he prepares to take the fort. Easier intended than done. If you've ever been to the town of Pilot Knob in the Arcadia Valley you'll know it's surrounded by hills, fairly sizable hills, one called Shepherd Mountain. So he gets his foot soldiers, his cavalry, his cannon up on these hills, poised for attack, and he sends an emissary down to demand surrender. Can you see it?"

Tom said yes, he could. It would be a thorny dilemma for the Union commander as they were outnumbered ten-to-one.

"You got that right. The garrison commander was none other than Brigadier General Thomas Ewing, brother-in-law to General William T. Sherman, the scourge of Atlanta. Ewing was a force to be reckoned with, and rather than bring out the white flag or turn tail and run, he chose to stand and fight. But he had a big thing in his favor and he knew it. The fort, an earthworks, occupied a strong defensive position. It weren't no big fort, but it had walls nine feet high and ten feet thick, and surrounded by a dry moat nine feet deep. Impenetrable as they get. On top of that, there is a large, open field all around the fort, about three football fields in every direction, few or no trees, a clear field of fire at any approaching force. They've also got channels into the walls, ports for rifles and for looking out. It is going to be one hell of a battle.

"The attack came as one big assault from different directions, one brigade over the top of Pilot Knob, another over the summit of Shepherd Mountain, another advancing through a valley between the two. Now, not all the Union troops were in the fort. There was a sizable bunch in that open field I mentioned, but after a spell, way outnumbered, they were driven back to the fort. And though Shepherd Mountain was a ways off, the cannon deployed there did manage to do some damage to the fort. The main assault, though, was over that field. Thousands—thousands!—of Johnny Rebs, swarming, firing, howling that Rebel yell.

"As you can imagine, they were cut down before they could ever reach the fort. And even though they saw their comrades falling all around, they still kept coming, so far as they knew, into certain death—that's how much they believed in their cause."

Or blindly caught up in the pack mentality, thought Tom. Lemmings going over a cliff.

"Just one brigade reached the fort itself, plowing through a hail of cannon and musket fire, only to find the earthworks too steep to climb. The Yankees had these primitive but effective hand grenades and tossed them over the walls, repelling those troops around the moat. The Rebels fell back, carrying their dead and wounded, and prepared for another assault the next day. They say Price lost ten percent of his men that day, around 1,200, but no one knows for sure. I do know that Ike Fortner lost his left arm just below the elbow. I know because I met him when I was six and he was eighty-four. He come up from Arkansas for a visit, brought this rifle and give it to us as an heirloom. You see it's got his initials here on the stock.

"Anyway, what happened next was the humiliating part. As I said, the Confederates were preparing for an onslaught the very next morning. They were building ladders to scale the walls, checking and double-checking all their cannons for serviceability. They had a bonfire going in the valley, the purpose being to keep an eye on the fort. Well, Ewing he was one wily son of a gun, and he decides now is a good time to skedaddle. He can't see defending this fort any longer, he's got bigger fish to fry. What he does, he plans their escape in the night. Around midnight they begin to exit the fort. Stealthy as coyotes, they sneak undetected through an area right between two enemy camps, the soldiers probably fast asleep, exhausted from the battle. Guess the bonfire didn't help. Before leaving, though, they had put all the supplies and armament they couldn't carry in the fort's powder magazine, and they lit a slow-burning fuse to set it off."

Talking about it as though it happened yesterday.

"It was a risky move, because the Rebels hearing that explosion could move in to investigate, find the fort deserted and light out after them Yankees. But Ewing, he felt he had no choice because the military man in him just couldn't allow the enemy to gain control of his resources. Well, the powder magazine did go up with a hell of a bang, and it didn't matter how close the Yankees were when that happened because General Price didn't send his men to investigate until daybreak."

"Let me guess," said Tom, "they were livid at being duped."

"Oh, livid and then some. His officers were shamed and demoralized that Ewing had escaped through their lines and urged Price to pursue them. Price declined, his army already decimated, his dream of taking St. Louis shaken."

He looked to the lawyer and saw that he seemed attentive, appreciating the story as he should.

Actually, Tom was thinking about Randall's manner of speech, countrified, different inflections on vowels, kind of a drawl but not a Southern drawl. Though he was only one county removed from home, the difference was striking. Different dialect; different style of dress, some guys wearing cowboy hats; different attitudes judging by the bumper stickers he'd seen. Different culture, too. Randall was all right, but some of the characters he'd glimpsed on the way here, whew, like something out of *Deliverance*.

"History fills in the rest," Randall concluded. "Price's troops headed northward toward St. Louis, but eventually turned west and headed for Jefferson City. The capitol was too well-fortified so they kept on westward, fighting their way to Kansas City. There, the Battle of Westport was a resounding defeat for Price's army. Then, they went into Kansas and fought and lost the Battle of Mine Creek. By the time Price got back to Arkansas he'd lost over half of the men he'd started with back in September. How he got to be a general I'll never know. Ewing, on the other hand, was considered a hero, his exploits at Fort Davidson made headlines, and he was personally commended by Abraham Lincoln. The Union casualties from that battle numbered only twenty-eight."

"Every one an American."

"Come again?"

"Every person who died in that war was an American, didn't matter what side they were on. I've always thought it was a huge waste of life."

Randall considered this, took on a sober mien. "Soldiers on both sides inspired by patriotism," he said, "Yankees to preserve the Union, Rebels to defend their homeland. And the real tragedy of it? White Christian men at battle with other white Christian men, their same God looking down on them both as they dispatch each other with mighty wrath and terrible fury and the Big Man in the Sky shaking His head in dismay. Can you see it? But the lives those boys gave weren't wasted, no sir, because they believed in something, and with the Confederates it was a way of life that they thought was going to be taken away from them. That, and they couldn't stomach no Northerners telling 'em how to conduct their affairs. They were proud and brave and willing to die for what they believed in. You can't take that away. So, to answer your question, am I willing to put myself on the line in this matter. Yes sir, I am and I do it for great-great grandpa Ike and all he stood for."

Tom Consolino patted Randall on the shoulder. "That's great, Mr. Fortner. I am happy to be your lawyer. Now, just a few more things and we're done here. How many in your organization?"

Randall gazed at Tom, pencil in hand, ready to write on the yellow legal pad resting on the counter top. "Well, there used to be so many we could fill a stadium with our gatherings, but now it's probably just a few hundred scattered throughout Missoura and Southern Illinois and down around Arkansas. Tennessee and Kentucky have some, too. Membership's fallen, it's true, and it's these young people. They just don't have the same fervor—I think that's the right

No Big Thing

word. They just don't have the fervor, the fire in the belly that we had in our day. Too busy with monster trucks and doing the boot scootin' boogie in the honky-tonks to care about upholding traditional American ideals."

"I mean, how many in your inner-circle? In other words, you are the lead plaintiff but on the complaint it will say 'Randall Fortner et al'. That's Latin, et al, it means 'and others'. So who else will be joining you in this lawsuit?"

"Oh, I got you. Let's see, there's my wife, Eveline, my daughter Rebecca and her husband, Cy. There's my two grandsons, Jamie and Birch. Dalton Hankins down at the repair garage. Maybe Clinton Ragsdale over at the rendering plant. Oh, and my brother, Lance. But he's away for a while."

"Just so he's around if and when we need him to testify, and that's a long way off."

"Oh, yeah, he'll be available."

"All right, next on the agenda. It's just a thought," he ventured, "but it seems to me, using the name Ku Klux Klan, well, it stirs emotions. It could be seen as inflammatory. Why not adopt the highway in the name of this place? Old South and Southern Heritage Museum sounds nice. Just an idea."

"Nah," replied Randall, "we'll keep her the way she is. I'm not one for change."

—12—

Late October, Randall took his old 12 gauge Winchester to a meat shoot. Meat Shoots also called Turkey Shoots were going on all over Jefferson County come fall. For whatever reason they were always on Sunday afternoons and these shooting contests were usually advertised by roadside signs, sandwich boards, and whatnot, often hand-lettered: Meat Shoot Sunday Vfw Post 1287 Free Chili. Venues were VFW and American Legion posts, rod and gun clubs, fire halls, parish picnics, and just about any place organizers could set up targets with a background clear of human habitation. Some said that the shoots were practice for deer hunting season, which of course called for rifles not shotguns. But never mind that, a lot of these guys didn't hunt anyway. Like Randall, they just enjoyed being outdoors on a beautiful day like this one, drinking beer, socializing, shooting at small cardboard targets 25 yards distant. It was skill to be able to pepper the target; luck to land a lead shot smaller than a BB dead center on the crosshairs. Two bucks a shot, 15 shooters per round. They shot for pork loins, steaks, bacon, every winning package enough to feed a raft of people.

Randall turned his red-and-white Ford F150 into the long gravel drive that led to the Foothills Coon Hunters Club. Window open, crooked elbow at rest, he could hear the reports up in the distance. Something about the sound of a shotgun in the fall just made you feel good. Up at the clubhouse, he parked on the grass with everyone else. He noted Dalton Hankins' Lincoln among the twenty or so vehicles. There would be many friends here.

Randall did the routine: First, a beer, then bought chances for several consecutive rounds, then went around saying "Howdy." His first round was M; they were now in Round I. About a half-hour wait.

There were picnic tables with shotguns laid out lengthwise, breeches open, spent targets scattered around, some with pellet holes so near the crosshairs you couldn't believe they didn't win. He walked through the picnic tables, guys and a few gals sitting there, joshing, gesturing, comparing target cards from past rounds. Was it his imagination or were some regarding him a bit queer? He saw Dalton over there, dipping into a styrofoam bowl with a plastic spoon. A big pot of chicken soup inside the clubhouse, take all you want.

He laid his Winchester next to Dalton's Browning, sat down across from him. Dalton nodded hey and blew on his soup, piping hot. Then, pointing his chin to the Winchester, "How you 'spect to win anything with that ol' blunderbuss? Don't even have a choke."

No Big Thing

"Oh, I win every now and then," wry smile forming at the corners of his mouth. "Took home a slab of bacon last year. Pure luck, I admit. This a WingMaster, early model, it's great for duck hunting, not so great for meat shoots. So what the heck, I don't expect to win, not with all these tricked-out barrels, chokes that hold a pattern tighter'n a cow's bunghole. But if I do it's just that much more satisfying."

They talked about this and that for a while then Dalton asked about the Highway thing. Any forward movement? Randall told Dalton he got a lawyer to challenge the State over their decision. This lawyer was drafting up a complaint which would soon be served on the state Highway Commission and the case would be in play.

"Well, that's good news," said Dalton. "I was hoping you'd take it to the next level. But this is gonna drag out, I suppose, and lawyer bills can really add up, bury you in debt. Maybe we should do a fundraiser. I could call around, what do you say?"

"Thanks, Dalton, but no need for that. This guy is doing it free of charge. Says it's an important First Amendment case. That's what he specializes in."

"Really? Wow, you lucked out finding him. What's his name?"

"Tom Consolino, out of St. Louis."

Dalton said nothing, looked away for a bit then looked back at Randall. "That name sounds Italian, probably is Italian."

"Yeah, so?"

"Well, if he's Italian, he's probably Catholic."

"Yeah, so?"

"We don't like Catholics, remember? They're not Christian like we are. They're slaves to that monkey in Rome. They worship a hundred different saints, some of them actual criminals and degenerates. Mary, too, call her the Blessed Virgin."

"Well, this one seems all right. We didn't talk about religion at all. Maybe he doesn't go to church. Besides, he's doing us a huge favor."

"With a name like that you can bet your boots he grew up Catholic. And even if he's fallen away they still get married in the church, and have their kids baptized in the church. Look, these people come over as immigrants—no money, uneducated, willing to rob and steal to keep their huge families afloat. And God help the poor bastard who wanders into one of these neighborhoods. Talk about high crime areas. Standard of living set at the lowest bar. C'mon, Randall, can't you get a non-ethnic lawyer from some other reputable law firm?"

"No, I don't think so." He cocked his head toward the shooting stand. "I hear my round being called. Guess I'll get over there with my blunderbuss. Wish me luck."

A Few Days Later Randall got a letter, envelope addressed by hand, postmarked Fletcher, a pig-shit town over near Johnson Shut-ins. He opened it, a single sheet of white typing paper, folded in three. The anonymous author had scrawled: Hey You Racist Old Fart We Don't Need You at any More Meat Shoots.

—13—

At The Same Time, 50 miles away, Tom Consolino was drafting the complaint that would be served on the Missouri Highway Department. Because it was a constitutional issue, the denial of free speech, the case had federal standing and would be heard in U.S. District Court – Eastern District of Missouri, which was the federal courthouse in downtown St. Louis. The same venue where Dred Scott had been decided 135 years before. Well, same court, different courthouse which had since been rebuilt. For this case, Tom had to make a few strategic decisions right off. Like whether he wanted the case in equity to effect court-ordered relief, that is, get an injunction to stop the prohibition against his client. With a case in equity there is no jury. It's up to the court to fashion almost

No Big Thing

any remedy it sees fit; both parties could walk away unhappy. Or, he mulled, do I want to ask for damages on top of it, try the case before a jury? He had done other First Amendment cases, and had been awarded handsome judgments which nearly caused his clients to swoon. Here, it wasn't much of a dilemma. All he had to do was ask himself, Do I really want a jury to to decide the constitutional rights of a group that is, shall we say, less than popular?

The basis of the lawsuit was fairly simple. It is a First Amendment right to join the Adopt-A-Highway program. By opening the program to the public and selling it as a way to advertise good citizenship the State had created a public forum. The voluntary collection of litter was not the free speech, it was the ticket to the program. The free speech was the sign placed on a public thoroughfare holding up this or that certain group as good citizens, neighbors you might like to have. Randall Fortner and his confederates had been denied that for no valid reason.

It took him most of one afternoon to draft the complaint, checking case law in the office library every so often, returning to his cluttered desk in an office at the end of a long hallway. He had a good feeling about this one, sure that he was on solid ground in his allegations. It was as if the Founding Fathers had given him their blessing.

Tom Consolino then applied for a summons to accompany the complaint. The State, essentially a nameless faceless entity, may not be sued in federal court. Therefore the style of the case read *Randall Fortner et al v. Sheila Cowan in Her Official Capacity as Chief Financial and Administrative Officer of the Missouri Highways and Transportation Commission.* When everything was ready Tom called his process server and told him he was going to Jefferson City. The process server, a roughshod fellow in his 30s who could've passed for a hodcarrier, said, "But that's a hundred thirty miles each way."

Tom said, "I'll pay you mileage as well. How much do you charge?"

The server said, "I don't know... thirty cents a mile or thirty bucks an hour. Something like that."

"Figure half a day, four hours. One-twenty sound good?"

"One-fifty sounds better," said the process server.

And so the State was served, the case engaged. It made the papers again.

The press had fun with this new development, the Klan actually suing the State for their supposed right to beautify the highways. As if that would really happen. Nonetheless journalists and headline writers seemed to have stored up their bile for such an occasion. "White Trash Wants To Pick Up Trash" scorned the *Mound City Tattler*, itself a sleazy tabloid. "Just because there are no laws against hate-mongering doesn't mean it shouldn't be stopped dead in its tracks," opined a scathing editorial in the *Hillsboro Sceptre*. "Elijah Lovejoy should be turning over in his grave about now ..." snarled the editors of the mighty *St. Louis Post-Dispatch*. Elijah Lovejoy was a Presbyterian minister and newspaper editor who, in 1837, was murdered by a pro-slavery mob across the river in Alton, Illinois. Martyred for his abolitionist views and willingness to broadcast them. Tom Consolino became known as "the Klan's Counselor."

THE UNFOLDING SITUATION and attendant publicity had Pine Grove buzzing and also had the unexpected effect of polarizing certain patrons of the Grain Elevator & Mercantile. Surprising because the established attitude seemed to be that Pine Grove was the sort of place where people may not relate to the Klan, but they don't get worked up about a Klansman living among them. In truth, until this current brouhaha, Randall hadn't been viewed as anything but a helpful and affable merchant. But now the controversy surrounding him was forcing certain people to weigh scruples against practicality. For local farmers to take their corn or soybeans elsewhere would be a great inconvenience. Any farmer rankled by Randall's actions would have to be pretty lathered up to boycott the place.

No Big Thing

The regular customers, the ones who came to buy certain household needs—that was a different story. They could just drive into Acadia, spend their money in some other place that didn't pledge allegiance to the Confederate Battle Flag.

Eveline first noticed the drop in revenue around the beginning of the year. When she mentioned it to Randall along with her theory of why it might be happening, he shrugged it off, saying it was likely a seasonal thing. Truth was, Randall suspected there was some repercussion to the pending lawsuit. He wasn't naive about such things. In fact, he was fairly astute about anything that concerned his livelihood—at least when he didn't have those clouds in his mind—and he himself had noted the conspicuous absence of several regular customers. People he knew or suspected were outright liberals, people who casually mentioned something they'd heard on NPR or reminisced openly about demonstrating during the Vietnam War. Those folks weren't around any more. The Clinton supporters, well, they could go either way on the matter. Some of them as liberal as a 60s folk singer.

The story had legs and kept on going for longer than the regular three-paragraph news item, spreading outward to periodicals in neighboring states. Look what was happening in rural Missouri, the Klan rearing its ugly head. What next? The American Communist Party marching in the Macy's Parade?

—14—

One Morning in May, raining steadily, a car drove up, headlights cutting the gloom. A black Cadillac with a magnetized facsimile of the Confederate flag stuck to the rear door panel. Missouri plates. Randall knew exactly who it was and he grabbed an umbrella and went out. The driver rolled down his window and asked him to get in.

"Whyn't you come in the store?" said Randall, standing there, windshield wipers beating a tempo. "I got coffee on the hot plate."

The man wagged his jowly face. "Nah, the drive up, I'm all coffee'd out."

Randall walked around the Caddie, saw there was a passenger in the front so he got in the back, collapsing his umbrella and laying it on the floor. The interior smelled of stale cigar smoke and a fresh fart.

Jim Ed Burnett turned around and offered his hand. "Just move those robes aside. That's it. Nice to see you, Randall. It's been too long. This here's Corey Walton, heads up the Northern Arkansas chapter. We're on our way to the Annual Nathan Bedford Forrest whoop-de-do in Evansville, Indiana. Thought we'd take a small detour and come see how you're doing." Said it like he didn't give a damn how Randall was doing, but had some other thing in mind.

Corey Walton pivoted in his seat, regarded Randall. Didn't offer a shake, but gave a thin smile, void of goodwill. The face, framed by a flat top and small ears, was that of cadaver, pale and waxen. Judging by demeanor alone, the man was as severe as a lanced boil.

"So, Randall," said Jim Ed, "looks like you've been a busy boy. The papers full of your exploits."

Randall adjusted his six-foot-two frame to get more comfortable. "Well, yeah, I reckon, but it it's no big thing, just a legal action aimed at the State, hoping they'll finally see things my way. Our way."

"Yes sir," agreed Jim Ed, "I see what you're up to, and I want to have a word with you about it. You and me, we go way back. I was telling Corey on the way up what a wild man you used to be. Back in Cairo, the White Hats, me the deputized leader and you my lieutenant. And we knocked some heads in those days, didn't we? Had those hell-bent crazy niggers running for cover, wishin' they'd never started something. I remember we was in an alley over off Bluff Street, middle of the afternoon, as many of them as there were of us. And I recall seeing you tear into one of them bucks, one of the biggest, by god, and just take that boy down. You tore into him like

No Big Thing

he called your momma a cheap date. Heh, heh. You was wailing on him until his face looked like dog meat, and I had to pull you off or you woulda killed the son of a bitch. And we didn't need that, killing, just teach 'em a lesson they wouldn't forget. You remember that day?"

"Yeah, sure do," said Randall, shaking his head in amazement, "crazy times." In fact, the memory was hazy at best, a cloud cover obscuring it. But if Jim Ed said so.

"And the levees around the town on both the Mississippi side and the Ohio River side. It was a good place to burn crosses, remember?"

"That's right, we did that at night."

"Well, it's got to be at night, otherwise you lose the dramatic effect. Do you remember what you told me one evening as we were standing on that levee? You swore it as an oath."

"No, Jim Ed, can't say as I do."

"You said, and I quote: 'There is no finer calling than to be a Grand Knight of the Ku Klux Klan. We are God's chosen, far superior to the mud races, and I'll die for the right to profess that.'" Jim Ed got a bit misty, wiped at the corner of his eye. "Gotta tell you, man, that about had me in tears."

"We said a lot of things in those days," offered Randall. "You were always talking revolution, how we were going to rise up against the Zionists, start our own government."

"Yeah, and too bad that didn't ever happen," scowled Corey Walton. "Now the highest positions in business and government are run by Jews and Jew-lovers."

"But back to you," said Jim Ed. "The Randall Fortner I once knew had a firm idea that our organization has a chain of command. We are a para-military outfit and as such we definitely have a chain of command. Do you agree?"

"Sure, Jim Ed."

"Well then, why the hell are you acting on your own in this matter? What made you think you could initiate this clean-up-the highway thing without first consulting me, your recognized leader?"

Before Randall could answer, not that he had any good answer to give, Corey Walton interjected. "Jim Ed, hope you don't mind me sayin', but sometimes I think you're a little too much on the mild-mannered side. Here, let me give it a go." He turned around all the way, leaned into the back seat, a foot from Randall's astonished face, and boomed, "JUST WHO THE HELL DO YOU THINK YOU ARE, STARTING THIS ON YOUR OWN!"

The force of it damn near blew Randall's hair back.

Suddenly Randall felt confined. He went for the door handle.

"Where you goin', brother?" said Jim Ed.

Randall didn't answer, just climbed out of the Caddie.

Corey Walton got out, too. Jim Ed decided that he'd join them as well. They all three stood on the side of the Cadillac, engine running, windshield wipers swiping, Randall edging away from Corey Walton, putting Jim Ed Between them. Randall had nearly forgotten what a shrimp Jim Ed was, the top of his slicked-back hair about even with the roof of the Caddie.

"Well, here we are standing in the rain like a bunch of damn fools," offered Jim Ed.

"He can't talk to me like that," said Randall.

"Well, it's true, Corey does get a bit worked up when he senses insubordination. And that's what this is. You should've come to me first. You know that. And here I've been going around trying to explain the situation without having all the facts and information at hand. Makes me look kinda stupid, and I hate looking stupid. Jeez, man, you put me in a bind."

Randall held Jim Ed's accusative stare; he wasn't about to apologize.

"Just don't do it again," added Jim Ed.

"And in the meanwhile you in disgrace," spouted Corey Walton, glaring. "For a period of one year, you hear?"

No Big Thing

"Okay," said Jim Ed, palms out, "now that bygones are bygones and we're all getting drenched, I will say something positive. And that is, this thing that you did? It sure as hell got us some publicity, and good or bad it don't matter because any publicity is good for the organization. It tells people we're still here, gets them thinking about us. Hell, we've even had a few new members because of it."

Here, and to Corey Walton's dismay, Jim Ed put his arm around Randall's shoulder, walking him aside for a bit of privacy. It was a reach—literally—for Jim Ed to buddy up to Randall; Mutt and Jeff, they were. Jim Ed wiped the raindrops from his face, gave a wolfish smile, said with a murmur, "So, brother, things are looking up. You just keep up the public relations work and keep on badgerin' the State of Missoura to let us have our sign and you keep me abreast of the developments, hear?"

"Sure thing, Jim Ed."

"Oh," lowering his voice even more, "and you ain't in no disgrace period. That's just Corey talking."

"I don't think I even know how to be in disgrace," Randall said. "Can't very well kick myself in the rear, can I?" Jim Ed chuckled, and walked off.

He watched the Caddie's rear lights pull away through the puddles in the gravel parking lot, and two disparate thoughts came to him practically at once: The first, *did I really do those things?* The second, *dang I left my umbrella in the car.*

FEBRUARY, 1994

THE CONVEYOR BELT OF JUSTICE moves slowly, but somehow federal cases move along a mite faster than those in state courts. The State had been served and the Assistant Attorney General filed her response to the court: The State denies any discrimination and they would say as much in court if need be. The attorney for the state highway department came from the Office of General Counsel under the governor himself. His name was Peter Van Vliet and right from the start he relished the assignment: Put a bunch of backwoods yahoos back in their place, under the carpet with the rest of the cockroaches.

Peter Van Vliet worked closely with Sheila Cowan. The first thing they decided was to tighten the existing guidelines and regulations for the Adopt-A-Highway program. They gave the administrator of the program, Sheila herself, the power to deny any applicant, either a person or an organization, who had a "history of discrimination" or had "a history of violence."

"Can we do this?" asked Sheila, skeptically. "Grandfather in these guidelines? I mean, they didn't exist when the lawsuit was filed. We're just making it up as we go."

"We can do whatever we want," said Peter Van Vliet with an air of hauteur. "Let them contest it if they want. We'll put it to the judge." He gave Sheila a conspiratorial wink which made her a bit moist in the panties, for by now she was infatuated with this handsome, virile lawyer with a wedding ring on his finger. Off and on, over the course of several months, they worked together in her office, scheming, plotting, trying out various lines of defense. In the middle of one brainstorming session, they decided that they might think this through more clearly in the lounge of the Holiday Inn over on Bolivar Street with a probable adjournment to some beckoning suite above. They would see to it that opposing counsel didn't stand a chance.

No Big Thing

On a Cold, blustery mid-winter's day, Tom Consolino drove to Jefferson City to take the deposition of Sheila Cowan in the offices of the highway department. A bland institutional room was reserved, pitchers of water and cups set on the long conference table, swivel chairs in their places, the blinds drawn to deter distraction. The court reporter arrived with her dictation machine, followed by those to be deposed. No plaintiffs needed to attend. Opposing counsel, Peter Van Vliet, was there for moral support; he was not expected nor allowed to contribute any responses to Consolino's questions. At precisely ten o' clock, the proceedings began.

After Consolino had gone through the preliminaries with Sheila Cowan, the stating of full name, job title, how long she had been in this position, the scope of her responsibilities, etc, he got down to business.

Looking her straight in the eye from across the table, "Ms. Cowan, please tell us what does 'history of discrimination' mean? And how far back does this go?"

Sheila explained as best as she could what the term meant and, as far as how far back it went: "all the way."

Tom Consolino nodded. "I see. Well, the Catholic church has a history of discrimination. On the basis of gender they won't allow women as priests. And the Boy Scouts of America, the number one adopter of highways in your program, says 'No Girls Allowed'. You'll have to admit that combined membership between these two bodies is vast, and that's a whole lot of people who would not qualify to participate in the Adopt-A-Highway program based on your revised guidelines."

"No, not that kind of discrimination," insisted Sheila. "You know very well what sort of discrimination we're talking about here. The kind that's based on race, one group victimizing another group because of the color of their skin. We want to condemn that by refusing to let such hate-based groups into the program. It's that simple."

The lawyer for the plaintiff gave her a quizzical look. "First off, race is not a scientific term. There's no set criteria for what constitutes this race or that race. It's a cultural term. But that's somewhat moot to this proceeding. The more germane question is who gets to define what makes a hate group? It sounds like you and the state highway department have decided to be the arbiters of such a designation."

Sheila looked to Peter Van Vliet seated beside her. He leaned over and cupped a hand over her ear, mouthing something inaudible. She straightened herself and said, "All you need to do is read any objective account of the actions of the Ku Klux Klan and you'll come to the conclusion that they are a hate-based group with a history of discrimination and even violence against African-Americans, Catholics, Jews, and various other groups they deem objectionable."

"Um hm, yes, your point is well-taken. Now, going back to my previous examples of the Catholic church and the Boy Scouts and the nature of their well-known discriminatory practices. I contend that discrimination on the basis of race, for lack of a better term, and discrimination on the basis of gender are equally egregious. Two candies in the same wrapper."

Silence for a few moments. "Is that a question or a comment, sir?" asked Peter Van Vliet.

Tom Consolino smiled at his own foible. He tended to wax philosophical. "A comment, I suppose." He picked up a copy of the departmental regulations and pointed to the section detailing the Adopt-A-Highway qualifications for participation, which he had highlighted. "These regulations are so broad they could exclude anyone who has served in the military, the National Football League and the National Hockey League. I intend to show that Ms. Cowan as head of the highway department is bent on using these dubious regulations to exclude *only* my clients. So, there's my question: What would you say to that?"

Sheila Cowan was quick to reply. "We deny that the regulations are broad, they are specific enough for our purposes. And to the accusation that we are singling out your clients, despicable as they

No Big Thing

are, it's just the way it came down. It's the KKK today, and it may be some other hate group tomorrow."

"But my clients are the first group you've ever turned down, correct?"

"That's right," said Sheila.

"Because they don't meet the qualifications in these regulations that have been revised since their initial application, yes?"

"That's right," said Sheila.

He heard the smugness in her voice and it irked him. "Okay, let's move on. The regulations say any applicant to the program whose membership demonstrates or has demonstrated 'a history of violence' will be denied participation. Well, back to the Catholic church, of which I am a member, one of millions worldwide. I ask, have you ever heard of The Inquisition?"

Sheila shifted in her seat, looked to Peter Van Vliet who offered no counsel. "Um, no, I think that was before my time."

The deposition lasted an hour and ten minutes with one bathroom break. Tom Consolino thought it went pretty well. He had her squirming more than a few times. After the stenographer had left and the legal pads were put away and just before he was about to leave the room, Sheila Cowan cleared her throat. It was an attention-getting clearing of the throat and Tom thought maybe she wanted to say goodbye.

"Now that we're off the record," she said, flatly, "I'd like you to know that it will be a cold day in hell before my department will ever permit a bunch of bedsheet-wearing hooligans to clean up our highways." Then, smiling quite insincerely, "Thank you for coming."

—16—

THERE WERE FEWER than a half dozen black families in Pine Grove and they all came to the Grain Elevator & Mercantile for sundry supplies. And they were made to feel welcome—well, at least they were not made to feel *unwelcome*. But now that it was known that the proprietor of this establishment was a member of the feared and hated Ku Klux Klan, some of them stopped coming. The ones who still did business there did so with trepidation as if Randall or Eveline or Junior Bannister, the part-time clerk, would snatch them from behind, truss them up and take them to the nearest tall tree.

They didn't rightly understand. Randall Fortner had seemed like such a nice man. Why would he want to advertise himself as being in cahoots with this Klan society? Like to set race relations in Pine Grove and Jefferson County back about 50 years. Just to bring up the name of this white man's club, a secret society with scary intentions, to hear it on the street, see it in print, was enough to stir emotions and they were emotions better left unstirred.

There was one, a woman in her early 20s, who had never come around and was now coming around. Randall and Eveline took notice right away, for she was very talkative and quite inquisitive, asking all sorts of questions. Not just about the products on the shelves but about the weather, where were the good fishing holes, who was the best carpenter in town. How did the corn crop this last year compare to other years? Had they seen The Tonight Show lately, and wasn't Jay Leno just the funniest? And so on. Despite her utilitarian attire and common appearance, they could tell she was educated by her vocabulary and the considered manner in which she expressed herself.

Eveline took to her more than Randall did, he not being one for frivolous conversation. Agriculture was not a frivolous topic. He could chat all day about crops, for instance. The effectiveness of so-called experimental seeds, the prudence of fall plowing, and more, much more. This young woman was willing to talk farming or at

No Big Thing

least listen, but Randall felt discussing these things with someone who was not a real farmer was just wasting his breath. The woman, for her part, seemed to know just when she was making a pest of herself and would leave. But she would always be back, rolling up in her beat up Toyota Corolla, spending maybe a few bucks per visit, buying mostly the homemade beef or venison jerky, which was slightly moist, the way she liked it.

She didn't divulge much about herself. Her name, Tyra Singletary, told Randall and Eveline a certain amount about her kinfolk. The Singletarys were an established family with a place out on Old Slave Road between Pine Grove and Enterprise. Jim Singletary, most likely her dad, was in the store often enough, for he ran soybeans on 30 acres out there. The family, four or five generations, had been there since the Civil War. First as slaves under a man named Mullins, then for several decades as indentured servants, then as sharecroppers, and finally, some 40 years ago, as land owners. The family also had a herd of White Faced cows, which had garnered many a prize in the livestock pens at the Jefferson County Fair over the years. Randall once mentioned to Eveline that the Singletarys were a prime example of what coloreds could make of themselves if they put their minds to it and their backs in it.

So now they had this friendly and somewhat nosy black woman frequenting their store, a fairly big woman clomping around in hiking boots, wearing rolled-up Levis and pullover sweatshirts with the Mizzou Tiger or the Southeast Missouri Redhawk emblazoned on them. Hair in cornrows, sometimes covered by a Boonie hat, eyes expressive and intelligent. She was broad-shouldered, wide-bottomed, with a husky voice and a ready laugh. She looked as though she could put in a days' work out in the fields.

But manual labor wasn't her thing. She was academically-minded, having recently graduated from Mizzou with a degree in sociology and a minor in psychology. Her ambition was to be a policy-maker some day, either at the state level or in Washington D.C. Perhaps an adviser to a president. She intended to to obtain a graduate degree in either history or sociology and then get her doctorate in public policy. She had six applications out right now for the fall semester, all to top drawer universities, and she felt confident that she would get in one of them. And she was asking for a scholarship. Why not? She had several things going for her: A 3.8 grade point average from Mizzou; an excellent record of extracurricular activities including two years on the student newspaper, *The Maneater*; a household at or near poverty level; and, her ace-in-the-hole, she was African-American. A minority. A female minority. *Look out, Duke, here I come!*

While waiting for the acceptance letters she knew would come, Tyra Singletary needed something to do, a stimulating diversion. Of course she'd heard about Randall's bid and all it entailed; it had the other black families all in a dither. But Tyra was not appalled at the idea of a white supremacist doing business only a few miles away, she was quite intrigued. She found herself quite curious about Randall Fortner and others at the grain elevator, thought it might be interesting to start hanging out, see what she could pick up. What could happen, she wondered. They'd either tell you to leave or they'd put up with you and inadvertently let you glean bits and pieces of intelligence regarding their attitudes, their outlook on life. Could be a gold mine, in the sociological sense. Tyra began to see the Fortners in a cultural anthropology light, much the same way as Margaret Mead likely viewed the primitive tribes that she encountered. Tyra would study these racists assiduously, keep notes on the sly, form opinions, contrive theories, and maybe some day they would be a topic of her dissertation.

Her plan was to get them used to her by making small talk on mundane topics. Then when the time was right, get to the bone of the matter. The pithy issues of race.

The opportunity came one Thursday afternoon. Just Tyra and Randall in the store. Randall unpacking a box of mole traps, and Tyra, nearby, had the *Post-Dispatch* spread out on the counter.

"Amazing," she remarked loudly enough, "it says here that

No Big Thing

they're considering removing the Confederate flag from the State House in Little Rock, where it's flown for a hundred and nine years. Some state senator has submitted a bill, but it's likely to get killed on the floor. The governor himself sides with the senator, agrees that it's time. This is what he says: 'I know there's a lot of feelings on both sides as it relates to the flag, but if we ever hope to heal as one people and as citizens of one state then, yes, I think the flag should come down.' Wow, that's a bold move, don't you think?"

Randall had stopped unpacking and was listening intently, although looking at the floor. He walked over to where she stood. "Let me see that." She moved aside and he read the article for himself.

Finished, he shook his head dismally, said, "It's a sad day for Arkansas when something like that is seriously considered. Those folks whose ancestors fought for the Confederacy got as much right to that flag as they do the Stars and Stripes. To even talk about removing it is a slap in the face to the memories of all the men who died fighting for what they believed in."

Was he talking to himself or to her?

She ventured a reply. "I suppose that what they believed in is and has been offensive to black people all these years and now, finally, they're getting around to doing something about it."

Randall, standing beside her, now addressed her directly. "If they put it to a vote by the people, that flag would be up for another hundred years. It's not a symbol of oppression, as some say. It represents our heritage, a reminder of a way of life that's been lost. Almost everyone understands that."

She fired back, "But you have to admit that if you were a black person, seeing that flag flown in a public place, on government property even, would make you cringe. You'd start believing that the lawmakers didn't have your interests at heart, only the interests of whites who relate to that flag. You'd probably think: What next? A new round of Jim Crow laws?"

Randall gave a snort of indignation. "That's being sensational.

That senator who's trying to instigate this … this *thing* is probably black. He's just looking to make a name for himself, and this is an easy way to do it. Some things you don't mess with. What this amounts to, if it were to happen, is erasing history. That's right, it would be the same as pulling down the World War One monument over in Acadia. That war never happened. Or gathering up all the history books and blacking out every mention of the Confederacy. Can you see that happening? No, you cannot. The whole notion is ridiculous."

He was about to walk off when she said, "There are those who would say that people who insist on keeping that flag flying, despite the ugly feelings it may prompt in people of color—they would say that those people are obstructionist, even racist." Choosing her words carefully.

He looked at her, a frown spreading across his visage. "Or just set in their ways. You know, I get tired of saying I'm not a racist." Pausing here, pulling up a thought.

"Are you a black person?"

"That's obvious."

"Are you a proud black person?"

"I am."

"Would you be ashamed to say that?"

"I do say it any chance I get."

"Well then, it shouldn't come as any surprise that I feel the same way."

"Okay," she retorted, "I get your point. You're a proud white man with loads of sentimental attachment to that flag, but like it or not times are changing and that flag will come down. It may not be this year or next year, but it will come down because that's the way society is heading."

She was thinking she may have gone too far.

He came back without hesitation. "Then society is pretty thin-skinned, it needs to get over itself!"

No Big Thing

She wagged her head. "Ain't gonna happen, Mr. Fortner."

"That politically correct thing you hear about, huh?"

She swallowed. "That's right, your flag will end up being a casualty of that. The deciders of what is correct and acceptable are not numerous but they are in high positions. They see something that rubs on their liberal sensibilities, something they deem morally offensive—and your Confederate flag is a perfect example—they agitate and agitate until that thing is gone. From the public sector anyway."

Shaking his head from side to side, slow about it, he started to say something, then went to staring off. Tyra had sense enough to let him be. After a bit, he said, "What a pickle. I don't want to believe it, but deep inside I know it's true. You can't push back the tide. But I hope you see that there's something very wrong here. Like I said, you put it to a vote, that flag remains. I *know* Arkansans, their heroes are the heroes of the Confederacy, and the majority of them respect that flag, want it there. Shoot, that isn't racist, not one bit, that's the people talking. What's wrong with that?"

Tyra enjoyed the role of instigator, although she was not malicious. She felt like her work was done here so she left the question hanging. She folded the newspaper and put it back in the rack. She took a leather wallet from from her back pocket, said, "I'll take some of that venison jerky, you don't mind."

He walked over to the big glass jar on the counter, opened it, took out a couple pieces, started to wrap them in wax paper.

"Oh, no need to wrap it," she said. "I'll just eat it now."

He handed it to her and she tendered the money. Their eyes made contact and they smiled ever so slightly, a mutual feeling that they had gotten to know one another.

LATER ON he and Eveline were having supper, the two of them at the kitchen table, sun going down, the days' work over. Eveline said that her visit with the podiatrist went all right; he measured her feet for custom orthotics. He also suggested occasional foot rubs for the pain and discomfort.

"Foot rubs are a luxury," she commented, "cost a pretty penny, too. I guess you don't know anyone who could soothe a woman's feet, do you?"

Randall, cutting into a medium rare sirloin, looked up. "You wash 'em, I'll rub 'em. After supper."

"After supper, of course. Thanks. How was your day?"

"I had a conversation with that black girl who comes in almost every day now. We spoke of race and the Confederate flag. Seems there's a movement afoot to take it down from the Arkansas state capitol where it's flown for a century. We got into a discussion about that and it left me kind of blue."

"I hope she didn't try and bait you with that. That's a fierce topic for you and she to get into. She didn't needle you, did she?"

"You know, she never brought up the lawsuit with the State, even though she must know. She just made me see things a different way. Her perspective, I suppose. That, and the direction that society is heading and how it's going to overtake me and swallow me up before long." He paused, shrugged resignedly. "I feel like an old horse being put to pasture. I may as well go out to the barn and move in."

She reached over and placed her hand on his arm. "Old horse? Phooey! You show me a draft horse that can put in the amount of work that you do every day. No sir, you've got a lot of kick left in you. Don't let no one tell you any different."

They went back to eating. Then, she murmured, "Unsightly."

"What?"

"The woman is unsightly. That face could scare a haint."

"Oh ... maybe. Yeah, but that's neither here nor there."

She patted his arm, somewhat puzzled by that response.

No Big Thing

—17—

Birch Let Bowser Ride up front with him on the trip to Beaumont. The dog liked to stick his big head out the window and let his tongue flap in the wind. It was good that the day was warm enough to have the window open. March in Missouri was a temperamental month; you'd need a down jacket, stocking cap, and gloves one week and by the next you'd be wearing shorts and a T-shirt. You could get sunburned in March, you didn't take care. Birch wondered if Bowser's thick pink tongue could get sunburned.

They were on the way to see Patricia, Birch's mom, who lived some 40 miles southwest of Pine Grove. Patricia had left Pine Grove years earlier, and, after a long spell of Gypsy wandering, had landed in Beaumont, choosing a life of self-exile from her oh-so provincial family, Randall, in particular, whom she considered a blight on the human race. And while she had harbored a grudge against her father for the longest, she didn't dislike him enough to deny her only child the Fortner name. She sure wasn't going to give him the surname of that charming asshole who knocked her up way back when, then moved on. McGonigle. Edward James McGonigle, since dead from a rollover bulldozer mishap. Patricia lived alone and made her living as a seamstress with a small shop in the town. She was pleasant in disposition, well-liked by many, but had made it clear she wasn't in the market for "a beau." In her earlier life, she had gone by Trish. Here she was Patty.

Today was her birthday and Birch had called to be sure she'd be around. He had stopped at a Walgreen's on the way and bought a card and some presents that he hoped weren't too trifling. Some eau de cologne, chocolate-covered cherries, and a magazine, *Cosmopolitan*. He was tempted to get *Sports Illustrated*, thinking they both might read that. Then, the card: humorous or serious? He thought on this a while, narrowing it down to three, two of which were serious. He knew she would like whatever he presented, but, really, what was her true nature. And even more relevant, what was the nature of their relationship? He settled on one with flowers on the front that began, "Because You Are So Special To Me ..."

He wished there was a dad that he could visit. All he had was a picture he'd dug out of the trash after mom threw it away. Big open face, long hair, smiling like a jack-o-lantern. How different his life would've been had his mom and dad stayed together. Ed, his name, was no longer among the living, probably never even got to be called "Dad" by anyone. Conversely, Birch never had the privilege of calling anyone dad, and he felt incomplete because of it. Life was filled with loose ends and dead ends, he mused, one big ball of tangled string.

Down near Doe Run he crossed the Big River and saw the sign: YOU ARE NOW ENTERING ST. FRANCOIS COUNTY. He made the turn on a state highway and headed toward a piedmont off in the distance. Here and there roadkill dotted the road. Mostly raccoon, but also squirrel and possum and the occasional deer. In a few months there would be box turtles. It was a crying shame, roadkill. Here's this animal, minding its own business, trying to get from one place to another. It has the gall to step out on this asphalt ribbon and along comes this rolling behemoth, this monster, and suddenly its life is over. How's that for having a bad day? There was no point to it. Mindless carnage. Kill a box turtle because you didn't feel like swerving a little? They're like the nicest creatures on this earth, never did anyone wrong. Allow yourself time to react. For that very reason he rarely went over the limit. No hurry, there's lots worse names to get called besides slowpoke.

He could pick up KSHE way out here and he heard the beginning of "Copperhead Road," the bagpipes droning, and he turned it up. It was his favorite song, talking of "running moonshine" and getting over on the law, just the sort of recklessness that had got him into so much trouble during his rooster years. He particularly liked that part where the character who's telling the story, guy named John Lee Pettimore, says, "I volunteered for the army on my birthday / They draft the white trash first, 'round here anyway." Steve Earle singing with conviction, like it actually happened to him.

No Big Thing

Birch related, except there wasn't any draft when he joined up. He just had to git gone and the army was his ticket.

Then he rolled into the town of Clover Dell, and waited impatiently at the world's longest traffic signal. Looking at his watch, about fifteen more minutes.

In Beaumont, he pulled up on the storefront that read BUSY BEE SEWING & ALTERATIONS. He told Bowser to stay in the cab then went in. Patricia was sitting on the other side of the front counter, at her sewing machine, stitching what looked to be a bridal gown. There was another woman at another sewing machine further back in the shop. Patricia smiled broadly, arose from her chair, came around the counter and gave him a mighty and prolonged hug. Then, a playful shove back. "Well, look at you! Walking into my shop just like anything, like a movie star come home. And I thought you were done growing."

"Must be the good country living," he winked. "So how the heck you been?"

They decided to get Bowser and take a stroll, catch up along the way. She called to the woman in the back, "Thalia, I'll be out for a bit, be a sweetie and mind the shop. Thanks, hon."

Looking up from her sewing, waving bye, "Sure thing, Patty."

He told her about the community college, how it was a good experience, learning in an organized setting, meeting new people, being challenged mentally, enjoying some of the assignments. Barring any complications, he'd get his associate's degree in a few months.

"What then?" she wondered.

"Well, I don't know, really. Maybe go on to a four-year college, but that would depend on my finances. I could probably get a student loan. Or just stay put, maybe work for Grampa. That wouldn't be so bad."

She scrunched up her face at the mention of Grampa. "Nah, working in some musty old grain elevator isn't for you. You're meant for bigger things. What do you want to do? When you grow up, I mean." Chuckling lightly.

"That's just it. I don't rightly know. I like to write. I brought a story for you to read, an assignment from English Comp: 'My Life-Changing Experience.' I was thinking of maybe getting on with a newspaper."

Patricia stopped in her tracks. "Why, Birch, that is just the best idea I've ever heard! You'd make a great journalist, so thoughtful and observant. Always interested in what's going on around you. How's your punctuation? You've got to have good punctuation, you know."

"My punctuation needs work, that's for sure. I still can't figure out that semi-colon." Just then Bowser spotted a cat beneath a car and began to worry it. Birch had to grab him by the collar and pull him away. He'd just gotten the dog under control when a skateboarder came rickety-rack down the street and took a turn on the middling steep Rayburn Way, Bowser bounding after him.

"Shoulda brought a leash," said Patricia.

"Did you see his T? Long-sleeved T with writing on the back?"

"Not really, I was looking at your crazy animal."

"It said Skate Don't Hate, the 'skate' spelled with an S and the number eight. That's Cassie's creation, she designed it. He must've bought that at her shop. Small world."

"That's cool she can do that. How're you two doing?"

Now turning down Rayburn themselves, looking to retrieve Bowser. "Doing all right, I reckon. Now that I'm in school I see her less often, once-twice a week. A lot of times we'll just drive around in my truck. Sounds dumb, but we both like that."

"Sometimes ordinary things are the most enjoyable," she said, agreeably. "But the spark's still there? I know you guys been going out a long time."

"Yeah, the spark's there, but it's just, uh … different. Three years I'm gone, three years of her going off in her own direction, following this band, the Grateful Dead, getting all hippie-dippy while I'm on

No Big Thing

the other side of the world watching out for SCUD missiles. I don't begrudge her that experience, as messed up as it seems to me, but it's hard not to notice that we're marching to different drummers."

"Shuffling along is more like it. You're both young, you'll flow back together if that's what you both want. Don't try to force it, though. You may think that because you two have this history, it's always gonna be status quo. Same old feelings, same old desires, same old likes and dislikes. Neil Young has a line in one of his songs that I really like: 'I can't believe how love lasts a while, seems like forever in the first place.' If you feel she's pulling away spiritually, psychologically, then you've got to give her that. Then stand back and see what happens."

"Or just remind her that I'm the true love of her life and she can't live without me. Now where the heck is Bowser?"

They had come to a cross street and no sign nor sound of the dog. "Maybe he doubled back through the yards and is looking for us back up where we were." They about-faced and headed back.

Walking along, Birch reached out and squeezed her shoulder affectionately. "Happy birthday, Mom."

"Why, thank you! It was nice of you to come. You should come more often, bring Cassie if you like. At least she probably wouldn't run off like Bowser."

They walked on a bit more when Birch said, "You think you and Grampa will ever flow back together? Your words just now. I mean, it's kinda weird, you never being around during family gatherings."

"Well, that's a long story with a short answer: Nope, don't see that happening."

"You can't ever patch things up?"

"That wound is still open, and it's not going to heal in my lifetime."

"What did he do that was so bad?"

"You really want to discuss this? I'd rather not."

"Okay, I'll tell you what I think it's about. He clamped down on your love life because you happened to pick a Mexican as your bed warmer. You told him to buzz off, you were an adult and it was none of his business. He got all stern and said, 'If you can't abide by my rules, then you can't live under my roof.' So you packed up your stuff and out the door you went, never to return. I guess he got that message: Don't mess with Trish."

She laughed good-naturedly, said, "That's the very abbreviated version, and the only thing you got right was me packing up my stuff. First off, Eduardo wasn't Mexican, he was Brazilian. Not that it mattered to Randall because all he needed to judge a person was the color of their skin and seeing his daughter with a dark-complected guy—oh my god! The one time Eduardo showed up at the house, he brought me home from a dance, Randall just blew his stack, went into this tirade about how blacks and minorities were bringing down the standard of living for decent white folks. Did this in front of me and Eduardo as if he was imparting some great revelation! Did this like we cared about his bigot opinions. And it was ironic because Eduardo came from a very wealthy family, sugar cane growers outside of Sao Paulo, and he was getting his engineering degree at SEMO. So, actually, Eduardo should've been the one to look down on Randall, this arrogant bumpkin, consider *him* garbage. But he wasn't like that. He was intelligent and witty and considerate and I never saw him again after that day."

"You could've been living on a sugar cane plantation, sitting on a veranda, overlooking the fields, servants bringing you cocktails that I never heard of."

"Cachaça, it's the national drink of Brazil, and Eduardo's family grows the cane from which the drink is made. He gave me a bottle, had quite a kick. And you're wrong about Randall supposedly giving me an ultimatum. He didn't need to, I wanted to leave, *had* to leave. That wasn't the only crap that he pulled. He must've been drinking that day, because normally he wasn't that confrontational. Normally he just made all these insinuations about inferior races and majority equality and how things were in the good old days when white men ruled the roost. It would come up routinely in everyday conversa-

No Big Thing

tion—mean, ignorant pronouncements. It was like he's reciting the Bible according to Adolf Hitler. Who needs that?"

"He's not like that so much anymore."

"Do tell."

"He's definitely on the stump about white rights, but he's not pushing it down anyone's throat. He must've mellowed since you were living there. And some of what he says isn't just a bunch of warped ideas. Whites *are* being discriminated against. There's quotas in the workplace and in university admissions, you can only allow so many whites. No matter how qualified they may be, once they've met their quota, it's minorities who get the job or get in the school. That's not fair."

"The pendulum's swinging back the other way. It'll even itself out. But Randall reformed? You can't tell me he's no longer a card carrying member of the infamous White Sheet Society."

Apparently she didn't know about the squabble with the state highway department. "I guess he's still in the Klan, but I've never seen him put on a robe and head out to a cross-burning. Never heard him say the word 'nigger,' never known him to go out of his way to intimidate someone, some minority."

She laughed again. "But then we don't have many minorities in Pine Grove. No, he's still the same old codger, never stop believing that the white race is God's gift."

"Okay, this is what I get: He strongly believes in equal rights for white people, you're right about that. He sees the Klan as a channel for that, but he also sees it as a fraternal sort of organization like the Shriners, who, by the way, wear costumes just as silly as the Klan's. 'Hey, anybody seen my fez? I left it right here next to my twenty pound belt buckle.'"

Patricia cracked a smile. "So," continued Birch, "to Randall the draw is being a part of something with a bunch of other like-minded people. Birds of a feather. Only I don't think he's even active in the group. That was all in the past, and he's just coasting on what has been. He's also very much about preserving Southern culture and heritage. He's got this museum in back of the store—awesome, you really should see it—with all sorts of cool stuff like Civil War rifles and memorabilia, pioneer stuff, arrowheads galore, old books and documents. People show up and just give him stuff. I admire him for putting that together."

Patricia let that settle a moment, then, "Where did that dog go?"

"Probably back at the car by now. I'm not worried. The other thing is he's beginning to slip. Upstairs, I mean. I've been back a little over two years now and I've seen it coming on little by little. The signs are there for dementia or senility or Alzheimer's, one of those. I don't know how to tell them apart, maybe it's some of each. But it's sad, he'll start a sentence then stop in the middle of it, kind of drift off. He'll make coffee and then forget to drink it. He'll stand by a window staring out, and when you ask him what he's looking at he'll say 'Nothing' or 'I don't know.'"

"Careful now, that's me you're talking about," laughing at her jest. "C'mon, Randall's sharp as a tack, always has been. Misguided, yes. Blinded by idiotic rhetoric, yes. But senile? I doubt it very much, can't even imagine it."

"How about this: He thinks Lance is around, wonders why he didn't make it to dinner. You tell me that isn't half a bubble off."

"Yeah, that's a bit worrisome, I'll admit. I'll also admit that the very mention of my asshole uncle just sends me into orbit. Getting so drunk you drive the wrong way on the interstate and kill a car full of people, young people with their lives ahead of them. It just makes me sick to think about it, and I hope he rots in prison. Please don't ever mention his name again."

"That's fine, he's bad news in my book, too. But the thing I'm trying to work up here, is won't you think about coming around again? What if Grampa has some mental problem that causes him to suddenly go down fast? Then it'd be too late. You could try to make amends. We'd all support you. It could work if you want it to. Aren't

No Big Thing

you lonely just a bit way out here, away from all that you knew? You put yourself away out here. It doesn't have to be that way."

They turned a corner back onto the main drag. Her reply was taking too long. "Well?" he said.

Stepping briskly, "You know, Deadheads are a funny bunch, walk around in a haze of pot smoke, minds off on a cloud, believe in and practice free love. I used to know a Deadhead. He gave away everything he owned, bought a ticket for India to live in an ashram with some famous Yogi."

"Yogi Bear?"

"Yeah, that's him."

"No changing the subject, mom. What do you say?"

She halted, Birch too. They looked at one another. She shook her head very slightly in the negative, kind of a shudder. "I can't, son. To me, going back would be the same as walking head-on into a wall, not something beneficial or even practical. Maybe I'm just too proud to try to forgive-and-forget. I just don't have it in me. And I'm not unhappy here, so don't think that."

They commenced to walking again. Birch said, "Well then, that's that."

"I'm only an hour away. You come see me often as you like. We can go fishing for rainbow trout. We'll go to the Offsets, jump off the cliffs. C'mon, you used to love that place."

The Offsets was an old quarry in Fredericktown that had become a glorified swimming hole. He chuckled gleefully. "I used to think that was heaven. Literally. Hot day, cool water, cliffs all around. Swim, float, whatever, lay back and watch clouds go by. No finer place to be."

"We can relive it," she said. "Why not?"

He nudged her with his elbow. "Just like you could put aside your stupid pride and drop by the house for an afternoon visit," he said.

—18—

BOWSER WAS THERE, at the pickup, sprawled on the pavement
near the driver's side door, panting while licking a swatch of torn
denim like it was the treat of all treats. They said their goodbyes,
hugged once more, and Birch got in, the hound behind him. Patricia
watched them until they turned the corner and even then continued
watching until the deep rumbling sound of Birch's faulty muffler
faded. She went back in her sewing shop, said hello to Thalia, placed
the Walgreen's bag with the birthday presents and his essay in a
nook beneath the front counter and went back to work. At 2:30 she
took her customary break at a small table in the rear of the shop.
Taking a two litre bottle of Merlot from the fridge, she poured herself a goblet full and sat down to read. The composition was typewritten and double-spaced and had many corrections evidenced by
touches of White-Out and typed-over changes. She found herself
intrigued by the title and went on to devour the piece.

English Composition 202

Mr. Constantine

March 20, 1994

Assignment: Write an essay 4,000 words or less on a life changing
experience

MY LIFE CHANGING EXPERIENCE by Birch Fortner, Specialist 4th
Class US Army

I knew we were in for it when President George H.W. Bush told
reporters at the White House Press Briefing "This will not stand,
this aggression against Kuwait." It was August 5, 1990, and the
Iraqi Army had just invaded their neighbor country Kuwait. I was
a soldier stationed in Ft. Hood, Texas, not long out of Advanced
Individual Training, otherwise known as AIT, which is a ten week

No Big Thing

school where you learn your military specialty. Mine was infantry, a regular soldier. There were thousands of soldiers currently stationed in Ft. Hood, and I'll bet that very few of them had ever heard of Kuwait and now all of a sudden we were going there. We hadn't gotten our orders yet, true, but we knew what was in store. Bush was saying in no uncertain terms "You can't get away with this" and what is an infantry unit in the US Army if not ready and willing to go fight a war wherever the president says so?

Sure enough the orders came. It took five months because the US had to round up as many allies as it could to show the Iraqis we really meant business and so it wouldn't just be us over there and the rest of the world wouldn't see us as the one big bully on the playground. As it turned out the United Nations disapproved of Saddam Hussein's actions too, and there were lots of countries joining in the effort to stop the aggression but most of them were paper lions, showing up to the party with no more than a token force. I remember how France balked and said the thing wasn't worth fighting over, and the backlash that got, where, in this country at least, people started calling French fries Freedom fries. Pretty funny I thought, like saying, "That will teach you to bail on us."

So far as I know the Iraqis didn't have any allies. They were going it alone.

Anyway one cold morning in January 1991 my company, 240 strong, boarded a transport plane and flew to a staging area in Southern Kuwait. There were so many troops from so many countries there in one place you wouldn't have believed it if you didn't see it first hand. It was very interesting to meet soldiers from all over the world, share C-rations, swap stories, hear their unfamiliar dialects, and knowing we were all in this together it brought a sort of instant comraderie. The entire country of Kuwait is smaller than New Jersey and the Iraqis our official enemy were clustered around Kuwait City about 60 miles to the north. We were aware of one another, the coalition and the aggressors, and it was tough just waiting around for the shoe to drop. Of course the Americans had thought ahead and brought recreational stuff. There were games of touch football and volleyball in the sand, which was everywhere. That was maybe the worst part of the whole experience, you had to live with sand. You got it in your mouth, in your food, in your cot where it could even keep you awake at night. I am not a big fan of sand. We were in that staging area the lot of us for 12 days before the bombs began raining on Baghdad, really lit that city up. That was the official start of Operation Desert Storm.

Now you may think it was the Gulf War itself that was the life-changing experience, but it was something that happened to me in that war that really flipped me over, changed my attitude about certain people. That something involved another soldier named Cadence. His real name was Preston Bulworth, a country boy from Strawberry Arkansas. He was black as a coal chute at midnight and as good natured as they come. We had gone through boot camp together then AIT and then in the same company at Ft. Hood so it was natural that we had become friends along the way. I say natural with caution because truth be told it was not natural or usual for me to make friends with a black guy.

My family had raised me to believe that it was best to associate only with persons of the White race as they were better than the rest. Better in what way was never quite explained, but I always had a hard time believing we were superior in the intelligence department as I have known some really stupid White people. Anyway it was understood that Whites were just better. More fortunate is more like it.

Cadence got his name during boot camp in Ft. Knox when we did a lot of marching. Marching can be pleasant if you have someone to call cadence, meaning one soldier being appointed to keep the others in step by calling out in a sing-song way. The cadence you may have heard in movies is "your left, your left, your left right left." Over and over again, for a cadence really is a chant. Preston was a natural for calling cadence, he was always singing or humming any-

No Big Thing

way, so the top kick gave him the job for our platoon. His brother before him had been in the Army so I guess he had passed down some cadences that he had heard in boot camp, otherwise I don't know where Preston got them from. They were mostly about this fictitious guy named Jodie who was back in the hometown while you were off in the military digging foxholes and getting yelled at by platoon sargents. Jodie had taken your place and you were supposed to hate him for it. We'd be marching past the PX and Preston would call "Ain't no use in lookin back Jodie's got your Cadillac. Sound off *one-two* Sound off *three-four* Sound off *one-two* ... *three-four!*" Later he'd change it to a romantic theme. "Ain't no use in going home Jodie's got your girl and gone." If Jodie was not available Cadence could pull another from his song book. Marching past the base cemetary he would call "Close your eyes and hang your head we are marching by the dead." Or going past the movie theater "Standing tall and looking good ought to march in Hollywood." Preston with his deep strong voice really improved our morale, and he made us look good. It wasn't long before we started calling him Cadence.

Now we were in the Arabian Desert where marching would be impossible, at least it wouldn't look very snappy having to shuffle through all the sand. In the days leading up to the actual engagement with the enemy the men of the 25th Infantry Division were kept busy by policing the compound, picking up cigarette butts and candy wrappers and such. It was grunge work and we resented it, just wanting the show to start. Finally as I said the day came when the allies rained bombs on Baghdad and we got orders to move out. One of the things that amazed me was all the tanks they had brought over. So many different kinds, all deadly, heavy armor like you wouldn't believe, all of which had made its way across the ocean by sea and by air. It was well known that the Iraqi Republican Guard had plenty of firepower and these things called SCUD missiles so General Schwartzkopf had decided that whatever they had we would overpower it tenfold. Our job as infantrymen was to walk along ahead of the Humvees and tanks of the 2nd Armored Cavalry

Regiment to scout the unmarked dirt track on which they traveled, always moving toward the battle we knew would come. The going was slow as they were always having to stop to evaluate new intelligence that was coming through.

Cadence and I and a dozen others paced far ahead of a line of M1 Abrams tanks just amazed at the scenery which was basically non existant, just endless stretches of sand and dunes with a few weeds here and there but no trees and definitely no greenery. Someone said that hyenas once lived here but the Arabs had hunted them to extinction. We wondered why anyone would choose to fight to the death over such a Godforsaken place where you couldn't even build a house or start a neighborhood. Cadence said it was all about oil, there was oil beneath the desert and the US wanted to keep control of it under the Kuwaitis because they were our friends and if the Iraqis had it we wouldn't be able to buy it as cheaply and they might not even let us have some. So we walked along in front of and sometimes behind the tanks, me and Cadence and the rest, for about a week coughing at times from the exhaust and trying to bear up to the hardship, accepting that walking was what infantry does while artillery rides.

I am not going to tell every detail of that adventure, everything that happened up to the point where we finally did engage the enemy because this is not that kind of story and besides that would take about ten pages longer than this assignment requires. This story is about sacrifice and friendship and I'll try to keep to that.

We were parked on some desert track, the road to Al Abraq not far from the Iraq border. One white cloud in a bright blue sky. After zigzagging back and forth for quite a spell, like our commander didn't know where the heck he was going, the column settled down and waited. Twenty or thirty miles away the coalition air force was pounding the Iraqi troops and their artillery, you could hear it in the distance and at night sometimes it flickered in the sky like sheet lightning. This had been going on for many days and we wondered

No Big Thing

if there would be any Iraqis left for us to fight. I for one hoped the war would come to a quick end because I'd just as soon not be put in a kill or be killed position. I tried to see the Iraqis as bad people who need to be killed but I just couldn't. I guess I've always tried to see things from the other guy's point of view and I knew that they, the enemy, saw this giant sandbox as their turf and they were following orders from Saddam Hussein to reclaim it. You could look at it like we were encroaching on their territory, kind of like during our own Civil War the Southerners having to deal with Union troops running all over their lands looking for rebels to shoot, while they were just trying to farm. Some of them anyway.

We were now into February and dang cold at night to where you had to wear a couple sets of long johns. Cadence and I and two others named Denny and Mike shared a tent. It reminded me of camping out on the Black River back home only there were no hoot owls or tree frogs to sing you asleep. We had each other, though. In a situation like that you really get to know a guy. I got to know Cadence well, he was the first colored I ever really got to know. He would tell me about his life back home, how he had a girlfriend worked at the canning factory who was "purtier than a speckled pup," how he was going to go back to delivering produce for Mister Goggins and save up to buy his own truck so as to go into business for himself. I told him things about myself, too, some of them things I wouldn't even tell my drinking buddies back home.

One night we were lying there in our sleeping bags, lights off about to fall asleep and Cadence said, "You know Little Brother, they call the Iraqis sand niggers. What you think of that?" A while back Cadence had started with the Little Brother bit, it was his way of showing friendship and it was funny. I said I didn't care for it, that it was dismissing an entire army their capabilities their way of life and more based on some superficial thing like their physical appearance. Then I thought that if my Grampa had heard me say that he'd flip his lid.

One of the others, Mike or Denny can't recall which, said it was what you call a mis-gnomer because niggers have nappy hair and these guys did not.

The other one, Mike or Denny can't recall which, said it didn't matter we had to call them something and sand niggers was pretty good, good as slopes, the name for the gooks who fought us over in Nam.

What started as a simple question was becoming a philosophical discussion and I for one was feeling uneasy. Racial problems in our unit were practically non-existant, we know we're all soldiers working toward a common cause. If there is any outfit in the world that is totally equal opportunity and turns a blind eye toward race it is the US Army. Still, we had been drinking earlier, lots of it and liquor tends to bring out the bluster in a man.

Cadence sat up on his cot. You could see the whites of his big eyes. He said, "I'm with Little Brother here, it's demeaning is what it is. What have them Iraqis done to us that you want to 'dis them without even ever having seen 'em? And if you gonna call 'em sand niggers then maybe I should look on them as my brothers. We'll be niggers in arms." He laughed and Mike and Denny laughed too but it was a nervous kind of laughter.

Even though he had covered it up with laughter his comment was dead serious, I could tell, and I felt the spite in his heart, the sting of his shame. That was Part One of my Life Changing Experience.

We got the word to move out and we all mustered at 0600 one frigid morning in mid February. Tanks were idling and the artillery guys standing around having one last smoke before climbing in. We had yet to see one enemy combatant just some Bedoins on camels every once in a while heading who knows where. Word had come down from on high that a major coalition offensive was underway, troops advancing on all fronts. There were reports of thousands of Iraqi deserters, probably the smart move if you ask me. It was supposed to be a three pronged attack, one aimed at Kuwait City

No Big Thing

where the Iraqis were holed up probably living like kings, a second to the west targeting the large Iraqi column which was on the move to somewhere, and the third to the far west to outflank the just mentioned Iraqi lines and sort of squeeze them into submission. We were slated to be a part of the third push to outflank them. We didn't know then that the Iraqis were just itching to surrender.

The two units, infantry and artillery, rumbled along through the desert only the honchos knowing our precise destination. We were all cammied up in our desert fatigues, all prepped for action. Later that day after breaking for lunch we came upon what looked to have been a village of stucco buildings with flat roofs built around an open plaza with a dried up well and some busted cement benches and tables. There was a Pepsi sign lying in the rubble. The place had been shelled who knows when but it was definitely uninhabited now. The captain said to take a couple platoons and go through every structure to make sure the place was really empty. Then we fanned out in pairs, holding our M-16s in firing position across our chests ready for anything. My partner was Cadence and we went into one hovel after another hearing only the crunch of our footsteps on the hardpack. Here and there were odds and ends that the villagers had left when they fled and we were taking a few moments to study them. There was a book in Arabic with pictures of planets and we found some cooking utensils. There were plush animals now grungy and toy soldiers that once belonged to a kid.

Cadence was saying something when we heard movement on the outside around the open doorway. I put my finger to my lips shushing him and we stepped apart rifles pointed at whatever was out there. Slowly we edged toward the doorway still hearing something out there. As we came out into the light nerves on edge we saw six guys in Iraqi uniforms their arms in the air all bunched together saying something like "Shlama! Shlama!" which we took to mean "I surrender." They were a tattered bunch and as docile as cattle. We couldn't believe our good luck. Using pantamine we had them turn about and implying we would shoot them if they did not obey we marched them past the rest of the open-mouthed grunts and presented them to the captain.

The captain was very pleased and said he would give us a commendation. He then sent for the Iraqi translator who came licketysplit. We stood around as the translator the captured soldiers and the captain had a three-way conversation. The captain wanted to know where was their unit. How far or how many days away? Which direction? How many were there? The Iraqis were in no way uncooperative in fact they were all talking at once, eager to give up their comrades' position, and pointing off into the shapeless terrain where they supposedly were. The translator conveyed all this to the captain and added, "Now that they have spilled the beans, their words, they want to know if they can get something to eat."

The captain got the artillery colonel on the radio and after talking for a minute he clicked off and pointed in the direction that the captives had indicated. "That a way, boys," he said, "it's a good day for hunting Iraqi."

The whole dang convoy turned about and we headed off on a new course perpendicular to the one we had been on. As we plodded along in the sand word came down and was passed along that an Iraqi SCUD missile had hit the Army barracks in Dhahran killing 28 of our soldiers. This was terrible to think about and it gave us pause in believing that the enemy was soft and had little fight left. That evening with maybe five miles behind us we made bivouac in the trough of some dunes. In the morning the sky was murky and the sun had a hard time peeking through. We had just got underway again when a breeze picked up and before long turned into a howling wind. The wind carried sand, tons and tons of sand, and we realized that we were in one of those sand storms we'd been told to expect. The unit brass decided to keep on going despite the fact that visibility was practically zero. While the tank crews were inside their machines and out of the brunt of the storm, we the infantry were trudging along in it. We didn't need to be told to pull our caps

No Big Thing

down over our ears and wear the wraparound shades they gave us for this sort of situation.

After a while of very slow going we heard a shot and then a whole series of shots which sounded not that different from our M-16s. As I said visibility was very poor and we couldn't tell where these shots were coming from so there was much initial confusion at least among the small band of guys around me. "What's going on?" I called to Cadence. "I think we're being shot at!" he said, shouting because the wind and sand were not only cutting down vision but making it hard to hear too. The convoy had halted and we hunkered down behind a Humvee and waited for the platoon leader to come along and tell us what next. The shots were coming more often now and we heard some rounds pinging off the tanks. How dumb were these guys, we wondered, hoping to take out a massive armored tank with standard weapons, like a fly attacking a bear. They were just firing to be firing hoping to hit something, that's how desperate they were. "Is that all you got?" shouted this one goofball, Spec 4 Nichols into the wind.

Then we heard the sounds of our weapons, the M1 Abrams tanks and the Bradley Fighting Vehicles giving them all they had. The desert must have exploded with all that firepower, not that we could see a thing. Not wanting to be left out we popped off several rounds of M-16 fire from the prone position, aiming at nothing in particular but liking the sound of gunfire and feeling that we were at least doing something.

The convoy began to move again and my platoon picked themselves up and moved with it. It seemed we were going serpentine but in this vortex it was hard to really know. It was so bad that some of the guys were holding hands to keep from getting separated. Enemy fire had slacked off and it seemed the danger was past. I went to my hip to get a stick of Big Red and my fanny pack was gone. You might think it funny that a soldier in a war zone would have a fanny pack, it surely was not standard issue from the Quartermaster. But I really liked my fanny pack and had all sorts of needful stuff in it like chewing gum and fingernail clippers and eye drops and a pocket volume of the New Testament and chapstick and aspirin and letters from my girl Cassie back home. I called to Cadence at my side, asked if he'd seen my fanny pack on the ground back where we were. He said no, he had not, but he would go back and look. He knew how much I depended on that thing.

"Are you crazy?" I said. "No way you're going back there. I can live without it, I'll get another one." Before I could say any more he was gone. I was horrified that he would do such a thing and almost ran after him but truth be told I was afraid of getting lost in the storm. I walked on filled with much concern over Cadence. No one had ever tried to do me a favor as big as the one he was doing, the dumb cluck, and I hoped and prayed that he would come back all right.

Then everything stopped, no one could say why. We stood there waiting for something to happen. The sandstorm was finally winding down and some guys removed their caps and sunglasses and squinting in the broadening daylight began to shake themselves off. Behind us there was some commotion and at length we could see a couple medics trotting along with a stretcher between them. On the stretcher was a body and I knew it would be Cadence. My heart was pounding as they got up close and I saw that it was Cadence and that he was not dead. I rushed over to the stretcher-bearers and asked what had happened. They kept trotting along huffing and puffing and shook their heads that there was no time to answer questions. Cadence saw it was me and lifted his head and smiled.

"Hold it here, boys, just for a sec," he said.

"Why not?" said one medic to the other. "It's not an emergency."

"I don't know," said the other, "he could go into shock."

"But he's so heavy and I'm winded. Let's stop for a little while, okay?" They stopped, still holding the stretcher by its handles but grateful to catch their breath.

Cadence had my fanny pack tucked between his legs. "Take it," he said. I took it and put it on.

No Big Thing

"Mission accomplished," he said, his voice kind of raspy. He was bare chested and his left arm was at his side dressed in gauze and bound with Ace wrap, the tips of bloody fingers poking out. It looked bad.

"What did you do?" I asked. "What happened?"

"Ain't gonna get no purple heart for this," he answered. "I was reaching, Little Brother, reaching for your property laying there half covered in the sand and didn't see the tank coming." He laughed good naturedly like he always did, then hawked up something and tried to spit on the ground but instead it hit the medic's pantleg. Cadence grabbed my arm with his good one and said, "How can you not see something as big and mean as a tank, I don't know but it plumb ran over my hand and arm. Hurt like a bugger."

I was starting to cry, I'll admit it, when the medic said that's enough, we have got to get to the mobile ER up the way, get your buddy some help.

They trotted off and I jogged with them for a ways, keeping Cadence and his mangled limb in sight, wanting him to know that I was indebted to him and would never forget his kindness as foolish as it was. And that is the other part of my Life Changing Experience.

I figure you cannot have a Life Changing Experience without being open and receptive to new ideas that are coming your way. In the sands of Kuwait I learned that a man is defined by his actions and what is in his heart, and not what someone else says he is.

There were battles to come and I saw enough dead on both sides, but what happened that day with a soldier named Cadence will stick in my heart forever.

—end—

At the bottom of this last page Patricia saw the grade received, an encircled A, and the handwritten teacher's note. "Apart from run-on sentences, sporadic misspellings, and flawed punctuation, this is outstanding work! Would you be willing to read it to the class?"

"Mm, mm, mm," she cooed, finishing the dregs of her wine. Then she murmured something else, something she never thought she'd say because it was more of a thing that men would say to their sons when they were proud of them, and not so much women. "That's my boy," she said, "that's my boy."

—19—

Up on the Pulpit the Reverend Marsten Pinkard wiped his brow with a hankie and went back to his sermon which was nothing less than a tirade. He looked out over the crowd, most of them familiar faces, the pews and benches of the Pine Grove Baptist Church filled to capacity with the faithful come to hear him hold forth on the advertised topic: Protecting Our Way of Life In An Unfair World. Rev. Pinkard knew he had hit a home run with this one, because, the week before, the sign out front of the church had read "Preaching The Bible As It Is To People As They Are," and hardly anyone had showed up.

He flourished a folded newspaper before the attentive flock. "And just to drive the point home," he orated, "here is an article from the *St. Louis Post-Dispatch* telling how a group of white firemen are thinking of filing a lawsuit against the City of St. Louis claiming that the city discriminated against them by doing away with the results of a promotion exam that no blacks had passed. The fire department says it got rid of the test results because it was concerned that no black firefighters and only two Hispanics received passing scores. The fire chief himself says he was worried the test was somehow flawed because it had, says here, 'such a disproportionate effect on minorities'. Huh. Well, isn't that considerate of the chief? Maybe he'll decide to dumb the test down so any dropout can pass, and then we can thank the chief when the next class of firefighters are

No Big Thing

too dense to hook up a hose and our houses burn down as a result. I ask you, could it be that those minorities who failed the test just didn't pay attention back in fourth grade when they were supposed to be leaning the basics? Could it be that they squandered the brains the good Lord gave them and now they want a break because of it?"

Hallelujah!" someone shouted.

"It's God's truth!" from another.

Rev. Pinkard had always wanted to be a firebrand just like the Reverend Basil Manly Sr., plantation owner and president of the University of Alabama in the antebellum days, one of his early heroes. Pinkard shifted his considerable girth, took a breath, and continued in his clarion voice. "They call this affirmative action— people, policies or measures designed to protect groups previously denied equal standing. Don't get me started on that! It might look good on paper, it might appeal to guilt-ridden liberals in the big cities. But we here in Pine Grove will not have the wool pulled over our eyes. We know just what this affirmative action really is, nothing less than a payback for past mistreatment of blacks and other minorities. But we didn't mistreat anyone. Maybe our great-grandparents did, but that's in the past and we are here and now. We should not be asked to pay for the misdeeds of our ancestors."

"Hallelujah!" came the chorus.

"They got pushed to the back of the bus and now they think it's our turn to get pushed to the back of the bus? I don't think so. The laws that congress made are clear. Everyone is protected from racial discrimination. Not just blacks but whites. Not just brown skins but whites. Majority equality, that's what we're talking about, and that's not racist, people. That's just being fair. All Americans are protected from all forms of discrimination, even white men.

"You know, I could have called this sermon 'What's this country coming to?' I'll give you an example. A white woman in Texas filed a federal lawsuit against an assisted living center claiming she was discriminated against and harassed by Hispanics because she didn't speak Spanish. That really boils my broccoli, people. It's her god-given right to speak the language she was born with, not some foreign tongue! What's this country coming to?"

"Ruination!" came the response.

"Using racial quotas to increase minorities on college campuses even though those minorities are not academically worthy. What's this world coming to?"

"Pity our children," wailed a woman in the front pew.

"It just ain't right," cried a fellow in bib overalls. "It's un-American is what it is!"

A hand was raised, its owner fidgeting in his seat like a schoolkid. Whitey Jinkerson. Pinkard knew the man as a sort of trouble-maker, at least a perturbance in the congregation, and had serious doubts that he was really a Baptist. Some thought him slightly deranged, Pinkard knew, there was talk about him keeping possums under his porch. Pinkard leaned forward from the pulpit and peered downward. "Yes, Whitey, what is it?"

Whitey cleared his throat theatrically and said, "Isn't it true, that old saying, if we didn't have double-standards there would be no standards at all?"

Pinkard was taken aback by the impertinence of the remark. "Uh-huh. No, Whitey, I haven't heard that saying, it's new to me and I'm not sure how to respond. But thanks for sharing that."

Picking up where he left off, "Now, we have a situation in our own little town, where one of our citizens has been denied participation in a state-sponsored program because of his beliefs and those beliefs are directly tied to him being a proud white man who projects Christian values. I think you all know who and what I am talking about. This is yet another manifestation of that devil's work, affirmative action, which we must condemn and, yes, oppose in any way we can. If we truly examine the state highway department's motives we will then see—"

"But why does Randall Fortner need permission from the State to

No Big Thing

clean up the highway in St. Louie?" asked Whitey in a whiny tone. "If he wants to pick up litter, why can't he just do it on his own and do it right here? Main Street could use some sprucing up, you ask me."

Rev. Pinkard dropped his head and sighed. Now he was sure that Whitey wasn't a Baptist; Baptists were supposed to answer the preacher, not interrupt him. Moments passed as the congregation waited. "It's the principle of the thing, Whitey. It's just one more example of liberals trying to foist their twisted agenda on god-fearing people." He looked to a prim middle-aged man off to the side, sitting in a high-backed chair facing the pews. Paul Brownlee, the sexton.

"Paul," he intoned, waggling an index finger, "please come here." When Brownlee got there, Pinkard cupped a hand over his ear and whispered, "Would you please escort Whitey downstairs and get him some coffee and doughnuts until I am finished? Thank you."

After the service, Rev. Pinkard, looking resplendent in his purple-and-gold brocade vestments, stationed himself just outside the entrance to the church where he could personally greet any exiting member who cared to be greeted. Cy and Rebecca Wainscott were now speaking with him, lavishing praise on a thoughtful and meaningful sermon well-delivered, when Randall appeared solo. The three acknowledged him and went on with their pleasantries, concurring wholeheartedly with the reverend that life was just so unfair and instead of saying 'Oh, well, what are you going to do about it?' it should be taken by the scruff of the neck and roundly thrashed until it cried uncle. Randall stood there, stetson in his hands, patiently waiting for them to get through so he could say something to Marsten. Finally, his daughter and son-in-law had said their piece and turned to depart. "See you back at the house, dad," said Rebecca.

"Well, Randall," said Marsten, extending his hand, "I trust you gained some satisfaction from that sermon."

Randall looked down upon Marsten's pate, bald spot glinting in the sun—he was a full head taller than his old friend—and said, "It was quite decent, inspiring in parts, but if it's all the same to you I'd rather you kept my name out of it. I never have appreciated being the center of attention."

—20—

MEANWHILE IN ST. LOUIS the mood in the offices of the American Civil Liberties Union was cautiously euphoric, if that is even possible. A ruling from the U.S. District Court had just been handed down: The Missouri Department of Transportation's refusal to allow the Klan to participate in the State's highway cleanup program was unconstitutional. MoDOT's counsel, Peter Van Vliet, had vigorously argued in as many ways as he could that under the federal Civil Rights Act the State could—in fact, was obligated to— refuse certain applicants whose agenda was to "further or subsidize racial discrimination." Tom Consolino, in fine form, argued just as vigorously that the First Amendment barred the Department of Transportation from denying an application because it disagreed with that organization's political beliefs. There it was on official US government stationery, signed by a judge, entered into case law: The First Amendment trumps the Civil Rights Act. Tom Consolino and his colleagues, Keepers of the Flame of What's Fair For One is Fair For All, were vindicated. The rest of the population, however, was fit to be tied.

Never mind that the court's decision, which would lead to signs on public property advertising the Klan's work, would be a black mark on a state that has come far since the civil rights era. Never mind that modern St. Louis had a decent record of blacks and whites, by and large, getting along pretty well and this ruling had the potential to mess that up. Never mind that certain state lawmakers were irate over the decision, shouting that the Klan's "longrooted history of civil disturbance would now be regurgitated like a

No Big Thing

sour burp." Never mind that the NAACP, the Urban League, and other like-minded organizations marched on the courthouse chanting slogans and flourishing damning signs until certain clenched-fist militants in the group took it too far and the police had to break it up. Never mind that the average African-American citizen imagining himself or herself passing such a sign on the highway would be greatly offended, feeling shame, anger or betrayal depending on their temperament. And the African-American community in St. Louis was very large indeed.

Never mind all that because the court had spoken.

The mood in the ACLU offices on the second floor of the Old Post Office in downtown St. Louis was cautiously euphoric because the case wasn't yet settled. There would be an appeal, of course, and the lower court's decision could be overturned by a panel of judges who saw things differently. The run-up to appellate court could take another year or two, depending on how crowded the docket was.

PRIOR TO THE LOWER COURT'S RULING, the case was also aired in the media. There were radio and television interviews, the principals clarifying their positions to talk show hosts, stressing the validity of their arguments, speculating on the ultimate outcome, etcetera.

The local NPR affiliate KWMU had Tom Consolino in the studio and Sheila Cowan on the line for a live feed to "All Things St. Louis." Host Byron Gottlieb led off the session with an obvious question Sheila was prepared for: "Why exclude the Ku Klux Klan from the Adopt-A-Highway program? Don't they have the same rights as anyone else?"

Sitting comfortably at her desk in the state capitol, Sheila answered practically by rote. "The Adopt-A-Highway program is not a free speech issue. We want to recognize groups that are doing a good community service, and that is at our discretion. It's not everyone's constitutional right to participate in a highway beautification program. In order for this program to work it has to be taxpayer run and state run and it will not work if just anyone who feels like it gets to put up a highway sign."

Byron Gottlieb looked across the audio console with its many knobs and levers to the fellow in slacks and maroon polo shirt. "I think the 'Klan's counselor,' as he's been dubbed, will have a different take on that. Mr. Consolino?"

Consolino leaned into his microphone like he was kissing it, and said, "Actually, Byron, it most definitely is a free speech issue. By opening the program to the public and selling the program as a way to advertise good citizenship the government had created a public forum. All right, let's be even more clear: When government takes a place that traditionally has not been open to free speech, the roadside along the Interstate, then government has created a virtual public forum, opening the door even to those considered detestable. Government cannot viewpoint discrimination. Once they've opened the program for people to express their goodness then bureaucrats can't pick and choose which groups they approve of based on their own highly subjective beliefs or arbitrary moral sense."

"Who gets to decide what a hate group is, is that it?"

"That's at the core of the issue, yes."

"What say you, Ms. Cowan? Would the clear distinction of a 'hate group' make this decision easier? Once an organization is categorized as such should their right to free speech be restricted?"

One-hundred and thirty miles away Sheila Cowan tried to imagine the scene in the studio. She imagined that Byron Gottlieb was in cahoots with Tom Consolino, the two of them sitting there smirking, hoping to trick her into saying something stupid so they could pounce on her. "It's not what I say, but what the Missouri Transportation Department says. And what it says and strongly feels is this is a taxpayer-supported program run by MoDOT and we have a responsibility to both taxpayers and to the public interest. If anyone is deciding that the KKK is a hate group it is history, history and public perception. This particular group has a history of illegal

No Big Thing

behavior, violent behavior, racist behavior, and that's why we've tried to exclude them. It's one thing to talk and think a certain way, it's another to act on it. Obviously, the KKK has a history of acting on their beliefs which has caused harm to many people. The distinction isn't whether MoDOT agrees or disagrees with the group's set of beliefs, but whether it is in the public interest to exclude their participation." There. She felt like she nailed it.

"I see," mused Byron Gottlieb, "you're taking it up a notch, raising the bar of criterion to reflect the 'public interest'. Okay, well and good. But that begs yet another question in the same vein as the one just asked: Who then gets to decide what is in the public interest?"

Sheila bristled at this. What was this guy, some pint-sized provocateur? "I feel like I just answered that question, Byron."

"Maybe you did, maybe you did. We'll see. Mr. Consolino, what of the notion raised by MoDOT and its supporters that the State is in effect being forced to endorse the Klan by erecting a taxpayer-funded sign crediting it for good citizenship along the interstate?"

Tom Consolino puffed audibly into the mic. "I don't think allowing people to participate in this program is an endorsement," he answered, "but if it is look at all the people government is endorsing. Is it endorsing the Model Railroading Association and the Eastern Missouri Bow Hunters Club and all the churches and political groups who take part? Is it endorsing Winnie's Antiques Emporium? Is it endorsing the Shriner Hospital? They've all got signs. In fact, my client is the first and only group ever turned down by the program."

"Yes, yes," said Byron Gottlieb, "that is quite the controversy and we are here to hash that out. Can you both stay for a bit while we take calls from listeners?"

Tom Consolino reached over and touched the host on his sleeve. "Byron, if you don't mind I want to add something before we take calls. Putting up a sign with the Klan's name on it is an opportunity to discuss the need for racial tolerance. Censorship isn't going to make the Klan's bad ideas go away. Democracy isn't painless. The discomfort we feel at seeing the Klan represented as part of the program is the price we pay for our freedom."

THE MORE FRIVOLOUS media circus, from wacky television reporters to radio shock jocks, took their own facetious shots at the situation. Melvin "Mad Dog" Rush, morning personality on OLD SKOOL 105-FM, stole a line from the weekly tabloid and called it his own, telling listeners that before long they would be treated to the comic spectacle of "white trash picking up trash" on the interstate south of the city. Liz Jackson, "Anarchist Of The Airways," on KPOW 780-AM started a charity drive to collect old, worn bedsheets, "the grungier the better, to help out those poor destitute Klansmen who can't afford to buy their own." But the most alarming utterance came from the public-access television sector when Jabbar Moskowitz-Bey, broadcasting live, invited all "righteous citizens with a handgun lying around" to "take out any white devils" that may be found in the vicinity of the Klan's clean-up area, "if and when that happens." Moskowitz-Bey was more than an hour into his rant when St. Louis metro police along with the FBI battered his door, dragged him kicking and screaming from his basement studio, brought him to the FBI office on Market Street, frog-marched him down a long corridor and into an interrogation room where they kept him twiddling his thumbs for 24 hours while deciding whether to charge him with intent to commit a hate crime or inciting a riot or both.

But the ruling had the unforseen effect of backfiring on the ACLU. The Adopt-A-Highway fiasco falling in favor of the KKK was heavily publicized and very much rankled a considerable faction of liberals, some of whom were generous donors to the organization. Although they knew deep within their hearts that the ACLU was about defending any person or group whose civil rights had been tread upon, they just could not bring themselves to be open-minded enough to accept that the Klan deserved even one man-hour spent

No Big Thing

toward its aid. Thus, letters began to pour in to the ACLU office, the authors strenuously objecting to the defense of such a hateful group and asking that their name be removed from the membership rolls. The Missouri affiliate of the ACLU lost about 25 percent of its membership and nearly one third of its budget.

For Tom Consolino the situation turned personal whenever he went out and about on The Hill, the Italian-American enclave of St. Louis where he made his home. He very much enjoyed strolling along the tree-lined streets past the shotgun homes built in the early 20th century for the Italian and Sicilian immigrants who flocked to St. Louis, many of whom found work in a nearby quarry, Cheltenham, that extracted high-quality clay for brick-making. He would walk past the Big Hall Club where generations had held their celebrations; past Rose's Bocce Courts where, beneath an arbor of grape vines, they smoked and drank and played the beloved game all day and into the evening; past the offices of *Il Pensiero*—The Thought—the newspaper printed entirely in the vernacular with news and views both local and from the Old Country, now in its 66th year. To Tom, these brick-and-mortar buildings brought a stirring of pride, knowing they were and always would be links to the world his grandparents knew, to his unique heritage, a testament to the determination to forge a good life in a new country.

But now, since the court's ruling, Tom found himself somewhat guarded on his walks. Denizens of The Hill, neighbors, people he knew in passing, shopkeepers, strangers even, were actually accosting him, asking or demanding that he account for his actions in defending this despicable group that was in the news.

"Ku Klux Klan, what kind of stupid name is that?" harangued old man Fortino outside of the Marconi Bakery one Saturday afternoon. Tom had come to get some of their wonderful canolis for a family gathering, but they were already sold out. "A bunch of grown men running around in bedsheets, scaring decent people. Cattivo persone!" He spat on the ground. "Cattivo! They are bad people. They hate Catholics, believe we're no better than the ignorant, lazy blacks. Why you want to associate with that, huh? People start thinking you may be one of them."

Tom knew Pete Fortino only as a retired carpenter with a good pension, a member of the Tuesday night bocce league at Rose's. He knew that if Fortino saw fit to castigate him in public then half of The Hill was thinking of doing the same. He considered the stooped figure before him with his piercing blue eyes and four-day stubble on his cheeks, and he said, "Mister Fortino, I know it's hard for you to understand, but this group, as horrible as they may seem to you, has had their civil rights violated and someone must offer assistance, legal aid, because the courts do not smile upon any petition that is not backed up by a lawyer who knows what he's doing. Capisci? So judge me if you wish but please know that any smudge on my reputation is just guilt by association with the First Amendment."

Fortino shrugged as though to dismiss whatever it was that Tom Consolino had said. He then gave a sort of derisive snort, turned on his heels and walked off.

Not even five minutes later he ran into Ginny Mazzola, retired school teacher and aunt to his wife. She was coming out of DiGregorio's with a bag of groceries. They said hello, and she made no bones about tsk-tsking him right there on the sidewalk. "This thing you're involved with, this coming to the aid of a certain organization," she began, "I know it's your job and all, but can't you see that it's having a deleterious effect on your family? Our family. We have become the subject of talk in this community, and that, young man, is a wound we should not have to suffer."

"I'm sorry for any embarrassment I may have caused," he told her, genuinely contrite.

The old woman waited for something more, a disavowal of his chosen profession perhaps. It did not happen. "Yes, yes, the world we live in is changing ... or maybe not changing at all if we afford that group the opportunity to stand out and be recognized. Allow them to show their colors as if this were the antebellum South and

No Big Thing

what they stand for is perfectly acceptable when it is not!" Ginny had been a high school history teacher and was well up, if not fired up, on discrimination in America. "This thing," she concluded, "the way it has played out, is reminiscent of flag-burning—offensive to many but legal nonetheless."

The slow crucifixion by innuendo was not letting up. Tom Consolino did not at all appreciate being put in a position where he had to defend himself, either that or choose to ignore the often testy person confronting him. To ignore would be rude, and to defend was getting very tiresome indeed. Then, a few months later, October, at the Columbus Day Parade on The Hill, Tom found the note on his car. It was a beautiful day, a Sunday, perfect for post-parade festivities at Berra Park, all the fantastic food and good wine and old friends one could hope for. Tom had tried several wines both white and red from the various kiosks that were set up on the fairgrounds, and by two o' clock he was quite tipsy. He had to get home anyway because his wife, Connie, was going to a Tupperware Party and he would watch little Mario, his precocious nine-month-old.

Through a rousing chorus of "Funiculi-Funicula" he bade his pals goodbye and made a loopy zigzag course to his Escort parked on Macklind. He almost drove off before seeing the note, but then got out, walked around to the front and lifted the windshield wiper that held it in place. He unfolded it with mild curiosity. Oh boy, here we go again.

The dispatch was typewritten and at the top it had a drawing of an outspread palm in black, like a warning, and a dagger dripping blood. It read, "You are accused and hereby convicted in absentia of aiding the enemy, the people who tormented our ancestors. It seems you don't know your people's history otherwise you would not be associating with these low-life spooks. We doubt that you have heard of the Herrin Mine Massacre, but it's not too late to learn. Check it out and you'll see what evil your friends have done, what pain they have caused. Let someone else defend them, a WASP like them. Not an Italian-American. You have brought shame to our community!"

It was signed The Sons of the Black Hand.

The following day at lunchtime Tom walked four blocks up Olive Street to the Downtown Library. He approached the librarian behind a desk in the Main Hall, a space so large and majestic it would not be out of place in the Palace of Versailles. He told her the topic and asked for a starting point. She hit some keys on a bulky computer, read what popped up on the the the screen, and scribbled something on scratch paper. Try this for starters, she told him. He walked off in the direction of the stacks. One selection was *Bloody Williamson* by Paul M. Angle. The other was the archives of the Marion Illinois History Preservation Society.

He spent much of the afternoon in the library reading up on the horrific events surrounding the wanton killing of immigrant coal miners in Williamson County, in 1922. What they did to these poor miners you wouldn't do to a dog even if it had snatched your juicy ribeye from the supper table. Many of these miners were Italian, true, non-union workers hired out of Chicago, but there were Poles and Irish and Lithuanians as well. The bull-headed mine owners had decided to use scab labor to defy a strike organized by the United Mine Workers; it was like lighting a fuse to a powder keg.

The first day of the attempted strike break, the striking union miners shot at the strikebreakers going to work. After that, they laid siege to the mine. The next day, union miners killed 19 of 50 strikebreakers and mine guards, many of them beaten and tortured by both strikers and local citizens who had fallen prey to bloodlust. The coroner later ruled that the strikebreakers were killed "by unknown individuals," and put the blame on the coal company itself for setting up the situation. Eventually six men were indicted, and their trials ended in acquittals.

Of course the Klan was behind it, and the Klan had a very strong presence in that part of Southern Illinois—Union and Williamson Counties in particular. There had been gatherings of Klansmen said to be 5,000 in number. Perhaps the majority of the membership

No Big Thing

were down-to-earth farmers and tradesmen, but the professions were also represented. The ranks were rife with law-and-order types such as police chiefs, constables, prosecutors and judges, which meant Klan politics held sway in those jurisdictions. The Klan professed and practiced racial intolerance, sure, but Tom began to see that the Klan was all about upholding the law, too. Certain laws, anyway. They were staunch defenders of the Volstead Act.

Apart from those hapless immigrants brought down from Chicago, there was already an established Italian community in the area and the men made their living in the mines. Most of the foremen employed by the mine were Klansmen, overseers who exercised Draconian control over the miners who often didn't speak English and had no will to stand up to the abuse. Both on the job and off, there had been a history of Klansmen clashing with these miners, making sure they understood their place: the bottom rung of the ladder. The Italian miners despised the mine bosses, essentially a private police force, calling them "dirty laundry" and "bedsheets".

Tom read with interest an excerpt from the Marion Illinois History Preservation Society. "Williamson County was a fertile field for the growth of the KKK. The area was predominantly fundamentalist Protestant and fervently patriotic, and these factors contributed to prejudices and intolerance. They also contributed to fanatical support of the Prohibition laws. Herrin had a ready-made scapegoat in its Italian miner community, as these people were foreigners, Catholic, and habituated to wine; many of them became bootleggers after the Volstead Act. Many citizens believed that the Klan offered a way to clean up Williamson County and redeem it from its shame. The KKK supported the work of Protestant churches in the community and stood for the 'highest ideals of the native-born White Gentile American citizenship, which held to be the tenets of the Christian religion; protection of pure womanhood; just laws and liberty; absolute upholding of the Constitution of the United States; free public schools; free speech; free press; and law and order.'"

So that was their platform, huh? Except for the qualification of native-born White Gentile, and that business about protecting pure womanhood, whatever that was, Tom thought that it sounded on its face like a club with the right kind of ideals. Just don't expect an open bar at the meetings.

Yes, on its face it sounded idealistic and even noble, but peel away the well-crafted language and their credo was the height of hypocrisy. Did upholding the constitution entail lynching black folks on the flimsiest excuse?

On his way out he passed a lectern with the Encyclopedia Brittanica opened and beckoning. He flipped to the Bs and looked up Black Hand. There it was, three paragraphs' worth. The Black Hand or *mano nera* was an old extortion racket used by some Italian immigrants to squeeze money out of other Italian immigrants who were better off. Threats of bodily harm were conveyed by means of a letter similar to the one Tom had gotten. Instead of a dagger dripping blood, there might be a drawing of a hangman's noose or a smoking pistol, but the message would be the same: Pay up or we'll mess you up. The tenor Enrico Caruso had received a Black Hand letter demanding $2,000. Caruso paid.

These Black Hand people, whoever they were, weren't shaking him down for money. No, they hoped to make him "pay" by dangling sordid historic accounts in front of him, trying to shame him into contrition. Trying to throw a guilty conscience over him, hoping he would see fit to publicly condemn his clients. Well, it wasn't going to work. He'd checked into it and seen that that his clients—their grandparents, anyway—were very bad actors indeed. It had affected him, yes, but not to the point where he'd had an epiphany. He now came away feeling as though he had done the right thing; he had been true to his profession. He'd kept his soul.

No Big Thing

June 1995

Spud Got The Idea from watching reruns of *The Dukes Of Hazzard*. Why not have a Daisy Duke lookalike contest at the saloon. It'd be a huge draw, get the women to show up and the men would swarm the place. He could charge a cover, too, three bucks a head. Hell, make it five but just the guys. The women are bait; you don't charge the bait. Spud liked his idea so much he went to the shelf behind the bar and poured himself a nice Bacardi and Coke. There would have to be a cash prize for the winner, fifty bucks ought to do it. He would be the final judge but audience response to the contestants as they walked onstage would have a bearing, too. Hoots and catcalls were always encouraged. It would be understood that "lookalike" didn't necessarily pertain to the face, not many women around here looked like Barbara Bach. It would be more about the sexy attire and the curvacious bodies that squeezed into that attire. Spud envisioned his place filled with wall-to-wall knockouts—goodies busting out, sashaying around in come-do-me high heels. It would be a new era for Spud n' Velma's. The Playboy Penthouse of Pine Grove.

Around seven they began to show up, women in small groups, some bringing their boyfriends. The weather cooperated for the event, ungodly hot with that humidity make you think you're in the Congo or somewhere. Spud himself was at the door, collecting money from the guys and ogling the women. He was pleased at what he saw on the gals, denims cut-off at the crotch, leather-tooled belts with fancy buckles, tube tops, tank tops, or blouses tied off well above the waist and just below the bosom. One not-so-attractive woman had the nerve to wear a bikini and as much as Spud liked that, even starting to feel a lump in his pocket, he had to tell her to go home and change. It wasn't fair to the others. The old lech was handing out adhesive-backed name tags and telling the gals to put their names—real or fake, either way—on them so as to initiate conversation and so the crowd would know who was who when the judging time came. Most did write their true names before sticking the tags on their shirts or back pocket of their cut-offs, but some got clever and wrote not very subliminal messages like Low Bred Slut and You Wish!

Birch came with Jinx just after eight and the parking lot was almost full. They paid their five bucks at the door and walked over to the keg of Busch on ice that Spud had the foresight to get, knowing that the bar would be swamped. The keg had its own bartender—well, a human ox in a Red Man Tobacco cap pouring into plastic cups at two bucks a pop—while the bar had two guys behind it. When it came to revenue Spud didn't miss a trick. The Red Dog Ramblers were up on the stage, playing covers in a haze of smoke, some of it weed. Two guitars, a fiddle, pedal steel guitar, standup bass, and a drummer, all synced in to a rousing version of "Jambalaya." One of the guitars was an old Martin and had a real nice twang to it.

They hung out around the stage for a while checking things out, liking what they saw, Jinx shouting over the music that Spud should do this more often, Birch saying it was better as a one time thing. Then they went over by the pool tables, their usual haunt, and made talk with some aspiring Daisy Dukes, cue sticks in their hands. Birch sidled up to the brunette, name tag You Wish! and asked if he and his buddy could play the winners.

She looked around to her friends. "What do you think, girls, do we wanna play these jokers, show 'em up good?"

One of them, tall and striking, stepped over to Birch. They were eye to eye, equal in height. Birch liked tall women. She gave him a look like she was inspecting a ham at the supermarket. Made a point of broadcasting her reply. "Well, I don't know, guess it depends on how well he can handle his stick."

Birch read the name tag on her way low-cut blue-and-yellow gingham blouse. He stepped back for a better look, top to bottom. Not bad, not bad. He chin-pointed to the name on her blouse. "Should

No Big Thing

I call you 'Occasionally' or 'Promiscuous'? Well, don't much matter. But I've gotta warn you, showing cleavage like that is looked down upon here."

They all had a good laugh and agreed there was pool to be played.

The girls were up one game on the guys. The first game was over in no time at all with You Wish! a/k/a Jolene sinking a stripe on the break and then sinking five more in a row. Jinx and Birch knew they were up against some talent, a lot of guys who played at this same table weren't half as good. But then those guys didn't show a pair of gorgeous melons when they leaned over to take a shot. Birch had a passing moment of guilt thinking certain salacious thoughts about Occasionally Promiscuous whose real name was Tiffany. More than once he had to remind himself that he had a girlfriend, a good one, and that she might come strolling through the door any minute now.

The Ramblers were now caught up in "Honey, Don't," the singer doing a pretty good Carl Perkins. Jolene studying her next shot, a bank of the six into the nine and hopefully into the side pocket. She lined up the shot, using her cue stick as a kind of azimuth, squinted at the arrangement of balls, hunkered down, eyes at table level, took a few practice strokes. "Well, here's hopin'" she said.

"Whoa, that sure looks like a tricky shot. Mind if I try?" Jolene turned, miffed. The stranger already had his hand on her cue stick, smirking vulgarly, showing some nasty dentition. "Aw, c'mon," he said, winking at Birch a few feet away, "I can miss just as well as you can. But I ain't gonna miss, nosirree." He wrested the stick from her and leaned into the shot.

"Hold it, Buster!" said Jolene, moving to stop him.

The man paid no attention but took the shot, banking the six into the nine and sending it into the side pocket just as nice as you please. He straightened up, rested the stick on the toe of his boot. "I'd pat myself on the back if my arms were any longer," he told them, still amused. He stood there arms at his side, looking from one puzzled face to another, waiting for something to happen.

"You wonder why they let some of these jerks in," said Jolene, making a move to grab the cue stick, the guy turning, blocking it.

"Probably snuck in," tried Tiffany, "couldn't even cough up five bucks. Look at him," she piled on, "you gonna grow your hair long least you could do is comb it. You look like a friggin Sasquatch."

"And bib overalls?" from Jolene, queen of snide remarks, "that went out with mesh tank tops."

The stranger just grinned even broader. "Keep it coming, girls, I love being flattered."

Jolene shook her head in disdain. "Oh, let's just go, leave this jackass to whatever his stupid game is."

"Bye, loser," sang Tiffany, giving him the middle digit.

"He's such a loser, he doesn't even know he's a loser," concluded Jolene.

They turned on their cowboy boots and made for less hostile territory not even saying goodbye to Birch and Jinx standing there with hands in their pockets.

"Jeez, Billy, why you wanna be that way? Drive them chicks off? It ain't like we meet a couple a good ones every day here."

Billy said, "Jinx, the day you score with a Daisy Duke is the day monkeys will fly outta my ass. Look at yourself in the mirror, would ya?"

Birch hadn't seen Billy Goldie in quite a while, the last time being in the Hillsboro Lock-up, after their arrest for B & E. He saw that Billy had gotten even seedier, looking like one of those grizzled prospectors you saw in some old movie with Henry Fonda. He had a blond chew-stained beard so bushy that birds could make nests in it. Birch called him out on that last remark. "Look who's talkin', Mister Suave and Debonair here. Shoot, *you* look in a mirror—the thing'd break to pieces." He shook his head, like what's the use. "You're a piece a work, man, but I guess you know that."

No Big Thing

Billy shrugged. "When I wanna talk to the fair sex, I'll talk to 'em. Maybe even nice. When I want to talk to men such as yourselves, hey, it's time for the girls to hit the road."

Birch gave it some thought. "Uh-huh. You wanna talk, fine. But let's finish the game, you and me. Five bucks to the winner."

"There's a plan. You even got five bucks?"

Jinx went for another round while they continued the game without much banter. Birch was on a roll and soon they were down to the eight ball, snug against a far bumper. "Down to the wire," said Billy. "Just like the old days."

Birch paused his shot. "The old days? You mean the good old days of thieving in the countryside? Robbing homes while the people were away, maybe an unattended church here and there? Wondering what we're gonna do with our loot, usually less than fifty bucks? Those old days?"

Billy chuckled. "Don't forget them cars we boosted. I've still got that sixty-three Impala, 'member that? Keep it tarped out back a my trailer. You think it's still hot?"

Birch took his shot, ticking the eight only to set up Billy for the kill. "I think you should drive it around and find out. Your turn."

Billy saw it. "I got to kiss that black beauty as soft as a butterfly's wing and send it home. Not an easy thing. You wanna make it ten?"

"I'll take a raincheck."

Billy reached in his back pocket, pulled a tin of Copenhagen, pinched off a chew. "You know, those days you like to mock—those capers—that was training, bro. Learning the ropes, finding your talent, see what you can get away with. You start out small, like you say, with homes and shops and churches and you move on to bigger things."

"This is what you wanted to talk about? I am so far from that life, and you're crazy if you're still in it."

"Oh, I'm in it, but I've graduated from burglary for peanuts." Lowering his voice, "I'm making and selling meth now. Big demand around here. I can look out on the floor right now and see a dozen satisfied customers. Got a few side hustles, too."

"You gonna take your shot or what?"

"Sure thing, bro." He miscued and missed the eight altogether. Chiding himself, saying, "You know, some plays eight ball with the rule that when it's time to sink it, you gotta at least hit the dang thing. We didn't establish any such rule. Still, you wanna count that against me, you can."

"No, keep playing. I wouldn't feel good winning that way."

"Nosirree, you'd rather stand around with your thumb up your ass, waitin' for opportunity to come a knockin'." He cracked a snaggle-toothed smile. "Or maybe pickin' up trash on the road is your idea of success."

"I don't follow," said Birch.

Billy sat on the pool table, scratched at his beard, thoughtful like. "Hey, I read the papers, listen to the radio. I know that the dang Supreme Court of this land just gave you boys the nod to go ahead and pick up trash. Good for you, bro—I mean it! If that ain't democracy in action, I don't know what is. Y'all must be pleased as punch. Beautify the highway, it almost sounds noble. And I 'spect you'll be the donkey doing the janitor work, ain't no real Klan 'round here to help out. But see, here's the thing. This litter pickup business is just symbolic. You get a piddly sign which says, 'Hey, here we are. You heard of us, you feared us, maybe you wondered what happened to us—well, here we are!' Yeah, that's a start maybe, but what we want is action to back up the symbolic part. And by action I don't mean bending over ten thousand times to pick up beer cans and candy wrappers, I mean getting out there and putting the hurt on niggers and spics and A-rabs and any other vermin we made the mistake of letting into this country. Make 'em understand this is not their place, make 'em see that it's better to go back wherever the hell they came from. You do that and *then* you can talk about bein' in the Klan."

No Big Thing

Birch gave Billy a thoughtful look, nodded slightly. "We did get the decision," he told him, "and it was sweet. Gramps was happy, we threw a party for him. And I will be the guy to go to St. Louis every now and then to play the grunt, as you say, but only out of duty to family, not because I believe the Klan is right or good. And you're talking to the wrong guy about that other—intimidating people for the heck of it, just because their skin's a different shade than ours or they speak another language." He paused, looked to the floor, then looked back at Billy. "It's just stupid. Bigotry, you know? Seems to me like every race or ethnic group has been the niggers of some place at one time or another in their history. This is America, man, the melting pot. Remember that from school? Or didn't you get that far? You want a sympathetic ear? Talk to Dalton Hankins over at the garage, I think he's all for bringing back lynchings."

Billy spat on the floor, the subsequent splat sounding contemptible. "Dalton Hankins can go piss up a rope. He's a fool who deals in propaganda and Looney Tunes conspiracies. Words. I'm talking John Wayne here—decisive, kick-ass, damn-the-consequences action." Billy gave a wave of his hand, shook his head in disgust. "Ah, what's the use?" He now leaned in, his words nearly drowned by the Rambler's booming version of Billy Ray's "Achy Breaky Heart."

"Look, let's put that aside for a sec, get to the bigger matter. My business is growing to the point where I can't do it all myself. Need a hand, bro, someone I can count on. That someone is you. What do you say? I'll do the manufacturing end, you take over the sales. There's a bit of driving to be sure and you got to know how to deal with bikers and other surly types, but the money will pour in like a spring flood. All you gotta do is spend it." He held out his paw. "What do you say—partners?"

Birch ignored the offered hand. "You know me even a little then you know my answer. I won't say how idiotic that idea is, I won't say what a fool you are for even thinking I'd come in with you. I followed you once, a dumb kid out for excitement, and I saw then what you're about. So, Billy, do me this favor, just listen up good: I am as done with you as I can be."

Billy withdrew his hand, curled his lip, said, "Well then, I reckon you're ready to get to the real work. Volunteer highway cleaner-upper, that's a profitable venture. Hope it suits you."

Birch went around the table, took his shot without hesitation, sank the eight in the corner pocket just as he called it. He looked to Billy, cocked an eyebrow, put his hand out. "I'll take my five bucks now."

—22—

BIRCH AWOKE to a sunny day and the plaintive call of a mourning dove outside the open window in Cassie's bedroom. Immediately he latched on to the words of an oldie but goody, "All Shook Up," specifically the part where Elvis says, "Bless my soul, what's wrong with me? I'm itchin' like a man on a fuzzy tree." He had never seen a fuzzy tree but imagined it to be all gnarled and misshapen like something out of a Dr. Seuss book. Birch was very itchy, intensely itchy; it had started the day before, incipient raised welts on his wrists and armpits, begging to be scratched. Which he obliged, lacking the will power to deny them. Poison ivy, he figured, probably got it from pulling weeds around Randall's house, a favor to the man. He'd gone there to get a pep talk prior to his maiden trip to litter patrol on the outskirts of St. Louis. You're doing this not for me, Randall had told him, not for any family member, but for a higher cause. People going to see you out in the open. They are going to shout things, ignorant words, taunt you. You don't pay any attention to that, hear? You just clean the place up, make it presentable, and then you come straight back and tell me how it went. This first trip? Jamie's going with you, you'll pick him up in the morning. Then he slipped him three twenties and said that he would very much appreciate it if it didn't all go into Spud Burke's pocket.

Higher cause, an alluring phrase. Randall never said what it was, and Birch didn't ask.

No Big Thing

Cassie had her bare back to him, lying there on her right side. He saw again the tattoo that took up the entire small of her back, a stylized sun with flares coming off, something you might see in an old book on astronomy or alchemy. In the center of this sun was a depiction of a bushy-headed bearded guy with round shades. That was "Jerry," according to the letters beneath. At various points of the emanating solar flares were other faces; "Phil," "Bob," and "Mickey," going clock-wise. At the base of the artwork was the caption in cursive: GRATEFUL DEAD TOUR – SUMMER 1991. As he studied the tattooist's handiwork he couldn't help but notice that he didn't do a great job on Jerry, looking more like a bewildered orangutan than a music legend. Cassie rolled over and put her arm on Birch's belly, lightly stroked the hairline there, little by little heading southward. He began to stiffen. "That's a fine way way to start off the day," he said.

"You assume too much," she said. "I'm not interested in picking up what you have. I don't have time to stand around and scratch my body all over."

"You didn't have a problem last night."

"That's because you told me your condition only *after* we did it."

"True love is exposing yourself to poison ivy," he said, nudging her arm lower down. She resisted. He fixed her with an imploring gaze. Those eyes. He could gaze into her smoky brown eyes all day long, drown in those pools of mystery, even as she said, "True love is making breakfast for your man. C'mon, into the kitchen, coffee for starters."

"I can wear gloves and a long-sleeve shirt, it won't get through that."

She withdrew her hand and moved off the bed. Standing there in panties that said FRIDAY on the front, although this was Wednesday, she made it clear *l'amour* was on the back burner for now. "C'mon, soldier boy, up and at 'em. Today is your big day." Soldier boy, her term of endearment.

He reached over and picked up something tactile and serpentine and forlorn-looking, half-covered by the sheet. "Here, this must've fallen off during the night. Does that happen a lot?"

"Another one?" she said, snatching it away from him. Threading it longingly between her fingers, she explained how they can can fray just like a rope frays, only she felt it was happening too often. "You must've pulled on it when you were on top of me. You were kind of rambunctious."

Was that admonishment in her tone? "Well, yeah, I had something to be rambunctious about. Sorry if I helped it to break off."

"Oh, never mind," she said and that was that. She put the dreadlock in her dresser drawer and walked off.

Things weren't the same between he and Cassie, he could feel it, a bruise in their sense of togetherness. Maybe she she felt it, too. It had been there for a while, but he would not bring it up. After all, it was only a suspicion. And if it was a valid suspicion, then what? Stand by and watch their relationship wither on the vine? Try real hard to make her happy, raise her above all else, make sure she knows that they were meant for each other? But she already knew that, or so she said many times over the years. Women.

He Turned Onto The Gravel and passed under the arch that spanned the drive telling visitors they were entering Bar None Ranch. As he pulled up to the long one-story ranch house Jamie came out wearing jeans tucked into cowboy boots, a black muscle T, and a banged up Cattleman's hat. Rebecca stood on the porch, dishtowel in hand, watching as Jamie climbed in the truck. She waved at Birch, and called, "Y'all be careful now." Birch nodded genially, waved goodbye, and they were on their way.

He was glad to have Jamie along. The kid could talk a blue streak, about eighteen different things at once, just prattle on and on, like to wear you out trying to keep up with him, but at least he made the time pass quicker. "What you got for us?" the first thing he said,

No Big Thing

nudging the cooler on the floor.

"Oh, you're gonna like it. Cassie made them egg and onion sandwiches, brown bread, a little mayo, salt and pepper. That'll be lunch, unless we eat 'em on the way there."

"No fried Spam?"

"Nah, she was out. Too bad."

"What else?"

"A six of Busch, should stay cold until we need it."

"Planning ahead. What's all this?" He lifted a white T-shirt from a pile on the seat between them. Unfolding it, he read the message aloud. "'I Picked Up Trash For The Klan And All I Got Was This Lousy T-Shirt.' Sweet, you gonna wear it?"

"Uh, no way."

"Heck, I'll wear it."

"Cassie's twisted sense of humor. Be my guest, you can even keep it." Birch patted some other articles, also on the seat. "Randall gave us these nifty orange safety vests. They've got this reflector tape on 'em, a glow-in-the-dark feature."

Jamie flicked an eyebrow. "I've always wanted to glow in the dark."

"Yeah, right, like we're gonna be working at night. And then some wooden pokes with nails at the end for picking up stuff without having to stoop down, and some old feed sacks to put the stuff in."

Jamie flicked the little hula dancer glued to Birch's dash, made her shimmy and shake. "We're all set then. So giddy up, Cuz, you can't get us there fast enough."

They settled in for the drive, radio blaring country, scenery fleeting past, Jamie chain smoking and Birch scratching himself. And jokes, it wasn't a day trip without jokes.

"You hear about the two Irish queers?"

"Can't say as I have," answered Birch, primed for the punchline.

"Oh, they're out there, Tom Fitzpatrick and Patrick fits Tom."

Birch laughed genuinely, they both did. "How 'bout this one? Did you hear about Evel Kenievel's sister? She's working as a car hop."

The reaction Birch expected didn't come, the joke obviously lost on his perplexed cousin. "Car hop? I don't get it."

Birch sighed. "Evel Kenievel would jump a bunch of cars and buses for the TV cameras, a daredevil on a motorcycle, and his sister's a car hop. At a drive-in. Comes and takes your order, comes back with a tray of food. It's a play on words. I made that up myself."

"Hate to break it you, Cuz, but you better stick to laughin' at *my* jokes."

Then they stopped gabbing to listen to some Dwight Yoakum. Vigorously, Birch scratched certain insatiable areas—the rash spreading—making a note to stop and get some Calamine lotion. Jamie worked on creasing the crown of his hat, purchased mail order years ago from A.A. Callister Western Wear and Tack. He'd been wearing the thing since he could ride a gelding. Birch joked with him that if that hat still fit after all this time his head probably hadn't grown which meant his brain hadn't gotten any bigger either. After a spell of looking out the window, Jamie said, "You worried?"

"Nah."

"Why not? Might be trouble."

"Because Cassie threw the I Ching before I left and it said that the gods were smiling on us today."

"Oh, great!" Brief pause. "Excited then? You excited?"

"Not that either."

"What are you then?"

Birch looked at Jamie, expecting an answer that would somehow illuminate the situation. "I reckon that I'm a man on a mission with a clear goal in mind and the means to accomplish that goal."

"That's it?"

"Straight up, man, keep it simple."

"Cuz, I like that. Get in, get 'er done, get out." Jamie reached to open the cooler. "Don't mind if I do," he said, popping a can of

No Big Thing

Busch. He took a long first sip, sighed contentedly, leaned back in the seat and propped one boot on the dash. "So what the heck's an e-ching? Some kinda Chinese dart?"

WHEN THEY GOT THERE they saw there was little room to park on the shoulder and, besides, it would look as though they had broken down. They imagined interference by some good Samaritan or worse, police, so what they did was to find a residential street in the vicinity, homes backed up to the interstate, park there and hoof it in. All the way around, carrying their gear in the rising temperature.

They came up on the sign, modest as it was, proclaiming THIS HIGHWAY HAS BEEN ADOPTED BY THE GRAND KNIGHTS OF THE KU KLUX KLAN. They saw it was already defaced, someone having spray-painted a red X across the face. It was all dinged up, too, like someone had taken a pipe to it. Down at one corner, neatly affixed, was a bumper sticker, white with red-and-blue letters, a pair of tiny crisscrossed American flags: DAVID DUKE FOR PRESIDENT.

"I think that's one of Dalton's stickers," said Birch.

"I think you're right. Small world," said Jamie. "How long's this thing been up?"

"Couple weeks," said Birch.

"Well, another couple weeks we'll be out of a job 'cause there won't be nothin' left of it."

It was a pretty well-trafficked stretch of highway, cars flying by at 60-70 miles an hour, heading south toward Arnold and Cape Girardeau and Memphis and, beyond that, New Orleans. Every so often some driver would slow and gawk and even hit the horn. Sometimes a friendly sort of honk, like *beep, beep, thumbs up*. And sometimes not very friendly at all, laying it on, like *Go on, git! We don't want your kind around here.*

Their assigned area was an uninviting strip of turf and they were slowly making their way to the end of it. Two of the burlap feed bags had already been filled, mostly beer and soda cans and bottles, but also torn out pages of magazines, some machine parts, scrap lumber, busted toys, a headlight with wires, a car jack, a backpack with schoolwork inside, cereal boxes and mangled tin cans, a computer keyboard, and a decent fishing lure that Jamie called dibs on.

"Is it my imagination," said Birch, "that this part of the road has more litter than the rest?"

"It does seem to have more than its share," agreed Jamie. "You think people are dumping here deliberately 'cause of the sign?"

"Wouldn't surprise me," said Birch. "People come up with weird ways to show displeasure." They worked in silence for a while then Birch said, "I reckon I'm a hypocrite."

"How so, Cuz?"

"I'm a litterbug myself, throw stuff out the window as I'm driving along and never give a thought to it. But I don't like seeing litter and I sure don't like picking it up."

"Cleaning up after a bunch of thoughtless idiots, hillbillys raised in barns. Probably got no table manners either."

"Zero self-esteem," offered Birch. "Litterbugs don't care any more about themselves than they do about their environment."

"Isn't there a fine for littering?"

"Yeah, but nobody ever gets caught."

"What if they did? Get caught. Can you see a guy going up before the judge? 'Your honor, I'm sorry I pitched this old TV out on the highway. But you see, all it would pick up is *Matlock* and I'm tired of *Matlock*. If it was worth a hoot I wouldn't a throwed it away in the first place."

"Yeah," said Birch, grinning, "but like I said, that'll never happen. You'd have to dump a heap of trash, really blatant-like, to get the cops' attention. You know?"

"I'm sure it's been done," said Jamie.

"At least we're not picking up cigarette butts. I must've picked up ten thousand cigarette butts policing around the barracks where we

No Big Thing

lived during boot camp in Fort Knox."

"They probably told you it gives you character, right?"

Birch chuckled, "They told us if we missed one butt we'd land in KP for a week."

They came upon a twin mattress with its springs exposed.

"Must've fallen off a truck or car roof," said Birch, "someone moving."

"Don't tell me you're thinking about hauling this out?" said Jamie.

"It won't be hard, all we have to do is swing back around, stop on the shoulder for a minute, jump out and throw it in the back."

"Nah, this is above and beyond the call of duty. There's probably mice living in there, and then we take it home?"

"Well, that's a good point," said Birch, "we don't want to import any city mice to the country. Might throw the ecology off balance."

Then they heard a shout from the highway and at the same time a bottle went flying past them. They saw the source, a red station wagon tooling along with a guy hanging out the passenger window, screaming epithets and giving the finger.

"Guy's worked up about something," observed Jamie.

Birch picked up the bottle, a Busch longneck. He looked inside, saw the foam at the bottom. "Dang, if you're gonna throw bottles of beer at least make 'em full."

Ten minutes later the same car came by, moving considerably slower than the 40 mile an hour limit. Same guy in the passenger seat lobbed a lit M-80, and it went off at Jamie's feet. It's been said that an M-80 is equal to a quarter-stick of dynamite and while that's likely an exaggeration it did make a hell of a noise and kicked up a lot of dust. Jamie jumped like a kangaroo, the guy in the car laughing like all get out, yelling, "Where's your robes? Asswipes!" They saw the driver, too, flipping them off with a hand on an arm sticking up from the window. As they more or less puttered along, Jamie squeezed off a couple rounds, one of them shattering the back window. The station wagon stopped right there in the slow lane where it merged into the exit for Meramec Bottom Road. Cars and trucks behind them started swerving and honking. The station wagon had little choice but to move on.

Birch looked to Jamie, right arm down at his side, holding the pistol. Incredible. "Where'd that come from!"

"It was in my boot this whole time," said Jamie, looking happy with himself.

"Well, damnation, this isn't good. They're gonna come back, we gotta get out of here now."

"You wanna leave the job unfinished, fine with me."

ON THE OTHER SIDE of Arnold they stopped at a Cracker Barrel. Over sandwiches and iced tea they recounted their experience, how they hightailed it out of there, taking all their gear plus three feed sacks filled with roadside trash and junk, and, heading back, how they'd seen the red wagon parked on the shoulder and two guys beating on the sign with a carjack and a crowbar.

"Uncalled for," said Birch, a wry grin, "that sign never did a thing to them."

"Hotheads," said Jamie, "just looking for an excuse to get crazy. But we ain't gonna tell anybody what happened. I mean, shooting at 'em and all."

"Uncle Cy would tan your hide, that's for sure." A pause. "Well, as much as I'd like to boast on your behalf, tell everyone what a lucky potshot that was, I reckon I can keep it to myself." He popped the last of a club sandwich into his craw. The waitress came along and asked if they'd like anything else.

"Okay then, I'll get the check," she told them, but instead of walking off she began to study Jamie's T. "I Picked Up Trash For The Klan," she drawled, half-dubious half-suspicious. "Don't tell me y'all with the Ku Klux Klan." She pronounced it Cue Klux Klayan.

"No, ma'am," said Birch, "that Klan won't have us. We're with the Dumb Clucks Klan."

—23—

SHE HAD LEFT that morning fairly confident she would go through with it. The feeling had been tugging at her heartstrings for quite some time now: a mounting desire to end this estrangement and try to make peace with her father. Where did this notion come from? Well, Birch was egging her, true, but she wasn't sure if it had a specific source. She had read somewhere that forgiveness was the most human of attributes. To err was human, to forgive divine. But to forgive would she need to feel contrite? The drive up was filled with Patricia examining her conscience. She had walked out of her life, a relatively cozy situation, some 15 years ago as a reaction to Randall denigrating her Brazilian boyfriend for no other reason than his ethnicity. The unfairness of that action stung her emotionally, yes, but it was the attendant notion that her father and the entire Fortner clan were just so narrow-minded, so hopelessly country that she would never realize any dream that lay beyond the confines of Pine Grove, a notion which pushed her to the brink. Eduardo had a striking almond-colored complexion and spoke English with a strong accent to the point where you couldn't understand half of what he said—so what? Randall, so proud of his own backwoods heritage, could never see beneath the surface of a person. If they were Caucasian, by and large, they got a pass. If they were anything else—except Native Americans, he liked the "original people," as he called them—it was one strike against them. Eduardo was merely the current target of his bigotry; next week it would be some other person of color or someone holding a belief that he did not subscribe to. This was 1981, she was a fox, ready for action. She would not be stifled by parental bad vibes. She'd had enough, time to book.

One day she lit out, deciding none-too-reluctantly to leave her boy behind, in the care of her parents, hoping their conservative ways wouldn't rub off too much on Birch, a happy and hyperactive nine-year-old. "I don't know where I'm going or when I'll be back," she told Randall and Susan in the kitchen at breakfast. "Please watch over Birch and see that he grows tall and strong as a weed. Make sure he doesn't skip school and please don't try to make him eat succotash, as he hates it."

"He's a trooper," said Randall, "he'll be all right."

"We'll miss you, dear," said her mother. "You be careful out there, and call if you need anything but only if you really need something. Otherwise, we'll be content in knowing the world is turning and you're on it."

There was another compelling reason she had to get away, and it had nothing to do with Randall's intolerance. She was hooked on dope, had been for a couple years, snorting it, smoking it, whenever she got the chance. Actually, "hooked" was too strong a term; she thought of herself as an enthusiast. She didn't *have to* go through the motions of getting out-of-her-skull high, consorting with high school dropouts, becoming Party Down Wild Woman with each episode, she merely enjoyed it. Once a month had turned into once a week, but she had it under control. Sort of. Maybe her parents knew, maybe that's why they didn't try to convince her to stay. At any rate, she reasoned that removing herself from the source would solve the problem. As if Jefferson County had a monopoly on methamphetamine.

She was gone six years, first landing in a commune outside of Dennison, Colorado. After a couple years she decided that communal living with its back-to-the-earth mindset pervading everything from organic gardening to rabbit butchering to mate-swapping was for the birds. She moved on, finding a more enjoyable situation on the inlets of southern Puget Sound near Olympia, working on a sea farming operation run by the Nisqually tribe. They raised catfish in ponds, but the mainstay of Nisqually Oyster Company was oysters. As one of six full-time employees she was given a cabin which

No Big Thing

overlooked the Sound and soon became a birder for the prolific variety of waterfowl there. She was surprised to learn that oysters are planted as seeds called spat which somehow affixed themselves to plywood boards that were placed tent-like in the shallows of the inlets where the tides came and went twice a day. In that respect it was like farming, and she learned the skills of planting, harvesting, shucking, and packing the slimy oysters. Her biological clock set by the tides.

It was a satisfying existence with a purpose at its center, and, having weaned herself off meth, she blossomed. But of course someone had to come along and spoil it. That someone was an improbable character by the name of Farron Bird. At 34, he was a respected tribal member with a degree in aquaculture and was poised to take over the company from his ailing grandfather, Abraham Lincoln Bird. Right off Farron took a shine to Patricia, one which was not reciprocated. Still, he made advances, giving her special treatment, and showing up at her cabin uninvited with wine and crackers and kippered herring. Like the commune, this was a very cloistered community and she began to feel all eyes upon her. It was too bad she wasn't interested, she told herself, because here in Farron Bird was a ticket to a pretty nice life for the long haul. It was his hygiene or lack of it that bothered her. The man smelled like dirty socks, and his breath would wilt a flowering lungwort. Even his smarmy demeanor was odious. Once again, she felt up against it, so, in a sort of reprise of her somewhat hasty departure from the home of her parents, only more clandestine, she threw her meager belongings into the back of her Datsun and drove, leaving behind both the oysters and a paycheck due for $136. When she wanted to git, she got.

Meanwhile, back at the Missouri homestead, Birch had seen the the death of Gramma from an untreated dental abscess and the remarriage of Randall to Eveline. He was in high school now and running with the wrong crowd, or so Randall would say—and did say. Eveline tried in her own ineffectual way to mother him. Good intentions on her part, but she had never been a mother and was woefully out of touch with the appetites of teenage boys. She was unfailing in her encouragement, though, stressing that he had his whole life ahead of him and how certain reckless actions like plowing through hedges while inebriated behind the wheel of his 4 X 4 would likely put a crimp in his otherwise shining future. Her ministrations did not stick. Randall had decided that it was no good to impose unbending rules as he had done with Patricia. He was softening in his advancing years, more likely to sit down with the boy and try to talk some sense into his willful head than to lay down the law like some high-handed deputy sheriff.

At The Junction of Highways F and CC was a billboard decrying the theory of evolution. There was a depiction of an ape on all fours followed by a half-standing man-ape followed by homo erectus, modern man. The depiction was circled in red with a bold red X superimposed. The obvious message: Don't believe what established Science tells you. This billboard would have you call a certain phone number for "The Truth." Evangelicals, she thought, always trying to push their beliefs on you. Discontent until everyone in their sphere is brainwashed the same as they are. At least Randall was not that bad. He didn't proselytize, he mostly just reacted when your liberal beliefs encroached on his rigid, out-dated beliefs. A real dinosaur.

She drove through a terrain covered by rolling hills, about two-thirds hardwood and the rest conifer. It had started to drizzle and the wipers went to work. At length she came upon the sign announcing that one was entering Pine Grove. A footnote proclaimed the town to be the Home of Sue Ellen Watkins – Runner-Up 1987 State Spelling Bee. It was a Sunday so the family store was closed. She drove along Main Street noting any new shops that had opened since she was last here—what, four-five years back? There were none, although some were gone. She came to the place where she had grown up, a two-story eight room farm house with gabled roof, a stone chimney jutting upward. The expansive yard was contained by a rough-hewn cedar log fence, devoid of nails or bolts, timbers

No Big Thing

only, arranged in zigzag fashion. Randall's stamp. Ditto for the pair of Conestoga-type iron wagon wheels stationed at the entrance to the drive.

She stopped there, just into the entrance, turned off the wipers, put the car in Park. She lit a smoke, cracked the window, and sat there staring at the house, her home for some twenty years. The place where she'd kept ponies, where she and Rebecca had had dress up tea parties in the parlor, where she'd built an earthen bed of native flowering plants, where she'd eaten countless bountiful meals, dutifully done her homework every evening, where aspiring boyfriends had come to call, where she'd given birth to Birch with the help of a midwife. Through the blurry prism of rain on the windshield she looked to the window on the second floor, light-blue shutters on white siding, her old room. She wondered what it was now. A sewing room for Eveline or a study for Randall with his library and papers on the history of the Old South. A feeling came over her, wistful and tinged with sadness. The old saying about water under the bridge came to mind. It was too late to erase the hurt she'd felt, the hurt that was embedded in her like stubborn grit under the fingernails. Too late to set things straight.

Contrite? That was not a feeling to be summoned. No, her sense of it was more like rueful.

She stubbed her cigarette in the ashtray, put the car in Reverse, backed out, and went back the way she had come.

—24—

"Your Move," said Birch.

"How much to stay?" asked Jinx, pushing his meager cache of chips together.

"Buck-fifty is all."

Jinx pushed the little pile toward the pot. "Whatcha got?"

"I think I'll raise you another buck."

"No, you won't. I call. Whatcha got?"

"You first."

The two others who had folded watched with amusement as Jinx lay down his hand, one card short of a flush.

"That won't even get you the time of day in Timbuktu," said one.

"Pathetic," said the other.

Jinx raised his glass in a mock salute. "At least I stayed in. You bums fold at the drop of a hat."

Birch lifted a Busch longneck from the table, guzzled and forced a belch. With a flourish he lay his hand atop Jinx's. Two pair: eights and threes. He swept the chips—matchsticks—over in front of him. Grinning, "You play with the big dog, you're gonna get taken."

"Let's play something else," said one.

"Montana Red Dog, you know that one?" said another.

"Do I hear Crazy Eights?" from Jinx.

Birch swigged his beer to the end. "This dog is gonna hit the head and then I'm done for a while."

They were sitting in the back of Spud's, gambling on the sly. Big stakes, each matchstick worth a quarter. It was Fourth of July weekend, but nothing much going on that they wanted to do. A barbecue at the VFW Post, a parade over in Acadia with fireworks this evening. Maybe the fireworks, but for now it was drink beer and BS with the guys. The saloon, for that's what Spud's old roadhouse really was, starting to get busy with bikers and farm boys; it was more than a watering hole, it was *the* social hub for locals, mostly guys under 35.

Jinx left the table as well, and he found Birch over by the pool tables looking at a famous picture, titled *Custer's Last Fight*. It was a reproduction of course; the original limited editions commissioned and printed by the Anheuser-Busch Brewery like a hundred years ago were now worth a heck of a lot.

"There's a lot to look at here," said Birch. Jinx nodded and saw

No Big Thing

he was right. What incredible detail. Fighting to the death at close quarters, Indians with rifles and longknives and bludgeons, soldiers with rifles and pistols, soldiers being scalped, dead and dying on the ground, Custer in the middle of it, pistol in one hand, the other arm raised in defiance, and, in the background, a horde of mounted Sioux thundering in for the kill.

"It was a slaughter," informed Jinx, who knew something about the Battle of Little Bighorn, having once been to the site and heard the National Park Service guy's spiel. "The Sioux had their day, but it was one of their last. They went downhill from there."

"That Custer was a headstrong son of a gun, wasn't he? Lead all those men into a battle they couldn't win. Probably underestimated the strength of the Indians."

"Or had too much confidence in his own troops," offered Jinx, "every one to a man killed that day. They say if he'd come out of that fight, he'd have run for president of the United States and won. He was really ambitious."

"Ambition killed him. Reckon it pays off to sit back and chew on things for a while, not make any sudden rash decisions like blindly going up against several thousand bloodthirsty Indians. May as well play catch with a hornet's nest." He took a long pull off his longneck. "I think I'm going up to St. Louis, do a little litter patrol."

"Not today," said Jinx, "it's a holiday."

"Yeah, today, I'm in the mood."

"By yourself?"

"Yeah, why not. I know the drill. It'll be ... fun. Maybe."

"Well, for one, you been drinking all afternoon and because it's a holiday weekend there'll be cops all over the place, laying in wait like spiders, watching for drunk drivers. You don't need that crap."

He saw the genuine concern on his friend's face, a face that had always suggested slight feminine features although he would never mention that to Jinx or anyone else. "I'm not worried, I'll keep to the limit and be watchful."

"You're crazy, man."

He gave a dismissive wave of the hand. "I wanna do it and I'm gonna do it. That's all there is."

This was the old Birch talking, the one that got himself eleven misdemeanors by the age of 17.

"You trying to prove a point or something?" wondered Jinx.

"Probably am," said Birch, "but I have no idea what that point is."

"Don't go."

"I'm already gone."

Birch drove to his apartment over on Sumac—there was a tendency around here to name streets and places after trees, bushes and plants—and got his stuff. Litter-stick, trash bags, nylon safety vest. He let Bowser out and watched him do his business. He grabbed a beer from the fridge, saw there was just one left. He'd stop at the Quik Mart, score more beer and a fried-something sandwich. In terms of intoxication, he was in the zone, just right, sailing along about one-and-a-half sheets to the wind. He could pace himself and stay there all evening, maybe some peanuts to keep the balance. He thought of calling Randall, notify him, but then he remembered they were at the VFW thing. He vaguely recalled Gramps telling him about the State having some sort of, what? Protocol, yeah, a protocol says that MoDOT will be notified when litter pick up is scheduled, but this was a spur of the moment thing. To ask permission was not his style; ask permission you just might get turned down, and, besides, if he didn't get moving right now he might change his mind altogether. He gave Bowser a goodbye scratch behind the ear, grabbed his gear, looked at the clock on the wall: 3:40.

He rode the back roads out to the interstate, windows open, radio on KSHE, drinking beer from a styrofoam cup, the MARA-THON logo telling that it was coffee. He was feeling good about this trip, doing his duty without being asked, sacrificing his free time for community service, showing the world that the Klan kept its word.

No Big Thing

He had just crossed over the Meramec, the natural boundary between Jefferson and St. Louis Counties, when he saw the thing on the shoulder but partially obscured by weeds. It was one of those roadside markers, put up by friends or family to memorialize some fatality that happened, probably right here. You saw more and more of them these days, handmade, some fairly crude, others looking like the work of a master carpenter, but many of them very creative with custom touches relating to the victim and/or his lifestyle. He'd recently seen a white wooden cross about four-foot high with a bible passage and the guy's name: So-and-So "The Preacher." Like that. He had given these markers some thought and decided they had no place on a public highway. That's what cemeteries were for. These makeshift memorials—hard *not* to gaze upon—were a distraction and could cause accidents.

He slowed down for this one, a miniature Washington Monument, trying to read it, making out a name "Blackie" and a partial message "He Had So ..." He looked harder, the next word was "Much." So much energy? So much fun? when all of a sudden *bam!* the beer in his cup sloshed all over him as he bonked his forehead on the steering wheel. He looked at the big black pickup, way too close, its tailgate just on the other side of his windshield, and thought: Where did you come from?

Immediately he saw the problem, there was something going on up ahead and the right lane was backed up to a stop, a line of red brake lights stretching into the distance. Inattentive, he'd plowed into this Dodge Ram. He composed himself as best he could, mind racing at the thought of what to do when the cops came as they surely would. There was also the possibility the guy in the truck was a psycho. He found his insurance card in the pull-out ashtray where he kept it, and got out. The guy's face and body language told Birch he was harmless, reasonable, not the kind to go off the edge. Whew. Together they looked at the impact and saw that the Ram's big honkin trailer hitch had punched Birch's grill. There was greenish fluid dripping on the pavement, but not a lot which meant that it would be a good idea to move it off the road soon while he still could. A woman got out of the Ram and came back to look. She seemed the more take charge type and she suggested—just short of ordered—that Birch back up his truck a few feet. "Right now, you got your nose in our bunghole," she said. "We need a better look-see."

He did just that and they saw that except for some marring of the chrome-plated trailer hitch, the Ram was unscathed. No damage, no need to take it any further. "In fact, we need to move out," said the woman, "Jared here's gonna take me to dinner at that steak-house in the city." She gave him a squeeze. "Ain't you, hon?"

The queue had dissipated and yet he was blocking the right lane, the slow lane, traffic going around him. By now there was a green puddle beneath his engine. He got in, suspenseful as to whether it'd start. He turned the key, yes, there it was, that beautiful sound. Just before pulling out he looked over at the marker, fake flowers around the base, fully readable now: "Blackie – He Had So Much To Live For."

But the truck didn't want to pick up speed, it kind of limped along, sputtering and coughing. He decided to drive it on the shoulder until he got to an exit where he could pull off and call someone. He was almost to the Meramec Bottom Road exit when the flashing lights appeared in his rear view.

"It Could've Been So Much Worse," he told Jamie. "I could be sitting in the drunk tank right now instead of here with you. And thanks a mill for driving all this way to get me. I owe you big time."

"You're lucky you caught me, I was just leaving."

"I know, Spud said he had to send Dee out to the parking lot to get you to the phone."

Jamie popped a a can of Busch, indicating a partial six on the floor. "Go ahead, Cuz, it's all good now."

"Thanks, I could use one." He pulled the pop-top, the familiar and comforting *whoosh* of effervescence escaping from the can. They

No Big Thing

were well into Jefferson County, off the interstate now, following the two-lane blacktop home.

"Tell me again what happened, first time you were kinda sparse on the details."

He looked over to Jamie, eyes on the road, camo cap pulled down on his brow. "Where's your cowboy hat, you look like a doofus without it."

"I loaned it to Chuck Norris, now go on."

"Yeah, so I saw the light show in my mirrors and I pull over and wait for the cop to come up. After the accident I had the good sense to pitch what beer I had—get rid of the evidence, you know?—but I still have a cupful in the drink-holder so I chug that right quick and wait, thinking I'm probably going to the slammer. Cop gets out and walks up—"

"What kind of cop?"

"St. Louis County, red-and-white patrol car."

"Man, you're lucky it wasn't highway patrol, those guys are total bad asses. No slack do they cut."

"Yeah, so this guy, first he does the drill: 'Let's see your license, proof of insurance' and whatnot. He's looking at my license and I know he's gonna ask me what's wrong with my truck, why was I driving ten miles an hour on the shoulder. So I'm waiting for that question but instead he hunkers down and leans in close and starts looking *in* the cab of my truck, around where I'm sitting, which naturally makes me kinda nervous even though I don't have nothing illegal laying around. I figure he can smell the beer because a bunch of it spilled when I hit the pickup. Any moment I'm expecting him to say in that serious tone, 'Sir, you mind stepping out of the vehicle?'

"But that doesn't happen. So, finally he gets around to asking about the truck and I tell him the radiator got a leak and I'm trying to make it to that gas station over yonder so I can give it a rest and figure my next move. I can see he's still checking me out, being suspicious like every other cop. And I'm checking him out, too. It's still a tense situation."

"I can see it," said Jamie, "wheels turning in his cop brain: 'This guy's probably done something or holding something'."

"You're right, because then comes the dreaded question: 'Have you been drinking?'"

"Oh man, right into the furnace! This is a question any guy who's had a few hates to hear. Do you flat out lie or do you tell the truth—'Just a few, officer, but that was hours ago and I'm fine to drive'—say something like that and hope for the best."

Birch nodded, "That's what I did, admitted I'd had a couple. He could smell it, I wasn't about to insult him. So he decides he's going to do a field sobriety test. Ever had one of those? They hold a finger up in front of your nose, tell you to look at it."

"I heard about that, looking for some kinda eye movement shows up when you're drunk."

"Then they have you stand on one leg and try not to fall, something you couldn't do even if you were stone sober." He chuckled. "I couldn't keep my balance, I asked him if I could hop around. That'd help, I told him. Then, he's got me trying to walk a straight line, one foot directly in front of the other, like you're walking a tightrope."

"Circus boy."

"It was a challenge, believe me."

"Oh, Lord, is that you?"

"Sorry, must've been that chili I had, waiting for you."

Jamie fanning away the stench, "Rotten, like something crawled up in you and died."

"Denny's chili's nothing but beans," said Birch.

"Just don't do it again, Cuz, and open your window some more."

"Yeah, yeah, so I'm waiting for the shoe to drop, as they say, trying to read this cop's mind, what he's gonna do with me, and you know how they say that Asians have this hard-to-read face, like expres-

No Big Thing

sionless? That's how this guy was."

"Wait a minute, he's Asian?"

"Yeah, his nameplate said Nguyen—Vietnamese, I think."

"Nuh-guy-in?"

"N-G-U-Y-E-N. We had some in the community college, must be a common name for them. I guess they pronounce it 'Winn.'"

"Oh man, them ornamentals, they got it in for us whiteys."

"Not this guy, he was cool. He said that I *barely* passed the field sobriety test. He said he could impound my truck, run me in, slap a DUI on me easy as pie. 'But you didn't try to weasel out of it,' he said, 'you told me true and I appreciate that.' Then he pointed to the gas station over yonder, said I should drive over there, call someone and sit tight until they come to get me. 'How's that sit with you?' he said, 'and don't let me see your pickup moved until tomorrow.'"

Jamie shook his head in wonder. "I'll be a five-legged mooncalf."

"Not only that, but he had a gallon of coolant in his cruiser and we put half of it into my radiator. Then he sent me on my way."

"That was a fairy tale, Cuz, you just came out of a fairy tale."

"Don't I know it," said Birch, going for another Busch. He began to fidget and leaned slightly to one side. "Here comes another one—sorry 'bout that."

—25—

FIVE DAYS A WEEK, a little after four, Wells Coughlin, coming down I-270 East, took the I-55 turnoff and headed south for about four miles, over the Meramec River into Arnold where he lived with his two dogs and three cats. He worked at Maxwell Fabricators, had for 17 years now, a family-owned shop which took on almost any order from grommets to fire plugs to prison bars. Wells Coughlin was a cutter, shearing metal day-in day-out, with whatever tool was required for the job. He was particularly adept at wielding hand-held torches—oxyacetylene or plasma, either one—and he considered himself somewhat of an artist. Although not stand-offish, he tended to keep to himself and instead of having lunch with his coworkers, suffering lame jokes and idle gossip, Wells preferred to go off alone and read a newspaper or magazine with his Braunschweiger and pickle sandwich that he packed each day.

Wells Coughlin had been flying solo for a long time now, ever since grade school when he'd been diagnosed with strabismus, a condition in which the eyes do not align properly when perceiving an object. In Wells's case one eye looked right at you and the other eye looked off to the side. A handicap, to be sure, and while it prevented him from enlisting in the Marines, it did not affect his job performance. He could weld and cut like no tomorrow. His condition, however, was slightly disconcerting to some of the workers in the fab shop, and to lighten this unease they called him "Wall-eyed Wells" behind his back. They also called him Cog to his face, which was not a dig, just a nickname evinced by the pronunciation of his surname: Cog-lin. Almost all the guys had nicknames—Cujo, Butterball, Lugnuts—and Cog was better than most.

So Wells Coughlin a/k/a Cog was tooling along the interstate heading home on a Wednesday. Nice day, looking forward to firing up the grill, playing with the dogs, working on his collection, when he saw the sign. It wasn't there yesterday, but here it was bold as you please, telling the world that the Ku Klux Klan was still around. He'd heard something about this on the news, a legal battle come to a head, but he didn't realize the controversial sign would be part of his daily commute. As he passed the sign a feeling welled up, a powerful covetousness; he *had* to have that sign.

He got home, greeted the dogs which basically lived outside in his large fenced-in backyard. Throwing tennis balls, playing fetch, romping along with them, he still couldn't get that sign out of his head. He went inside, changed clothes, grabbed a cold one, and went back out, this time not for dog antics. He walked down the

No Big Thing

rows, inspecting each structure, making sure all was squared away. If a board had come loose, he carried a hammer and nails to tack it back in place. If the marker listed noticeably one way or the other, he would set it straight, using wooden stakes if need be. He did not touch up faded paint or lettering. Those were the personal work of the fabricator-artist and he respected that. Leave it be, let the elements take their toll. He was the caretaker, presiding over a collection of grief made manifest.

He remembered the circumstances of each acquisition. This one, a testament to "Nine Toes," and festooned with Mardi Gras beads—just the way he found it—he came upon after driving off the Brussels Ferry and heading upriver to no particular destination. It was bigger than most, a large white cross meant to be seen from afar, with not only the gala beads but a weather-beaten fishing hat resting atop the vertical beam of the cross. Cog considered this quite the prize to augment his then-meager menagerie and he wasted no time in uprooting it, carefully placing it in the bed of his pickup and concealing it with a tarp that he carried for such a purpose. That was three years ago and darned if the thing didn't still look good today. Or this one here, a marker for a biker he'd found down around Blackwell on a foraging excursion, a big old thing decorated with motorcycle sprockets and hung with a denim vest showing the guy's colors. "RIP Roadhog" it said. One thing he really appreciated about his collection: the variety. True, most of them were made of wood, in the configuration of a holy cross, that being the symbol of the prevailing religion. But there were also flat markers made of metal with the decedent's name stamped on it. Markers of plywood, propped up with two-by-fours, names or messages crudely painted on. His favorite saying on a purloined roadside marker: "One Thing Led To Another And Before I knew It—Time To Punch Out." He particularly liked the ones with quirky or poignant epitaphs, sayings they wouldn't allow in a cemetery setting.

He placed them in rows, giving them space to breathe. Sometimes, when a new one came along, he wouldn't set it right away.

He'd lay it on the lawn near the others and he'd think on it for several days, getting a feel for the vibe it was putting off. He might finally decide that it should go next to a certain other one around which the plots were all taken up. If so, he'd switch out an older one for the newcomer. It was extra work but worth it; Cog had a touch of OCD and to not place a marker where he felt it was best suited would really bug him. Like this one here, his most recent acquisition, plucked from the prairie grass along northbound I-55, not far from here, an obelisk with black letters etched into limestone. "Blackie – He Had So Much To Live For." It was more professional-looking than most, the work an artisan, possibly a stone mason or a sculptor. He was still debating where to place it.

Pushing fifty and never married, Cog very much enjoyed his hobby, as he thought of it—like stamp collecting only these collectibles were large and unwieldy and would probably get him in trouble if discovered. In fact, his main worry over his furtive enterprise involved being found out. Aghast at the thought, he had a vinyl privacy fence, the tallest he could buy at Home Depot, going around the backyard. Just inside this perimeter were stands of bamboo he'd cultivated, some of it twelve foot or taller. No busybodies were going to see his treasures, and likewise he never invited anyone over.

Cog got the gas grill going and threw on a couple of pork steaks. He put on his apron with the picture of a barbecue fork and the gagline "King Of The Grill." Some special marinade, some Kansas City Steak Seasoning, couple more beers, he was half-way to heaven. Still, that sign was in his thoughts. It would be a departure from the current line, but it was so unique, so compelling he couldn't resist. Monomania had set in. He looked to the older dog, Sambo, and Miss Kitty, the calico cat, sitting there at his feet, patient, knowing they would get some savory tidbits by and by. "What do you think, kiddos? Is tonight the night for a commando raid?"

"THIS ALL YOU GOT?" Billy asked the kid in aisle sixteen. The kid, busy stocking shelves in the COUGH & COLD section, looked up at

No Big Thing

the inquisitor and was taken aback. The large hirsute man standing over him—he was kneeling at the moment, organizing some Tylenol on a lower shelf—brought to mind an escapee from the asylum. That, or else another meth head hoping to score all the Sudafed in stock, a key ingredient in their noxious recipe. The kid whose name was Travis had tried meth a few times but now stayed away from it because, first, it gave him a bad taste in his mouth and, worse, he could actually feel his brain cells frying. So, working in an all-night Walgreen's and knowing the profile, he had seen his share of meth cooks come calling. This guy had the irritable look, the unhealthy complexion, and the rank smell—stale perspiration—of a meth freak. And he had "country" stamped all over him. Typical, thought Travis, they come up from the Boonies, hit the big box stores, usually late at night, buy as much Sudafed as they can, get back to their secret kitchen, extract the pseudoephedrine from the tablets, add a bunch more chemicals, and presto! A highly potent narcotic. A ticket to La La Land. A handy profit for jokers like this.

Travis saw that the man already had a couple dozen packages of Sudafed as well as the Walgreen's own version in his shopping basket. "No, if that's all there was on the shelf I think you done cleaned us out."

"Rats," said Billy.

Travis thought he might have a little fun with him, see how gullible he was. He stood now, facing the customer, all helpful. "Hoo boy, you must have a heck of a sinus infection," he ventured, "you got enough here to last you five years." Travis lifted a package from Billy's basket, studied it. "You know, you've got to be careful with this. Not too much at once. Says here, side effects, um, restlessness, nausea, vomiting, headache, and that's just the start." Holding the package close, reading, 'More serious side effects may include nervousness, dizziness, difficulty breathing, insomnia, fast pounding heartbeat.'" Indeed, the guy looked like a walking medical chart for half of those signs. Man," said Travis, "you must really be in misery to risk all that."

Of late Billy had shed the beard and cultivated a Van Dyck or goatee or whatever you want to call it so that it pretty much covered his mouth. But the teeth were in there somewhere, and Billy half-smiled a mouthful of stained nubs, stepped into Travis, got right in his face. Travis, now alarmed, tried to back up but only bumped the shelf behind him, bottles of NyQuil teetering. "I asked you a simple question. You answered it. I didn't ask you for a friggin medical opinion, did I?" The man got even closer, and Travis was terrified that this oaf would either kiss him or bite him. Travis looked around for help, saw none.

"Well, *did* I?"

"No, sir."

Billy put a bony finger on Travis' shirt, going for the middle button. "What's this?" And, when Travis looked down to see, Billy flubbed his nose with that same finger. He backed off, gave a wink. "Then mind your business and I'll mind mine. Cool?"

"Cool."

Billy Goldie had himself a pretty good haul. Three supermarkets and two Walgreen's yielding 84 packages of Sudafed or Sudafed knock-offs which were a little cheaper but still good. He would've hit Walmart but they closed at ten and he liked the late night-early morning runs, fewer raised eyebrows at what he was up to—not that what he was doing was illegal; Sudafed was an over-the-counter item, but seeing him with a shopping cart full, well, it would be clear to many that he had a lab. Nor did he want to make these runs too often so it was good that what he'd gotten tonight would last him another couple months. Driving home he recounted his encounter with that smart-ass clerk and laughed inwardly at the kid's quip that he must really be a mess to need all that decongestant. Okay, so that kid was probably wise to him, but did that kid have any inkling how cooking meth could be real work? It was such an exacting process you practically had to have a degree in chemistry to make it and

No Big Thing

have it come out right.

First thing, you had to have a decent kitchen and he had his trailer off in the woods miles from his house. Rule Number One: You don't manufacture where you live. But the trailer was not only his production plant, it was his home away from home, set up with amenities like a little fridge for food and beer, usually a fifth of Jack laying around, too. There was radio, coffeemaker, binoculars, some posters on the wall, cot and blankets in case he needed to spend the night. A loaded 12 gauge over & under over near the door. He would go there tomorrow after he had some breakfast. Rule Number Two: Never work on an empty stomach.

He would take his time, he was patient and he enjoyed the process. First, you separate the pseudoephedrine from the store-bought Sudafed tablets. To do this the tablets get ground up, he had a coffee grinder for that. Then they're mixed with an evaporation solvent like ether or Coleman camping fuel and the solution is then filtered and exposed to low temperatures to separate and remove the good stuff. He would have his red phosphorous ready, the stuff found on the striker plates of matchbooks. Tear off the striker plates and soak them in that same solvent already used with the tablets, the phosphorous now breaking down. Next, the pure pseudoephedrine is mixed with red phosphorous and hydriodic acid with a tincture of iodine. Now you add the mix to the cooking vessel along with the appropriate amount of acid. Then, add the base, a lye solution. The acid and the lye agitate each other causing a reaction that's called "the cook." Put the cooking vessel on the hot plate, the reaction speeds up. Liquid meth is now collected in a top layer, and will soon be "salted out," basically converted to a semi-solid. To do this a hydrogen chloride gas is bubbled through the liquid meth, which is poured through a filter cloth or coffee filter. Now it looks like a wet paste. This wet paste is left in the coffee filter which goes into a plastic funnel and placed over the mouth of a wide jar. Then you pour either acetone or ether over the paste to remove any discoloration for a clean white product. The paste is then dried, resulting in a chunky powder. They weren't doing Glass or Ice around here, you couldn't cut that stuff.

Simple? Not at all. Here he was, a high school drop-out, doing graduate-level chemistry!

This was the orthodox method. There were shortcuts to be taken, sure, but unless he was in a hurry to get the next batch out he tended to avoid those, adhering to Rule Number Three: If you're gonna do it, do it right. And it paid off because his customers often complimented him on the quality of his product—"bong-worthy," "righteous"—and the consistency of his product—"always a trip," "rush after rush" and worked flattery on him with the moniker "Your High-ness." He catered to seasoned drug users who knew intrinsically the quality of the dope by the first complimentary hit. Let other dealers cut their product with crushed up amphetamine or other fillers, he stepped down his product with MSM, a nutritional supplement for both humans and animals. That way they can get high *and* build up damaged cartilage.

Rule Number Four, Careful does it and you'll be here tomorrow, was the overarching rule, for if it wasn't followed you had nothing, not even your life. Thanks to his cousin and mentor, Ronnie Goldie, Billy knew how to cook meth at 17. But even the best of them are known to slip up, and Ronnie was burned alive when his lab exploded, fireballs shooting out the windows, his charred remains found in a corner of the backwoods cabin where he cooked. It was a closed casket. If Rule Number Four was followed then you've got your batch ready to weigh, measure into individual doses, and package for sale. The whole thing took two days and yielded thousands of doses.

Now Billy was winding down from a hit of meth taken earlier in the day, a dose that had been washed down with numerous beers and Jack Daniels at the Iron Horse Saloon, a stop he'd made on the way up to St. Louis. There were several joints along the way as well. In short, Billy was on the tail end of wasted and he had no business behind the wheel. He was thinking of his bed and how nice it would

No Big Thing

be to plop down on it, asleep before he hit the mattress. Asleep ... *dr-dr-dr-dr-dr-dr.* The sound jolted him awake in an instant before he could drive off the road. Thank god for rumble strips. He slapped his face hard thinking to ward off sleep.

"I'll be go to hell," said Billy to himself a minute later, driving along and seeing the sparks and glow of what had to be a welding torch low to the ground on the side of the highway. Wasn't this the place where the Fortners had their sign? And wasn't it 1:30 in the morning, an unlikely time for a state highway crew to be out. And that pickup parked on the shoulder, that sure didn't look like no MoDOT rig. "Looks like we got us a pilferer," he intoned, intrigue mounting, as he pulled in to the shoulder and began backing up.

The man was on his knees, his back to Billy, obviously engrossed in his task of cutting the sign off at the base of its galvanized steel twin posts. And sure enough, the final cut was made with Billy standing there. With a creak and a crash the sign toppled. He switched off his welding torch and stood up, still not aware of company. The man looked at the sign laying on the ground—his prize, his burden. He was thinking he ought to split before someone comes along. Thinking, too, about all the markers he'd snatched from country roads, how those were put there by private citizens who had no authorization to do so, they just assumed it would be all right and that their tribute to the dead wouldn't be violated or ripped-off. So, he showed them different. But this, this was state property and to cut it down and take it was probably grand larceny. He could go to jail for this.

Cog lifted the sign, it was heavy, maybe 70 pounds or more. Cradling it to his chest, he began trudging toward his truck when he heard, "You can just put that in the back of my van."

He turned, saw a figure not ten feet away, a shock wave going through his body. "Go on," said the intruder, motioning with his head, "that van right over there. I'll be right behind you, make sure you don't stumble."

Cog was freaking out, didn't know what to say or do. Was he

willing to fight the guy here and now for his hard-earned prize? This guy had to be unhinged, skulking around out here by himself. Maybe he was armed. Cog had a snub-nose .38 at home but didn't bring it, never imagining any trouble. Seconds passed. Finally, Cog responded by lowering the sign and resting it on the ground at his feet. "I don't want no trouble," he told him, voice quavering. "This here's the property of the state highway department and I'm an independent contractor 'sposed to remove it for repairs. You don't wanna mess with this."

"What kinda repairs?" wondered Billy, stepping in closer.

Cog, thinking fast, "Well, um, not repairs exactly, but a change of wording. This group's on the outs, didn't keep the highway clean enough, so I heard. The new adoption group is Mothers Against Drunks Driving, you probably heard of 'em."

"Yeah, I heard of 'em," said Billy, "bunch of old bags with nothing better to do than try to interfere with a man's god-given right to get tanked."

The man shifted position and Billy saw his face clearer now, something off about his looks. Billy shook his head like patience was a frayed rope, said, "You're lying through your teeth, bro', and if you don't get that sign over to my van right this instant I'm gonna let Jim Bowie here teach you a lesson." At that, he reached behind him and whipped out a hunting knife, like to skin a grizzly, its broad blade glinting in the filtered rays of a distant street lamp.

Cog felt his anus pucker and decided right then it wasn't worth it. After he'd done this lunatic's bidding, Cog stepped aside and watched dolefully as the van doors shut, the ignition turned on, exhaust coughing from the rusted muffler, the sound of gravel crunching, the van disappearing down the road, his coveted road sign with it.

No Big Thing

—26—

Terry Brannick Had Just walked out of Spud n' Velma's saying how he had to get home or the old lady would cook his goose, and now suddenly he was back. He went straight to the bar where a knot of regulars were conspiring to take the cash prize at the upcoming washers tournament. "Change your mind?" asked Terry's pal, Ron. "Good for you, 'bout time you stood up to that woman. Let me get you a drink, buddy."

Terry shook his head no, pointed behind him, thumb out like a hitchhiker, said, "You gotta see this."

They all filed out onto the porch beneath a tin awning. Soon others came out, too. It was a weekday around five; the entire happy hour cast of characters including Dee the bartender now stood around gazing at the spectacle in the parking lot.

"Well, what d'ya think?" called Billy. "She's a dilly, ain't she? C'mon over, get a closer look." He had the sign propped up against his van. Some of the guys did walk over, drinks in hand, shuffling around as Billy did his show-and-tell. It was three days after he'd relieved Cog of his prize, and he'd had time to think about what he wanted to do with it. He'd made his batch, was ready to move it, and it occurred to him that he could use the sign to attract an audience, potential customers. Work them like an old-time carnival barker and when he had their full attention, make his sales pitch. The sign was his prop, the several hundred hits of dope, his livelihood, tucked away in his van.

"Y'all wondering how I came upon this beauty," said Billy in his pitchman voice. "Well, I took it from some freak who'd cut it down and was gonna use it for spells of black magic. That's right, this wizard or warlock, whatever he was, was gonna use this here sign for wicked evil purposes, said something about summoning up demons. I stopped him like a tree stops a motorcycle."

"What do you want, a medal?" interrupted a smart alec name of Darrell.

Jinx, in the back of the group, was alarmed by Billy's presentation and decided that he would call Birch on the house phone as soon as Dee went back inside.

"Sure, why not?" said Billy, bestowing a crooked smile. "It can read 'Billy Goldie—Ass Kicker Extraordinaire.' Think about it for a sec. See, this thing is just an object, something made in a shop without much thought given to what it actually means. I see it for what it really stands for—white pride, a race to be reckoned with, a fraternal brotherhood with the right ideals and the balls to see those ideals acted out, no matter the cost or what's standing in your way. We gotta let 'em know we ain't playin' here." He paused, mulling this for a second. "You with me? Y'all don't know it because I don't generally broadcast my political views, but I am a Klansman at heart. I've read up on it and I believe those old boys were on to something."

Terry Brannick shot his hand up. Billy, dubious, stopped his spiel. "Yeah?"

Terry gulped. "You should take that sign over to the store, that's Mr. Fortner's property."

Billy snorted in disgust. "Mr. Fortner, my ass. You see what happened here? This sign chopped off at the ankles just like the Klan in these here parts. Randall Fortner's part of the problem. He'll make a big deal out of getting a sign put up, fight it out in court, get written up in the papers—you'd think he was the Grand Wizard or something, but he's a sham! He don't have the interests of the Klan in his heart, he's just doing it for publicity, self-glorification! Got an ego the size of Texas. Sure, he went and made an application for this here sign, he filled out a form saying he's a Klansman. Yeah, right, a Klansman on *paper only*." He looked at each and every jamoke, gauging reaction, thinking this must be what a preacher feels when he's addressing his flock. "I say it's time for a new era of the Ku Klux Klan, one that's not just wishful talk and bumper stickers but honest to goodness action. What do you say?"

"What kinda action, Billy?"

No Big Thing

"You know dang well what kinda action," Billy shot back. "The kind that puts spades and minorities on notice. They gonna tow the line or face some serious consequences."

"What's your middle name?" asked a guy named Kenny who hardly ever said much.

Billy just looked at him. This wasn't going the way he'd hoped. "What does that have to do with the price of donuts in Denver? It's Loudon, why?"

"Dang," said Kenny, snapping his fingers. "I was lookin' for Lee."

"Lee? Why Lee?"

"My momma told me that all the real bad-asses have the middle name Lee."

A fellow with a bird-like frame, looked like a scarecrow, spoke up. "I don't know, Billy, being in a club, just about any club, means going to meetings, probably paying dues, spending time with folks you don't really know. We ain't got the time nor wherewithall for that."

"Yeah," offered another, "it ain't like we don't wanna get out there and discriminate but there's so much else going on—"

"Like drinkin' and pool playin' right here," put in Ron, Terry's pal, having a bit of fun.

"And joke tellin', we do a lot of that," reminded another one, standing close to Billy. "Speakin' of which, did you hear the one about the Missouri farmer and the Texas oilman? Seems there was this Texas oilman heading up to Chicago, got off the interstate, got turned around and had to ask for directions ..."

Jinx, still in the background, saw that Billy was doing a slow burn, and he wondered how long it would be til the pot boiled over.

"Okay, okay!" spouted Billy, eyes scrunched shut, one fist pressed against his forehead, "have it your way. Jeez! I see I ain't getting nowhere. Well, on to other business. Anyone interested in getting their head up?" A conspiratorial wink. "Know what I mean?"

They headed back inside, the ones who weren't interested in getting their heads up with Billy. Jinx asked Dee if he could make a call.

Dee handed him the cordless, said to leave a quarter on the bar, ha, ha.

Jinx had to wait several minutes while Eveline went and got Birch who was "weighing some feed at the moment." Then Birch got on, asked what's up. "I'm over at Spud's," Jinx told him. "Birch, you're not gonna believe this ..."

—27—

"THIS MAKES ME SO MAD I want to spit." Sheila Cowan pursed her lips and frowned mightily. "Spit and curse and shout. Maybe punch a wall." She took a single sheet of paper from her desk, one that had just arrived by inter-office mail, crumpled it, and threw it with some force at her assistant. Stefan Piontek gave a startled cry as the missile glanced off his cheek. "Read it," Sheila commanded. Stefan rose from his chair, planted in front of her desk, and plucked the memo off the carpet. He began to uncrumple it. "Aloud," said Sheila, acerbically, "read it aloud, so I can be better humiliated."

"Okay, just let me smooth it out some. Here we go. It says, 'Looks like we lost a highway sign, the same as your department lost the fight to put it there in the first place. I'm tempted to say that you and your people are slipping, but I guess I'll just hold my tongue.'"

"What else?" asked Sheila. "I want it all."

"Uh, well," said Stefan, "the message is hand-written on the margin of a xeroxed news article, headline 'No Trace of Embattled KKK Sign.' Do you want me to read the article?"

"No, get to the closing."

"It says, 'Let's get together, Toby Shoemaker.'"

"Give me that!" Sheila came around her desk and snatched the paper away. She held it out at arm's length as Stephen cringed where he stood. "It doesn't say that, you idiot. It says, 'Get it together.' It's a goddamn admonishment, not an invitation."

"Sorry," said Stefan, "I have a touch of dyslexia."

No Big Thing

"I wish I had amnesia," she said, "so I wouldn't have to remember the day the Director of the Highway Department dressed me down in a memo. How I rue the day you came in here to show me that application sent in by Jed Clampett over there in Bumpkinville."

Rue, thought Stefan, that's an interesting word. He'd heard it before, its definition unclear to him. Why not regret? Rue must be a better choice, a certain kind of regret. More deeply felt? Regret marinaded in bitterness? Maybe it wasn't a variation of regret at all, maybe it was more a synonym for hate or despise. He would look it up later; he was always trying to improve his vocabulary.

Sheila was silent now, her back to him, looking out the picture window toward the river. Her corner office with its bank of sizable windows on two walls gave a panoramic view of the state capitol, normally a cheerful perception but not now. She began to move, pacing the confined area behind her desk, back and forth, head down, massaging one temple, still fuming but also mulling the thing over. Stefan saw she wore no shoes, hose with subtle fleur de lis accent covering her calves and feet. Today, she had on her "knock 'em dead power suit," as she called it, an attention-grabber from Donna Karan's spring line. A white silk poet's shirt that fluttered over a black calf-length skirt and cascaded over the lapels of a smart, fluid pantsuit. She looked as though she might be seen reading Yeats or Dickenson under a spreading maple somewhere on the capitol campus but instead she was having lunch this day with the governor.

Now she was staring out the window again, Stefan patient, biding his time. Finally, she spoke. "I can't have this thing continually coming round to bite me. Now, every other week it's in the shop. The cursed sign is battered, shot up with small arms fire—.22 rounds, just peppered! Spray-painted with hateful nasty words."

"Don't forget the acid, that was a genius move, took the finish right off."

"Now, it's gone altogether and it's such a high-profile fixture that if we don't replace it quickly there'll be talk and we'll be accused of flouting the court's decision." Off in the distance she saw a tow going by, saw the mounds of black protruding from the open frame of each and every tow. Coal from out west on its way to St. Louis. "And this is just the beginning," she went on, "it's going to happen again and again, a recurring nightmare, unless we figure out how to put it to an end." She pivoted, now facing Stefan, jaw set, arms crossed on her bosom. "There's *got* to be a solution. We've *got* to put our heads together and find a way to beat this thing."

Stefan nodded assent. This was his moment, he knew, his chance to shine. Kudos coming his way, all the accolades he could handle. "I've got an idea," he said.

—28—

BIRCH HAD SETTLED into his job as, well, factotum at the Pine Grove Elevator & Mercantile. And while factotum can be taken as a slight, there was nothing demeaning about knowing how to do a little of everything, and he enjoyed the variety of tasks. In a thirty-minute period he might be measuring out a length of rope, discoursing on the going price of veal calves, dipping minnows from the bait tank because the crappie were running, ringing up a pair of work gloves, or touting the merits of this supposed "100 Percent Guaranteed Squirrel-Proof" bird feeder. Yeah, right. Only problem was the squirrels didn't sign on for that. If he was never idle that was okay because boredom was hell. Even with no customers there was always something to put away, to clean up or rearrange, to order on the phone. Randall was there mornings, with his tea and packet of Sen-Sens, stationed at the check-out counter gabbing with every customer who had the time. Eveline showed up sometime after noon to relieve Randall who by then needed to get off his feet. He would either go out back to his museum and putter around or head up to the house for light lunch and a nap. Three-thirty or so, he would be back to relieve Eveline and finish up until closing at five-thirty. Birch worked the livelong day five days a week, but if he needed time off it was granted without a fuss. There were two back-up helpers, the

No Big Thing

aforementioned Junior Bannister, a strapping 17-year-old, and an older neighbor girl with a harelip, Addie, both of whom apparently had nothing else going and were almost always available on short notice.

Then there was Tyra Singletary, now in graduate school at Duke, and home for the summer. Once again, she had taken to hanging out at the store, not buying much of anything, but looking to strike up conversation with the Fortners and their customers. She hadn't yet used her talks with Randall for the stellar thesis she would need to graduate, but she was working on it. In fact, this thesis, incipient but taking shape by the day, percolated in her brain all the time, and she carried a small notebook in her back pocket to write down snippets of insight. She jotted surreptitiously so as not to alarm anyone, cause them to think she was some kind of investigative reporter secretly taking notes on them. Which, of course, she was. Still, her presence was not objected to and, in fact, because of her general good nature, it was welcomed.

Her thesis for a masters degree in sociology, tentatively titled, *Bigotry in Rural America: A Case Study of One Family*, now had two sections and a sub-section. But the title, she thought, was rather blah. She would have liked to come up with something really catchy like Margaret Mead's doctoral dissertation, *An Inquiry into the Question of Cultural Stability in Polynesia*. Maybe her piece could be called *An Inquiry into the Hearts and Minds of American Bigots Masquerading as Normal People*. Too close to Miss Margaret's title? She would be mortified if ever she were accused of plagiarizing the great woman's work. At any rate, she needed more material to work with. She needed for something to happen.

And so it was that when Tyra heard talk around the store of another round of trash collection, the last one having been aborted, she decided she would plead her case to go along.

"Nah, it's gotta be solo," he told her flat out, "it's better that way."

"Always good to have a partner," she countered, "I'll have your back."

169

"What, you think we're going into a war zone?"

"Oh, c'mon! You afraid to be seen with a black woman?"

"Is that what you are? I hadn't noticed."

"I'll bake some brownies to take along. How about that?"

"A bribe, huh? They any good?"

"Betty Crocker's best. I use walnuts and semisweet chocolate chips, they come out light in color. Blonde brownies, the best you've ever had. "

"Blonde. Are you putting me on?"

"No, are you taking me with you?"

He gave a grunt of resignation, said, "Thursday morning, eight o' clock sharp, I leave with or without you. Bring some gloves and a hat. And the brownies."

THURSDAY CAME and she was there, pulling up in her old Corolla, faded Burgundy in color, one hubcap, a busted taillight. A real beater. At least it had a working four-on-the-floor. Birch, on the wood-planked porch of the Mercantile, watched her park and get out. Then he watched someone else get out. They both walked up to him, boots and jeans and sweatshirt, for there was a slight chill this morning. The one he didn't know had a small black backpack. When she got up close he saw the writing on it: CAPE BRETON ISLAND. He shifted position, said hello and waited to be introduced. Tyra was circumspect, worried that he would call it off.

"Birch, this is Leah, my roommate back at Duke. When we made plans for today I didn't know she was coming, she's kind of spontaneous like that." They stood facing each other. Birch nodded. "Anyway," Tyra went on, "she dropped in and I invited her to stay for a while. Long as she wants, but it won't be too long because school starts in ten days. Anyway, she's here and she's interested in, uh, your work and I'm hoping you don't mind another ride-along."

Actually Birch found himself quite happy with the change of plan. Leah was a looker with a wavy crop of auburn hair pulled back and

No Big Thing

fastened with a rhinestone flower hairpin, green eyes that twinkled, and a light sprinkling of freckles on her oval face. There was a sense of mischief about her as well, something he'd like to get acquainted with. He shrugged, feigned indifference, said, "Would you like some coffee for the ride up?"

Dalton Hankins had done a good job in repairing Birch's F-10 after that mishap, and it was running in top form. The three of them were crowded on the seat, Tyra shotgun and Leah in between. A few times when Birch shifted he would elbow Leah and her coffee would slosh out.

"A fine host you are," she said, being funny, "hand out coffee and then make me spill it."

"I only brew the stuff," he said, "I don't provide the coordination required to keep it in the cup."

"Oh, you're quite the wit, you are."

"You're only half right about that."

It went on like that and between ripostes Birch learned that Leah Sampson was Jewish, grew up in Portland, Maine, the only child of a professional couple, dad's a lawyer, mom's a full-time fundraiser for charities. She liked outdoorsy stuff, and ticked off several pastimes that Birch associated with the privileged class—white water rafting, fly fishing, rock climbing. She was in her third year at Duke, wrapping up a doctorate in psychiatry. She hoped to go into private practice, "repair the damaged and fragile psyches of other rich kids." A blue-blood, a rare bird in his world, nothing like her in these parts. And he marveled that a woman like her even existed, nice to look at with smarts and athletic ability and a fresh if not bumptious outlook beneath it all.

Meanwhile, Tyra sat looking out the window at the passing scenery, brooding or lost in thought. When they asked for more brownies, Tyra was just a little chagrined to admit that she had eaten them all. Nor did she apologize. Bring her best friend and love interest on this stupid expedition and all she does is make eyes at studmuffin here.

And they kept it up, joking between themselves, leaving her out of the conversation. Not that she wanted to engage in such insipid talk.

"Jewish, huh? Where's your beanie?"

"Yarmulke, it's called yarmulke and I'll spell it for you so you don't get it confused with the motorcycle."

"Rice burners, you don't see those around here."

"Anyway, dear, I'm reformed Jewish. We don't wear beanies. Cartier Diamond-Paved Love Necklace maybe, but no beanies."

"Oh, give me a break," moaned Tyra.

They got to the site and, like before, parked on the residential street behind the designated area. Hiking in he couldn't take his eyes off Leah, pushing ahead, moving with purpose, her long wavy hair flouncing with each stride. He saw her as a leader, quite the opposite of Cassie, who probably would've been lagging behind on this little jaunt. And that was okay, he decided, some work point and others bring up the rear. Both were important to an effective operation. He wondered if a dauntless, self-reliant, over-achieving smarty pants was in the cards for a guy like him. There was a spark there, he felt it.

Once there they took off their outerwear, sweatshirts and jackets, for the day had warmed, and he was cheered to see a pair of points pressing against her Land's End lavender T. That was one thing Leah had in common with Cassie, anyway—no brassiere. They donned their safety vests and walked abreast the length of the field, picking up the usual detritus and stuffing it into burlap feed bags. Though the sign had been recently replaced, it bore the marks of renewed attacks—angry graffiti, dents made by tools unknown, small-caliber bullet holes. There was a bouquet of fake cemetery flowers wired to one of the steel posts.

By the minute, Tyra was having serious regrets about this whole thing, feeling that maybe it was a big mistake to invite herself, her presence easily misconstrued as a black person voluntarily helping this hated Klan outfit that terrorized other blacks. She wasn't that person; she was here to study the situation, make sense of it, write about it. Cars going by, seeing them, realizing who they were and what they were doing, laying on their horns. Not in solidarity either. She felt so, so ... on display.

WHEN THE ANTAGONISTS ARRIVED it was like a bad dream. They never saw the long black New Yorker park on the shoulder, never saw them get out. They only saw the trio walking toward them, advancing up the slope, walking fast as they could on the uneven ground, broadcasting malice even from a distance. A white guy, a black guy, and a black woman with a red Mohawk that stood out like a flare. Birch put them in their mid-twenties. Long shaggy mullet on the white boy, the black guy in a bulging muscle shirt sporting a bushy 'fro and tattoos on his arms and shoulders. The woman in pedal pushers, sandals, and T-shirt with an image of Bob Marley. If Mohawk woman looked like she belonged in a WWF ring, the other two had the bearing of traveling carnival roustabouts, a groovy look that turned to seed at close inspection. Three of them, three of us. Birch stood facing them, waiting.

Leah and Tyra went over to Birch, who put his arms around their shoulders, fraternal, like *You see us here, a working unit, we don't need any interference.* The trio came up, didn't say anything at first, just nodding or smiling in a nasty sort of way. It was weird, weird and tense. Serious unease in the air. Birch felt for the jackknife in his jeans pocket, knowing that his 42-inch litter stick with a nail on the end would better address any trouble.

Finally, mullet-head goes, "We were just passing through and I see you out here picking up and I see the sign, says this highway adopted by the Ku Klux Klan. And I say to Reggie here, now ain't that a hell of a coincidence, these folks picking up what looks to be trash in a place where the Klan 'sposed to be doing that? I say, Reggie, do you suppose they may be actual Klansman? Reggie says, I don't know, Ozone—that's my handle—let's swing back around and find out. See, Reggie's African-American, case you hadn't noticed, and he don't like Klan."

"We're just here to do a job," Birch told him straight up. "Not looking for trouble, man."

Reggie stepped forward, same height as Birch, looked him in the eye, glaring. "A job, huh? What if we did a job on you?"

Birch tensed, expecting the initial blow. He would let Reggie throw the first punch.

But Leah piped up. "You know what? We could all do the job together, what do you say? There's plenty of litter to go around, and afterwards I'll treat us to lunch at the restaurant of your choice. How's that sound?"

"The day I break bread with a bunch of racists is the day I kiss a pig," said Reggie. "So where's your outfits, you know, the white sheets and all?"

Tyra was electrified by all this, thinking how she would weave this encounter into a section for her thesis. *A Personal Account of Racial Hostility from Roadside Reactionaries*, something like that. She was already writing it in her head but she needed to insert herself into the action, validate that first person point of view. "Uh, we're not actually Klan," she told them, "we're just filling in. We're independent contractors. We found this niche, see? People adopt highways to advertise their business or their group, but then they don't want to do the work. They hire us to do it for them. It's not a bad gig." Tyra flashed a smiled at the strangers; she thought it a pretty good lie.

"Proxies," said, Leah, "we're proxies."

"Don't believe it," said Mohawk woman. "They're lying liars, you see and smell the Klan on them." She pantomimed an assault on her olfactory sense. "But what I don't get," stepping forward and almost touching breasts with Tyra, "is why a good-looking sister like you would allow herself to be seen out here doing this shit work for the

No Big Thing

white devil."

Tyra looked away then looked back again, saw anger flowing out of this woman. "Well, that misconception did cross my mind," she answered.

"It crossed your little mind, huh? Well, listen here, Uncle Tom-ette—that's what we gonna call you if you don't step away from these fools right now and come to our side."

Mohawk woman was a good four inches shorter than Tyra, and while she was laying down the gauntlet Tyra found herself wondering what she might be like in bed. "Uh, thanks but I'm happy where I am, and I don't even know you all."

"She don't know us because she don't wanna know us," said Ozone. "We're not her kind of people. No lie, we don't judge others by the color of their skin."

"We're not like that," spoke Leah.

Said Reggie, "Then what you're up to here, standing in for the Ku Klux Klan"—he made a face—"can't even say that without wanting to puke! This must be what you call a paradox, huh?"

"You call it what you want, but we'd like to get back to work," said Birch.

Mohawk woman turned her attention on Birch. "You ever hear of Sly and the Family Stone?"

"I heard a Stone Cold Steve Austin," he answered.

Mohawk woman harrumphed. "Sly Stone had this group, funk and psychedelic, played at Woodstock—guess you heard a that—and they had this song, 'Everyday People.' It goes 'There is a long hair hair who doesn't like the short hair for being such a rich one that will not help the poor one. Different strokes for different folks.' That's the message, can you dig it?"

"Mona, Mona," clucked Reggie, "you got to *sing* it or you lose the meaning. Here we go, you ready?" They all three chimed in, "There is a yellow one that won't accept the black one that won't accept the red one that won't accept the white one. And different strokes for different folks and so on and so on and scooby dooby dooby." They looked to their captive audience for some reaction.

Mohawk woman—Mona—spoke directly to Birch. "So that's what we're talking here, those lyrics mean something. Tolerance for other people, making room in your narrow mind for a rainbow of skin colors, their different ways—"

"I like Stone Cold better," said Birch, arms folded on his chest.

Mona moved in, stood there, fixing on him fierce-like. "Understanding and accepting that not everyone's like you and your racist friends," punctuating each word by jabbing an index finger an inch from his face, "coming to terms with the hate inside you ..."

Her words were lost on Birch. The finger-jabbing thing had tripped a trigger, and Birch could no better stop what he was about to do than he could stop a rushing locomotive. And she wouldn't let up, the accusatory finger right in his face, back and forth fast-motion, making him flinch. He grabbed that finger, bent it back and heard it snap. Mona turned almost white, her mouth stretching open in a silent scream, and for a second Birch thought of spitting into it. Then she dropped to one knee and yowled lustily. Reggie and Ozone turned on Birch.

Birch had his litter stick brandished, holding them off, when the patrol car pulled up, lights flashing, St Louis County Police written on the side. The cop, a tall white guy, jumped out, walked swiftly toward them, cap down on his brow, hand on his holster. All purposeful-like, doing his cop act.

Then they were all standing around the cop who had become the ringmaster of this circus, trying to keep them from all talking at once, trying to figure out who is the most culpable, for, damn it to hell, *somebody* was going to the station. Finally, having listened to both sides, he told the interlopers to follow him to the station so the victim could make her complaint and he led Birch in zip-tie restraints to the still-flashing cruiser.

"My dad's a lawyer, he'll get you off!"

No Big Thing

Birch turned, started walking backward so he could see the last of her. "It's too bad," he shouted, "I was just getting to know you."

"To be continued," Leah called, and blew him a kiss.

"Give me a break," said Tyra, rolling her big eyes.

In the squad car, the officer, nameplate BROYLES, was punching keys on a computer attached to the console. Routine check on the prisoner. In the back seat Birch fidgeted, hands cuffed behind, shoulders straining from the unnatural and forced posture. Officer Broyles whistled through his teeth. "Hoo boy, you got some priors, don't you?"

"All that's supposed to've been erased when I went in the army," said Birch, "that was the deal."

"I guess they didn't get it all," said Broyles, turning to look at him through the steel grate that separated captive from captor. "I was army," he said. "Where were you?"

"Iraq, Kuwait. Twenty-Fifth Division, infantry."

"How 'bout that. Twelfth Division, artillery, in and around Mosul."

"Saw some action, didn't you?"

"You better believe it, nothing like having blank permission to kill a bunch of sand niggers."

Birch only nodded and Broyles took that as approval. He studied his prisoner a mite more. He looked to be about his own age, good-looking, not stupid but probably a hell-raiser. Probably the kind of guy he'd enjoy having a beer with. "These women, I'm telling you, they can really press your buttons. If I've seen it once, I've seen it a thousand times. Get up in your face, eyes flashing, go off on you like they have a right to, throw out words, really hurtful, *make you* have to lash out, automatic like. That what happened up there with those jerkoffs?"

"Something like that," said Birch.

"What're you guys doing here anyway? You got the official-looking reflective vests, bags of trash to carry out. Your friend, the pretty one, said you all part of the KKK clean-up crew. Really?"

"You got it."

"Huh. I've thought about that," offered Broyles. "All these people up in arms about this so-called hate group being represented on the highway as if they're any worse than Parents and Friends of Gays and Lesbians who got their own sign down the way. What a crock. Fact, I'm glad you guys won your battle in court, glad to see you out there proclaiming, trying to make a difference in this dysfunctional world. Too bad I got to arrest you."

Birch just looked at him. Moments passed. "You know Officer Nguyen?" pronouncing it "Winn."

Officer Broyles got this look like he'd just swallowed a toad. "Yeah, I know that little slope, what about him?"

"Never mind."

—29—

SHE WAS HOLDING SOMETHING BACK, he just knew it, and he was imagining the worst. Another guy? Cancer? Wait—pregnant? That would be something to conceal until the time was right. Even as they talked he was telling himself that Cassie was knocked up and extending that revelation into a future scenario of a domestic existence. He and she and little Birch. Or Helen, he'd always liked that name. He looked at her behind the counter ringing up a tie-dyed T with a big peace symbol on the front and he imagined a tiny seed inside her, growing, dividing, developing. A life unto itself, stamped with their DNA. A miracle.

She bagged the shirt, thanked the customer, and watched him walk out. "Okay, where were we? Oh, you were telling me about the next step in your situation. You're out on bond now and there's no trial date, but you're meeting with your lawyer next week. What do

No Big Thing

you think he'll say?"

"Actually, I don't want to talk about it anymore. It's either boring or upsetting. It's better to put my mind somewhere else."

"You poor thing!" She came around the counter and gave him a hug. "I am so sorry this happened to you, you don't deserve it. I can see it's stressing you out. I can make some Chamomile tea, that'll relax you."

"How about a cold one? You got any beer in that fridge?"

"It's pretty early for that, isn't it? How about we go out back and do a number?"

He chuckled at the thought of getting high with her, because it would never happen. "To each their own, yeah?" They were still close, in a loose embrace. He put his arm around her, said, "You might want to cut back on the smoking now that you're in a particular condition."

She looked at him in great consternation. "What on earth are you talking about?"

Positively beaming, he said, "C'mon, you don't have to hold back anymore. Go ahead, mama, tell me."

"Oh, my god, you think I'm pregnant!" She burst out laughing, that staccato hyena laugh that was not one of her more appealing traits. "Well, that's news to me. Gee, I better phone my gynecologist, tell her she must've given me something other than birth control pills. No, silly, I'm not pregnant. No cravings for weird combinations of food, no morning sickness. My uterus is without child. Some day maybe."

Suddenly, Birch's fantasy popped like a balloon. His mind got off that track and went to another. "But you're keeping something from me, I could sense it right when I walked in."

She looked at him with genuine amazement. "Wow, you are clairvoyant, aren't you? Yeah, there is something brewing but I was having a hard time bringing it up because you've got enough to think about, enough troubles right now. Not that this is troubling," she was quick to add, "it's just a change for us, something that's come up."

He studied her face, looked into her almond brown eyes, preparing himself for whatever it was, wondering if ten seconds from now would he be happy or sad. "Yeah, well?"

"Yeah, well, you know Jerry died last month and it's been very very hard on us all. He was the leader, the founder and the glue of the band. The greatest jam band in the history of the world, and Jerry was just so, so spiritual, it was like being around Jesus. Yeah, like he was Jesus and we were the disciples. You'd watch him become one with the music—not just him but the band as a whole, and they would go off into their world, transcend into this amazing place, and they would take us with them—oh, I wish you could've heard them play, you'd know what I'm talking about."

He nodded to show he was with her, silently urging her to get down to it.

"So Jerry's gone and there's going to be this memorial for him in San Francisco coming up soon, and me and Amanda are going," getting excited now, "we're going to load up the van with merchandise and we're making as many Jerry Garcia Ts as we can make and we're going to have major fun *and* make a ton of money selling to other Deadheads." She paused, became somewhat pensive. "I know this comes at a bad time, but I can't predict these things. He meant so much to me, to all of us, it's like there's some magnetic force pulling me to this thing. There'll be a jillion Deadheads there from every state and lots of countries, too."

"A regular convention."

"Yeah, and I'd ask you to come but I figure you're stuck here."

It was a nice lie, but he knew she didn't want him to come. "Can't leave the county without permission from the court," he said.

He heard himself asking who will run the store, a question he really didn't even care to know the answer to, for he was busy thinking about Leah. Two weeks after the incident that got him arrested and he couldn't shut her out. Truth was he had growing feelings for

No Big Thing

Leah and he had come to Cassie with a guilty conscience and the half-baked intention of bringing it up. He had been wrestling with this predicament day and night lately, it plagued him far worse than his pending trial for felonious assault. Two women, different as can be—one familiar yet changing, the other fresh and beckoning. He knew it was really stupid, like romantic suicide, to tell your girl that you've met someone else, especially when that someone lived several states away and the whole idea of how it would work between them was murky at best. He did know that Cassie was a different person now, in contrast to the Cassie he had idealized while in uniform five-thousand miles away in the Great Sandbox. Still, he had loving feelings for her, perhaps out of habit, and yet his feelings for Leah were strong, too, maybe stronger. He felt like a man torn apart, his heart cleaved. Although grieved by the idea of hurting Cassie, he had come here prepared to confess a sort of cheating in his heart, admit that he was worried he didn't carry the torch for her anymore because if she was the one, the only one, he wouldn't have allowed himself to be smitten by someone else.

So she wasn't the only one holding something back. This news of hers relieved him. Her going away would give him more time to think on the matter. There was no need to bring up Leah a.k.a. "someone else."

A customer came in and began looking through a rack of T shirts on hangers. Cassie moved back behind the counter. "Mom says she wouldn't mind giving it a go, but that's half-hearted on her part. She's not that into it. If I don't find someone who's committed a hundred percent, we'll just close up for the duration. It'll be okay, we can pick up easy enough when we get back."

"When do you think that'll be?"

She shrugged. "Who can say?"

—30—

MRS. MOELLER put the coins in his palm and closed his fingers, making a loose fist around it. "Please take it," she said, "it'll make an old lady feel better." Birch peeked, saw two quarters. It would buy an apple in the cafeteria. The old woman looked up expectantly, her rheumy eyes glistening with gratitude.

Birch gave a half-reluctant shrug. "Who am I to turn down an act of kindness? But please know I'd wheel you to Kansas City and back if that's what you wanted."

She squeezed his hand affectionately. "I know you would, and just knowing that lifts my spirit. Thank you, thank you for being here, for doing this. You are an angel in disguise."

A stunted angel, he thought.

It had been a strange trip from that roadside altercation last month to being here now at the Jefferson County Home for the Aged. Leah had made good on her promise to call her father who in turn called up a favor on his old friend Aaron Goldfarb, founding partner of Goldfarb, Klein & Kline, a prestigious old money St. Louis law firm. Before he could even get supper—the jailers ordered out for the prisoners in holdover, usually the Colonel or Taco Bell— there was a lawyer asking to see him. He was promptly bonded out and driven to his pickup waiting on the residential sidestreet where he'd left it. The lawyer-chauffeur, a talkative sort named Larry Pickman who said his specialty was probate but not to worry he could switch horses, criminal law was just another wrinkle in the same cloth, gave him a firm handshake, told him to go home and try not to worry. His fate was in good hands.

"If you could just move me over to my bed, I'd like to lay down and watch *Jeopardy!* You know, I can get half of those questions they ask. I'm no dummy. I used to be a schoolteacher. Twenty-seven years,

No Big Thing

loved every minute of it."

"Sure, Mrs. M." He moved the wheelchair so it paralleled her single bed, the sheet and blanket folded down, ready for her to slip in. He locked the wheels. "You need help?"

"No, I can manage but thanks."

It was in the the papers: "Klansman Charged With Hate Crime." Reporters calling, coming to his apartment, asking for him at the store. Politely he told them to buzz off. What good would it do to tell the truth of what happened? They would spin it whichever way they wanted. The more enterprising scribes found ways to get to the busybodies and know-nothings of Pine Grove and the sordid details of Birch Fortner's checkered life were revealed, the more fantastic the better. How his grandfather used to gather the neighborhood kids for weenie roasts while demonstrating the art of cross burning. Talk that he'd once misdirected a carload of coloreds when they'd stopped at the store, lost and anxious. Instead of telling them how to get to the interstate, Birch had sent them to the clubhouse of the Wind Tramps and then laughed about it. Talk that he'd come home from the Iraq War with a necklace of human teeth. Talk talk. He was lambasted in print six ways from Sunday, and no matter what the outcome he would never live this down.

He bided his time awaiting trial. Twice he went to St. Louis and met with Larry Pickman, who was still optimistic about this mess. He had his best investigator on it; there were holes in the other side's story. He would open those holes so wide you could walk an elephant through. But what if it doesn't work, asked Birch, what if I'm convicted? What sort of time am I looking at? Larry assured him he wouldn't do any time at all, that he would walk out of that courtroom whistling Dixie—"that's a joke"—but if, big if, the court did find him good for the crime of felonious assault with a motive of hate, then he could get three years in a medium security correctional facility. That's *prison*, not jail, thought Birch, despondently, where there's no such thing as a nice day. But, please, don't even think of that, Larry told Birch, because I have a powerful feeling this thing is going to go our way. Besides, he added, I play raquetball with the prosecutor.

On the day of the trial and just before the trial itself, in a conference room outside Division 19 in the St. Louis County Courthouse, a bargain was struck on a handshake between Pickman and the prosecutor. The gravity of the crime was mitigated by testimony from depositions. Defense was able to show that Mona Kendricks, the victim—or was it instigator?— had actually made first contact, rudely poking Birch in the eye with a rigid digit. He acted in self-defense and she was lucky she got out of it with only a broken finger. The felony was removed, the "hate crime" taken off the table, and Birch pled to the misdemeanor of creating a public disturbance and a traffic hazard. He was given a fine of $250 and ordered to 30 hours of community service. Which landed him here, in Mrs. Moeller's sad little room so thoughtfully provided by the County.

"Will I see you on Thursday?" she asked. "That's my next appointment with occupational therapy."

"Yeah, so far as I know," he said.

"Good," she said. "I much prefer you over that nurse's aid. She takes the corners too fast, like to frighten me with her recklessness. Could you prop me up, please?"

"Sure thing, Mrs. M."

"Oh, look at that! World Geography for five hundred. 'This mountainous body of water is the largest lake in South America.'"

"Uh, I didn't know there were any lakes in South America. Lake Amazon?"

"No, dunderhead. Titicaca. What is Lake Titicaca."

It was three-thirty on a nice day in mid-November when he signed out. He had most of the court-mandated community service under his belt now and he was looking to graduate, as it were, by

No Big Thing

Thanksgiving. He would miss Mrs. Moeller and the other old souls who had found their way to this outpost, a decent enough place where they could burn the short wick of their lives comfortably even if they or their families hadn't saved for more upscale assisted living in a private facility. Watching afternoon TV is watching afternoon TV, no matter where you are, Birch reasoned.

He had no plan, nothing in particular he needed to do. Though there was something he'd been meaning to do, no hurry, just a half-baked notion in the back of his mind. Today was as good a day as any. He drove the state road to Spellman, the next small town over. He got to the destination and saw no vehicle anywhere so he didn't bother knocking. He drove out of the town, took a turn here, a turn there, trying to remember the way. It had been several years since he'd been there, before the army. Harvested fields of feeder corn and soybeans didn't offer much in the way of landmarks, and there were a couple wrong turns where he had to double back and get on track. Finally, he came to a T, a no name gravel road going in both directions. He took a right and it all came back. Just past the Diamond Feeds sign he saw it, a rutted track no better than a skid trail going into a forested area. He bumped along, branches brushing his truck. Then, a good ways in, he saw the battered beige trailer, a patina of mold on the siding, surrounded by a number of vehicles, many rusted out with flat tires, the hoods popped open. A testimony to a country boy's love of cars. He parked in a clearing and honked his horn. Let him know he has company.

Inside the trailer Billy was coming down from a two-day high and he was none too pleased at hearing a honking horn in his turn-around. He was laying on his cot, wondering which was worse—the godawful headache or the constipated feeling in the badlands of his digestive tact. He had just gobbled a fistful of aspirin and was waiting fitfully to more or less pass out. He threw the covers back and got up, cursing.

A door reinforced with plywood, PROPERTY OF UNION PACIFIC RAILROAD stenciled on it in red, swung open. Billy appeared with a shotgun cradled across his chest. With the bib overalls, plaid shirt, beat up straw hat, and of course the "shootin' piece" as a prop, he looked more like a hillbilly than ever.

"That thing loaded?" he called, stepping out of the pickup.

"Darn tootin'," said Billy. "You wanna see?"

"Nah, that's okay. I believe you. What you got going?" Birch approached as Billy rested the shotgun, coming off the porch and into the yard.

"Oh, little bit of this, little bit of that," grinning despite the shitty way he felt. "Practicing animal husbandry."

"Yeah? Helping sheep through fences?"

"You remembered."

"I remember a lot, got a ways to go before the old brain gets addled."

"You wanna beer?"

"Got some in the truck, but I'll be glad to take yours long as it ain't skunked."

"You never had no skunk beer from me."

"Seems like I did once upon a time."

"Well, if you did, you drank it anyway. Your palate don't know the difference between ambrosia and skunk beer. I know mine don't."

Billy went in the trailer and came out with two Busch tallboys already opened. "What brings you out here anyway?"

Birch took a long pull, came up for breath, then another. "Man, that's good. I hope I never lose my taste for this stuff."

"The good part of that is you can have all you want for as long as you want it, that brewery ain't ever going out of business. So what brings you here?"

"I was thinking of that sign you got. The one you took from that wizard. I was thinking I'd like to have it for my Grampa."

"Oh, I see," chuckling to himself. "Well, follow me." Birch followed to the end of the trailer and there it was, in a patch of nettles

No Big Thing

leaning against a tree. "She's a beaut," said Billy, caressing the finish, "a piece of history."

"Could you part with it?"

"I don't think so, it looks nice right where it is. It's part of the decor, you know."

"Look, I'll buy it. How much?"

"Shoot, this a collector's item. I'd have to do some checking, see what what it'd go for on the open market."

"How much, Billy."

"Three grand."

"Three grand?"

"That's how much you can make working for me in one month."

"Fat chance there." He made a sweeping gesture with one arm. "And I can see you're putting all that cash flow to use living high off the hog out here."

"Smart ass. Better save your cute remarks. It'll be even more after I expand my operation to smack."

"Why would you even think I'd wanna be part of that? That's not me, I told you at Spud's—"

"You told me squat. Turning over a new leaf, my ass. Once a player always a player." Billy blinked in the thin fall sunshine. "Why you want this sign so bad anyway? It ain't like you and the old man are some high and mighty members of the Klan proper. The *real* Klan as me and certain others without blinders on see it. Y'all just talk and no action. It's laughable. You'uns ain't worthy of this sign"

Birch shook his head no. "I can see where you might come up with that notion, Billy, but that's not right." He looked him square in his bloodshot eyes, wondering if there was anything there that he could hang an honest opinion on. "Actually, I've given it some thought and what I come up with—you ready?—way I see it, the Klan as it exists today has little resemblance to what it was in the beginning or even on up to the sixties when they were trying to keep the blacks out of the schools. It's assimilated—five dollar word—assimilated into the rest of society only society don't know it or won't admit it. Now I've never told this to anyone, it's just a bunch of ideas thrown together, a ball of string with loose ends. So bear with me, I may not make a lot of sense, but the Klan in the nineteen nineties is connected to or, better yet, part of all these other groups and walks of life that don't have all this bad publicity attached. I'm talking about Masons and Elks, your evangelicals, your living-in-the-past vets down at the American Legion and VFW, your law and order types, your bikers, lots of farmers and ranchers, the old coots who sit around the war memorial in Tom Griffin Park, and pretty much all Republicans—and this county is ninety percent Republican. You better believe they're all practicing some type of conservatism and that translates to hard work, fair dealing, flag-waving patriotism, fear of Jesus on Sundays, buy American, up-in-arms over the thought of the government taking away their guns but at the same time standing solidly on the side of law and order—with the exception of criminal elements like yourself. And yeah, you can add racial bigotry to that."

"I wouldn't put bikers in that list," offered Billy. "Too independent, a bunch of anarchists, you really can't pigeonhole them."

"Point taken," said Birch, "but what I'm saying is these conservative values seen in at least half the people living in this county are the same values traditionally held by Klansmen. From what I can tell the Klan has pretty much been about trying to live life upright, uphold the law. In fact, they've seen themselves as vigilantes, going out to right wrongs, as they see them. Somebody in the community not towing the line? Those old boys'll be out there, pay him a visit, offer some motivation."

"Now, *that's* what I'm talkin' about!" said Billy.

"If the law in town can't or won't do the job, well, by god, they'll see it done—not justifying anything here, just trying to explain it."

"The Lone Ranger," said Billy, enthused. "He was a vigilante, always taking the law in his own hands, coming to the rescue of this

No Big Thing

or that poor bastard. I seen the reruns of that show. Where was the sheriff when these people needed help?"

"So the Lone Ranger was Klan, that what you're saying?"

"Yeah, he wore a mask, kept his identity secret, I reckon he was. Puts a whole new spin on things, don't it? But not Tonto, he wasn't in the club."

"No, not Tonto. So, wrapping up here. The white robes and cross burning is pretty much a thing of the past, and, sad as it may sound to you, it's not coming back. But their ideology—another five dollar word—is all over the place. The Klan in these parts has, let's say fifty active members—hearing Randall talk, that's a pretty good estimate—but by my thinking there's fifty thousand *honorary* members. And I already said what I mean by that, the assimilation thing. The Klan's traditional set of beliefs are so mixed in with the beliefs and views of the average citizen you can't tell where one leaves off and the other begins. You see a guy pumping gas, you have no idea what he's about. Well, maybe you get some idea by his clothes, what sorta ride he has, how he carries himself, but you don't know the prejudices he holds, the judgments he automatically makes on people. But in this county it's a safe bet he's tending to be narrow-minded and conservative and he sure don't like change. He'll always vote to keep the status quo. But is he Klan or is he a Pentecostal preacher or is he some factory worker who listens to Rush Limbaugh? See, you don't have to wear a white sheet and lurk around the countryside to think like a Klansman. It's almost fashionable to flaunt your prejudices, like, 'Yeah, I'm a racist, so what?' So, in that way the Klan is stronger than ever. Make any sense?"

"I ain't one for making sense of much 'cept for that which gets my blood pumpin'." Billy drained the last of his Tallboy, then plucked a weed-stalk with a tassel at the end and put it in his mouth. "All that talk and I still don't know why you want this sign." He crushed the can in one hand and tossed it in the weeds. "Okay, tell you what, I'll flip you for it. You call it. You win, you take it. I'll even help you carry it out. I win …" He smiled wickedly.

"I sell my soul to the devil."

"Hah! Another way to put it: you come to work for me, be my number one."

"Forget that," exasperated, "I don't want it that bad."

"You come all the way out here thinking to cop this beauty and now it ain't no big thing, huh?"

Billy wouldn't budge, Birch saw that, but was he willing to fight for it? He was reminded of Jake Parsons back in Kuwait. Jake lived in the hooch next to his and was always over borrowing something. One day while Birch was out, he "borrowed" Birch's new Gillette, the one with three "surgical blades" that pivoted to match the contours of your face. Next morning, when he wanted to shave, it wasn't there. Birch confronted him, Jake told him to bite the big one. Jake had four inches and forty pounds on Birch and he wasn't a pacifist. Birch was resolute, that razor was his. He and Jake went at it, first inside the hooch, beating on each other, grunting, cursing, bleeding, then outside on the sand where the fight switched from fisticuffs to rassling and Birch won after Jake passed out from a prolonged choke hold. Thing was, he never did get that razor back.

"I'll fight you for it," he said flatly.

"Ho, ho! This is gonna be good! I was fixin to knuckle your head anyway." Billy threw his hat down and took a boxer's stance. They squared off, silent, side-stepping a little, weaving and bobbing in anticipation, eyes locked, each waiting for the other to make a move. Billy faked a punch causing Birch to react, then he laughed it off.

"Fooled you, didn't I?" Billy grinned, putting his hands in his pockets. "We ain't gonna fight, no sir. What I wanna take a chance on hurtin' my pretty face for? Ain't no one here but us."

"No one to impress, huh?"

"You got it, bro'."

Birch took out his wallet, extracted the currency, counted aloud. " … forty-five, forty-six, forty-seven bucks. There you go." He held it out, but Billy wouldn't take it. "Man, you are one tough customer," he said.

"I'm the seller, you're the customer," Billy corrected, "and like I said, that sign looks good right where it is."

Birch gave an annoyed snort. "You're trying my patience something awful." He dropped the bills at Billy's feet, and went for the sign, expecting him to step in. He went to hoist it but the thing was heavy and he knew right off he'd have to drag it out. That's what he started doing, heading for his pickup, the one post dragging behind, making a narrow furrow in the ground.

Billy got behind him, walking along, and, again, Birch was sure that Billy would try something. He called out, "You could help, you know. Pick up that other end, that'd be nice."

"You can call me Good Samaritan," said Billy, "but don't never call me late for dinner."

Birch felt the other end rising, the drag now gone, and he smiled.

ONE MORNING toward the end of the year Randall awoke and couldn't recall who the woman in bed next to him was. It alarmed him greatly, but it also embarrassed him because he knew that he should know her name and her relationship to himself. She looked nice enough, older but younger than him, long brown hair falling over a peaceful face, wearing a red flannel nightie buttoned to her neck, the trace of a mustache over her lip. Mouth open, she snored lightly, an even score without punctuation. His wife? He didn't remember being married, he didn't remember much of anything not even his own name. He got up quietly so as not to disturb her, found the kitchen, made himself some tea and went around the house looking for something with a name on it, something to prompt his recollection.

But this passed eventually ...

A New Tavern had opened a few miles out of town. In a previous life, the Funny Farm had been a grange hall. It was bought at county auction by a retired fire captain, fitted to its new purpose, and it now boasted twelve beers on tap, shelves of premium booze and fancy liqueurs, several of them coffee or mocha flavored. For entertainment there was a jukebox with selections to make you spin, an electronic dart game, Golden T golf, and a claw machine filled with stuffed animals, fifty-cents a try. Something to win for the kiddies or the sweetie. There was no kitchen, not yet, but there were bowls of popcorn on the bar. And best of all, to the growing troop of exclusively male patrons, there was a naughty bartender, Misty, with a loose shirt and nothing underneath who didn't mind flashing the guys every now and then. It was fast, as flashes are, two seconds tops, so if you were talking to the guy next to you or looking out on the floor, you would miss it and then have to wait for the next time. Every guy for miles around had seen Misty's glorious globes.

Dee, the bartender over at Spud n' Velma's, couldn't top that.

They were at the bar, two on stools and two more standing nearby, drinking and jabbering and keeping an eye out for Misty to lift her shirt. Birch, Jamie, Jinx, and Terry Brannick right now. Others had just left, lured by the games over at the far end of the joint. The place was buzzing. It was Friday happy hour, buck-fifty drafts and two dollar shots. Guys getting primed for the evening, whatever it was they did on an uncorked Friday. Or maybe they just go home and pass out.

The four of them enjoying the scene, taking it all in. "This place'd be perfect if there were some girls around," said Jamie, between girlfriends at present. The others nodded in solemn agreement.

"You want girls, take a class at the community college," said Birch. "I was practically the only guy in my history class."

"I hear yoga is a good way to meet women," said Terry Brannick.

"Yeah," said Jamie, "but those yoga babes are so into themselves

No Big Thing

they probably wouldn't give the time of day to a beer gut like you."

Terry shrugged. "Even a blind pig roots up an acorn now and then."

Jinx rubbed his own ample belly for effect and said, "If a beer gut was something to be shamed of we'd all be walking 'round with our heads down."

"Ain't that the Bible truth!" said Terry, slightly consoled.

The talk was lively and topics tended to jump around like a cricket on a hot stove.

"So what's happening with the roadside cleanup in St. Louie?" Jinx asked Birch.

"Done. Over. At least for me," lifting his glass in a toast to finality. "That thing was trouble from the get-go. "

I'll vouch for that," from Jamie. "I only went there once with you and dang if we didn't get into some bad company before the job was even finished."

Jinx's ears pricked up. "What happened?"

"Some peckerheads driving by thought they'd pelt us with beer bottles is all."

"So Jamie decides to use their moving car for target practice," said Birch.

"Hit 'em a few times, too."

"You didn't!" said Jinx. "You really brought a gun?"

"Better to have one and not need it than to need one and not have it," said Jamie. Pondering this nugget, they all took long swallows in unison. "And then Bruce Willis here goes up with a couple of feisty women and gets to be Public Enemy Number One." He looked to Birch, shook his head, like, I-still-can't-believe-it. "You are one lucky duck, Cuz. If it hadn't a been for that rich girl's daddy, you wouldn't be here on this barstool right now. You'd be in Potosi, mopping floors and watching your back every second."

"Yeah," said Birch, "no two ways about it, she saved my butt and

I'm grateful. You guys never met her—Leah, her name—but she's been on my mind ever since. We've talked on the phone a few times and she sent me a letter, wants me to come visit on winter break."

"Where is she?"

"Duke University, somewhere in North Carolina, I haven't looked it up yet."

"That's a haul," said Terry.

"Cassie still in the picture?" asked Jamie.

"There's the rub. I like Leah, I want to get to know her better, and the only way to do that is go to her, spend some time. But if I act on that Cassie and me are through, and I don't know if I want that either."

"Caught between two stools," said Terry.

"Flip a coin," said Jinx. "Let fate decide." Birch gave him a look.

"You *don't know* if you want that either. Listen to yourself, Cuz, if you're waffling like that you've already made up your mind."

"Yeah, suppose you're right," allowed Birch. "Cassie and me been kind of growing apart for a while now. Three years away made a crack in the relationship and that crack never really did get patched up, it just got wider and deeper. It don't matter all that much anyway. She's gone, left for San Francisco, some memorial for her hero, Jesus Christ—I mean, Jerry Garcia."

"It's been a while now, hasn't it?" asked Jamie. "How long does a memorial last? You gotta wonder what she's doing out there."

"Cassie's doing whatever Cassie does," said Birch, and they all accepted this remark at face value. Deadheads were enigmatic like that.

Said Terry, "But this Leah, she's a fresh start, and that's good. You create your own history together. Turn the page, why not? It won't be boring."

"Now he's a relationship counselor," said Jinx. "You charging by the hour or what?"

No Big Thing

Terry ignored him. "Thing is, long-distance relationships are a bitch. I know, I went out with a girl from Tulsa for three years, all that driving back and forth."

"You coulda met in Springfield, split the difference," said Jinx.

"She didn't like Springfield, said it was home to thugs and perverts."

Birch going back to where he'd left off, wanting to air it out. "You're right, Leah represents a novelty, I mean, she's nothing like the girls around here, dresses different, talks different, thinks different. Once that novelty wears off ... who knows?"

"She talks different, how?" wondered Jamie.

"Well, aside from the New England accent, which, I admit, kinda grates on the ears, takes some getting used to. Aside from that, she has these oddball words or phrases for certain things, what do you call that?"

"Slang?"

"Yeah, slang but not slang. Dialect maybe. Like instead of you or me saying 'She went to the hospital,' Leah will say 'She went to hospital.' Or she'll call a drinking fountain a bubbler. Or about the day all that crap hit the fan, she'll talk about the schwarzer troubles. 'You didn't start that mess, it was the schwarzers brought it on.'"

They all got a good laugh and Jamie said, "So, what's a schwarzer?"

"Got to be spooks," offered Eugene Belka—"Yuge" to most—who had just walked up. Yuge was a security officer on the community college campus, looked more like a lumberjack with his black bushy beard and Stihl chainsaw cap. "Schwarz in German is black. The speaker, whoever you're talking about, is probably Jewish and using a Yiddish term for the spooks."

"That right, Birch?" asked Jinx. "She Jewish?"

"Yeah, I forgot to mention that."

"Whoa, talk about novelty!"

Birch didn't like the way this was heading, them seeing his heartthrob as some deviant. "Yuge is right, two out of three of them were black, that's what she's talking about. But, funny thing," he mused, "we call them spooks and in the old days they called us—I mean, the Klan—spooks."

"Who called the Klansmen spooks?" asked Yuge.

"The people who didn't like them, I reckon. But that was in the old days, I heard Randall talking about it."

Said Terry, "Probably because they were scary-looking and they came out at night. Like spooks."

"That makes sense if you're talking about a bunch of white robes burning crosses on a hillside," said Jinx, "but how do blacks—the schwarzers—get labeled spooks?"

No one could say.

Jamie stood up, rolled his shoulders a few times, called for another round. "Thirsty work, sittin' on this barstool," he muttered. Then, looking right at Yuge, "You know what I don't get? These white power guys—supremacists, I hear 'em called—guys like Dalton Hankins who go out of their way to make a stink about it, they want blacks to go *back to Africa,* as if they could or they'd want to. But, hey, it wasn't *their* idea to get captured in the jungle like animals and get shanghaied to this country to be slaves on plantations. We brought them here against their will. Now we want them gone?"

"You're right," said Birch, "it's hypocritical."

"Ever been to Montana?" said Terry, "Lots of room there. They could all go to Montana and be among themselves. Boogie all night and sleep all day."

"It ain't about there being not enough room," said Yuge.

"What's it about then?" said Birch.

Yuge frowned. "Do I gotta spell it out?"

"Yeah."

"Well, like he said, some don't want 'em here anymore. They done wore out their welcome."

No Big Thing

"You say."

He gave Birch a playful nudge. "It's an act, isn't it? I know you're putting me on."

"No, man, I'd really like to hear why they got no right to be here after they fought alongside us in wars over the last hundred years. After they work and sweat or study hard in school and try to get ahead the same as any of us? You're gonna stand there and say they don't deserve to live among us virtuous white folks without having to worry about some yahoos tryin' to give 'em the boot?"

Yuge bristled. "You sure you're the same guy was in the paper for bustin' Aunt Jemima's finger?"

He looked down, wagged his head a few times, looked up again, straight at Yuge. "I'm just tired of all this ... everyday racism."

"I never thought I'd hear that from a Fortner."

Birch rose from his stool, went chest to chest with Yuge. "You just did, now take a walk."

—32—

SHE TOLD HERSELF over and over she wouldn't do it, she wouldn't perform the simple act of going to visit her father. Although she imagined it, and therefore it *could* happen. All she had to do was get in the car, drive the 50 miles or so over to Pine Knob, pull in the driveway, honk the horn, get out and say, "Here I am!" That was easy to imagine; what would happen next was not easy to see, her imagination failing her, fading out like credits at the end of a movie. Without anything of substance to imagine, she and Randall just sat there in silence, neither speaking nor looking at one another, a clock somewhere ticking insistently. Not a very warm welcome to a prodigal daughter. No, she didn't want to do it and yet, and yet, she did want to do it. That part of her that had been bricked up all these years was making trouble, starting to push against its confines, the mortar starting to crumble. But no tuckpointer could repair that kind of wall so carefully constructed over the years, a wall that held in self-pride and kept out thoughts of forgiveness. So there it is, she thought, if the wall around her heart that closed off Randall was breaking down and there were thoughts of letting him in, then it was only a matter of time before that actually happened. So probably she *would* do it, but she chose to put it off and put it off some more, all the while thinking, We're not getting any younger.

And then she saw the article in the paper.

Patricia pulled into the drive and honked before getting out, just as she'd imagined, letting them know there was a visitor. She got out of her car and met with a brisk wind. She walked to the porch, imagining them at a window, maybe upstairs, seeing her coming in her blue denim skirt, yellow lambswool crew-neck sweater, and Patagonia Trail Rider Fleece Vest, holding a bouquet of flowers. Well, the flowers were wrapped, just purchased on the way here, so maybe Randall and Eveline watching from inside didn't know exactly what it was she clutched, but they would soon find out. She also wore a Lady Stetson and hand-tooled cowboy boots, items, which, if she were true to herself, she'd admit she wore them today to please her father.

She rapped at the front door, seconds passing like minutes, straining to hear footsteps. It was a little after noon on a Sunday in February. There was no snow on the ground, but it was close to freezing. She had timed her visit for this hour, for she recalled a fine repast of pot roast every Sunday, the table always set right around two. Then again, the pot roast was the tradition of Randall and his previous wife, her departed mother. Maybe Eveline didn't do pot roast, at two or any other time. It had been so long and she felt so estranged, and standing here on the porch, an uninvited caller, the wind messing up her hair, that didn't help matters much. There was a pickup in the drive, probably Randall's. Maybe they'd gone to church in Eveline's car, though she vaguely remembered that church was earlier and should be over by now.

She turned the knob and pushed on the door. It cracked open.

No Big Thing

She called in, "Dad?" White plumes of her breath accentuating the silence. "Hello-oo?" She stepped inside to the foyer and the first thing she saw was a gilt-framed portrait of General Robert E. Lee, the man in full uniform, arms folded, three-quarter profile, hat removed, showing his thinning pate and bushy gray crop around the sides. Gazing off, thoughtful-like, toward some distant charge, the very definition of distinguished.

Some things don't change, she thought.

She walked through a hallway filled with more framed pictures, stopping to look at them and marvel how young they all once were. Her mother, however, was not included in this gallery, and she wondered whose idea that was. She heard sound coming from up ahead, music maybe. She walked on into the living room, the area dim but bathed with the pale light of a television show. There was someone in the easy chair, she could see an arm hanging down. She didn't say anything, just stood there. The show was *Hee Haw*, and she recognized Lester Flatt and Earl Scruggs, the original Foggy Mountain Boys, along with some other crackerjack musicians. They were doing Dylan's "Like A Rolling Stone," giving it a bluegrass touch. It seemed odd at first, incongruous, but when she remembered that Dylan had spent time in Nashville it made more sense. Had to be a rerun, she thought, because Lester Flatt died more'n fifteen years back. She was a fan; she knew.

She walked in further, circled the easy chair, saw her father asleep, his mouth open, a weep of drool hanging on his stubbly chin. His legs were covered with an afghan blanket. She shook him gently. "Dad. Dad?" He opened his eyes one at a time, and she could see that he was focusing. She thought she had better help him out, a prompt. "Dad, it's me, Patricia, come to see you."

This didn't register. He seemed to be in a fog and suddenly compassion welled up inside her. She took his hands and stroked them. "Are you all right?" she asked. He looked at her quizzically, seeing her perhaps for the first time. He shook his head in the negative, went to rise and she helped him to his feet. He stood there looking at the wall, now holding the afghan around his shoulders like a shawl. She hadn't seen him for many years, she didn't know what to expect. Again, she asked him if he was okay.

He looked at her with astonishment bordering on annoyance. "No, I'm not okay," he chided. "I'm trying to die. I've been trying to die all day."

She felt an electric shock pass through her system. Alarms sounding. Still, she wasn't one to get hysterical. She shut off the alarms and began to rationalize. It couldn't be true. He didn't look like a dying man, although he was shaking slightly. That could be some sort of old age palsy or maybe he was shivering from being cold. And if he was dying, would he be left alone in the house. Where was Eveline?

"Oh, Dad, c'mon now. You're not dying, don't scare me like that."

He seemed to ponder her and her words. Seconds passed as he appeared to study the situation, trying to make some sense of it. "How did you get here?" he finally asked.

"Why, I drove. I've come to visit, it's been a long time." She held up the conical parcel, pulled back the wrapping to expose the blooms. "Here, I've brought you and Eveline some flowers. A mixed arrangement," she added."

"That's nice," he declared, making no move to take them. "Who did you say you are?"

She was going to have to be very patient with him. "Patricia, I'm Patricia, your daughter. I've been living over in Beaumont these past several years. I'm a seamstress, I've got a shop there."

She saw in his eyes that he didn't quite comprehend.

"Patricia? Lance's kid?"

"No Daddy, *your* kid, *your* daughter. Birch's mom. Why else would I call you Daddy?"

"Would you tell him the sheriff's been by here looking for him."

She took him by the arm. "Tell you what, let's go to the kitchen. I'll put these flowers in a vase and make us some nice tea. How

No Big Thing

about that?" And she gently turned him about, steering him toward the hallway.

She found a box of Lipton Tea and put the kettle on to boil while Randall sat at the kitchen table looking at the flowers just now placed in a Mason jar. "Daisies and asters," he said, touching the petals, caressing the stems, "very colorful. Cheerful, too. Thank you, thank you."

"Happy to do it," she called from over near the stove. "You know your flowers, huh?" She knew this was so, as a girl, having tended to the multitude of flowering shrubs and perennials planted around the house. It was just something to say.

"Yes, that's true. Some people like to have a vegetable garden in summer, I like my flower bed. But these, all different colors and so vivid. Are they natural colors or are they dyed that way?"

She walked over to where he was, put her hand on his shoulder. "You know, you're right. Some of these colors don't seem to be something you'd find in nature."

"They look good anyway," he said.

"Yeah, they do."

She found it interesting that he could talk about flowers and not remember who she was.

Time went by. "Another cup?" she asked.

"Yes, but a bit more sugar this time," he said, making a pinch with thumb and forefinger. "This stuff is kinda bitter, don't you think?"

"One more tea with extra sugar coming up." She went to the counter opened another packet, filled the kettle, put it back on High. She was feeling better about him now that they'd sat and talked like normal people for a while. The fog that she'd found him in had mostly dissipated, although there were brief episodes of befuddlement, like wondering when Lance would get here. It would be easy to play along, tell him that Lance was running late—about twenty years' late—but she thought a dose of reality might perk him up.

"Lance is locked up, Dad. He won't be here."

He blinked a few times and said nothing.

"In Potosi, Dad, Lance is a prisoner, doing time for vehicular manslaughter."

"They probably got him busy. That's why he hasn't been around much."

"Dad, listen, *please*, he killed some people with his car!"

He scratched his stubbly cheek, seeming to ponder this. "That don't sound like Lance," he said.

"But it happened, he took innocent lives, young people." Her eyes filled. "It's just sad, every time I think about it I get so sad."

"Huh," he remarked.

She still wasn't sure where Eveline was. Randall suggested the beauty parlor.

"It's Sunday, Dad, the beauty parlors are closed, least all the ones I've ever known."

"Oh, that so? Well, I just don't know where she's gotten off to. She's got a sister in Ste. Genevieve. Maybe there."

"Yeah, maybe so,"

She brought the fresh tea to the table, placed it in front of him on a saucer, and sat down opposite. "Now, where were we? You were saying something about a feud with the highway department. You had to take them to court?"

He nodded vigorously. "Mule-headed pencil-pushers! They tried to keep me from putting up my sign. They said it was offensive, but it wasn't and the court said as much. I had a good lawyer and, believe it or don't, he took my case at no charge. He did it for the principle of the thing. The principle!"

"Yeah, Daddy, I know. I read all about it in the papers. It's an amazing story, all that finagling, all that fuss over a little sign on the highway."

No Big Thing

"That's what happens when they try to deny a man his freedom of speech," he said. Acting more lucid now.

"And I heard that Birch got in some trouble working for you up there."

"He did, that's a fact, and it could've been bad, real bad, like him being imprisoned. He was lucky to get that lawyer, that's for sure." He gave a chuckle. "Again, lawyers coming to save the day. I never used to think too highly of them, but now I do."

She nodded, took a sip of tea. "Well, now it's at an end, thank god. Won't be Birch or anyone else going up there to get in fights, have their troubles displayed on the front page of the newspaper."

"What do you mean it's over?"

"Oh, I didn't mean to perplex you, Dad. I thought you knew."

"Knew what?"

She reached in the side pocket of her skirt, took out a clipping, unfolded it, spread it on the table. "See here? The headline? 'Civil Rights Icon Has Last Word.' And it goes on to say how the state legislature has voted to name the stretch of highway adopted by a local chapter of the Ku Klux Klan the Rosa Parks Highway in honor of the civil rights hero from Alabama whose refusal to give up her bus seat to a white passenger in nineteen fifty-five led to her arrest and then a boycott of the Montgomery public transit system." She paused, looked for a reaction.

"Huh," he mused. She could see him thinking. "Well, there's a poke in the eye."

"Now, it doesn't say that your sign will be removed and your work there no longer needed, but I think it *implies* that because why on earth would members of the KKK be willing to work a highway named after someone who refutes everything the Klan stands for? You have to admit, it was a clever move. They couldn't beat you in court so they went a different route, got the politicians to intervene. They hated your sign, loathed it, and one way or another they were going to make it go away."

"Figures," he said, dejectedly. "There was a letter from Consolino, the lawyer in this case—came a few days ago, it's around here somewhere—and it said something like what you're telling me only I didn't understand it then and I put that letter aside. Hmm. Well, it's all right, I suppose. We had our moment, we took it all the way to the Supreme Court of the United States and they agreed with us, our position, and we saw that there is justice after all. We contributed to upholding the First Amendment, and they can't take that away from us."

She brightened. "That's a good attitude, Dad. I mean it, a real noble way of looking at it. You know what? We should take what you said and write a letter to the editor of the local paper, maybe they'll print it. What do you say? You get some paper and a pencil and I'll help you with it."

He shrugged, smiled agreeably, reached across the table and took her hand. The back of his hand dappled with liver spots. "Sure, I reckon we could write a mighty good letter, but first I gotta use the toilet." She watched him get up and start toward the bathroom. She called, "Dad?"

He turned, looked upon her, said, "Trish."

—33—

"HERE, IT's FOR YOU," said Eveline, handing him the cordless. Randall was in the middle of another rerun of *Hee Haw*, Dolly Parton singing something about love lost and he kind of resented the intrusion. He took the phone anyway, said hello somewhat tentatively.

"Randall, that you?" a voice boomed on the other end.

"Yeah, Jim Ed, it's me," he answered, reaching for the remote to turn down the sound.

"What's shakin', brother?"

"Oh, you know me, just takin' it easy, watching TV right now."

"Well, I hope it's something good, 'cause I've got something good for you. I'm down in Cape and I've got Dale Randolph here. Say hi, Dale."

"Hi there, Mr. Fortner," said another voice all chipper and friendly-like. "Glad to make your acquaintance. Jim Ed speaks highly of you."

Jim Ed came back on. "Randall, I know you want to get back to your show so I'm gonna cut to the chase here. Dale's a public relations man, got a degree in marketing from Oklahoma Baptist University. He works to improve the image of companies and organizations—hell, even individuals if they want to hock their homes and sell their daughters. Kidding! Well, his fee *is* steep, that's true, but he's worth it. So, I'd heard of Dale and the great things he's done. Remember that squirrelly televangelist got caught sexing it up with another woman wasn't his wife? His followers started abandoning him in droves, the coffers drying up with no more 'seed offerings' coming in. Dale got in on that, started troubleshooting, and two years later that goggle-eyed son of a gun is back in the catbird seat. So, I called Dale 'cause I felt we not only had an image problem but we also had a great opportunity in that one of our members has had a lot of media attention and I wanted to know how we might capitalize on that."

"You sound like you're in an echo chamber," said Randall.

"We're on speakerphone."

Randall didn't know speakerphone from speakeasy, but he listened as Jim Ed went on.

"This mess that you're involved in with the State—first, they say you can't have the sign, then you and the lawyer saying 'You can't treat us no different than anyone else,' and taking it to court and winning by god! And the State saying, 'Okay, you showed us so here's your dang sign but don't think we like it one little bit.' And then you and your kin trying to hold up the bargain, making efforts to keep that highway spotless, free of trash from the thoughtless litterbugs who have no respect for nothing. And only to be confronted by some roving band of mongrels out to terrorize, make us look bad in the public eye. Your grandson stepping up, defending himself *and* the glorious organization he represents only to be arrested and have his name—*your* name—besmirched. Hate crime, my ass. Well, it all came out in the wash. He acted in self-defense, the charges are dropped, and those instigators are forgot, but not, I say *but not* the Fortner family name."

Jim Ed paused and Randall thought maybe he should say something. "Yeah, that's about the long and short of it, Jim Ed. You summed it up nicely, you did."

"I got a talent for that," agreed Jim Ed. "Anyway, what me and Dale were thinking is that now that you're in the public eye, now that your name is out there with a certain recognition attached, we want to, as I mentioned, we want to capitalize on that."

"You want to take advantage of me?"

"No!" blurted the other voice, this Dale. "Well, yes," he hedged, "but not taking advantage of you. Utilizing the situation, is the way I'd put it. You see, Mr. Fortner—may I call you Randall? You are presently what we in the business call trending, and that's a good thing because we can use that as a platform to get our message across. In other words, Randall, we would like to market you, turn you into a spokesperson for the Klan of which you are a member in good standing."

"I'm already a spokesperson for that."

"That's right, you are," said Jim Ed smoothly, "but what we propose to do is crank it up a notch. We want to portray you as a hero to the cause, we're going to bill you as 'The Man Who Wouldn't Take No For An Answer.' They want to name that stretch of road after this uppity nigger woman? They think they can do an end run around us like that? Fine, but we've got our ace-in-the-hole and his name is Randall Fortner. You will be the counterpoint to Rosa Parks. She wouldn't take her seat at the back of the bus, and our Randall wouldn't cow-tow to the State."

No Big Thing

"Stood your ground," confirmed Dale. "The public will recognize that noble trait and they will warm to our cause."

"We should see membership increase," from Jim Ed, "more gatherings, overall enthusiasm. It's going to be a new era. What do you say?"

Randall saw that Dolly was now joined by Porter Wagoner and they were performing a duet. Their lips were moving but with no music or lyrics. He really wanted to hear the song. He reached for the remote and turned up the volume just enough. "I don't want to do it," he told them. "I don't like a lot of publicity."

"What?" said Jim Ed. "After this sincere and heartfelt pitch you gonna turn us down? Let's try it again: We have a situation here where we need you to step up and just, well, show yourself. All you got to do is talk to a few media people."

"Ones that we've selected," put in Dale. "You won't have to answer any embarrassing questions."

"And we'll coach you," said Jim Ed.

"I've got the press release ready to go out," said Dale.

"Don't forget the photos," said Jim Ed.

"Right, we need to schedule a photo shoot for the billboard part of the campaign. Billboards with your image spread out strategically from Hannibal down to Cape Girardeau."

"We'd love to cover even more territory," explained Jim Ed, "but those dang billboards are expensive. You'd think they were built of precious metals or something."

It was probably a good song and he was missing it. Randall turned up the volume even more. There, that was better. He could hear Dolly now, Porter strumming along, singing with her: "Can't keep it a secret, everything I feel is written on my face, I can't hide my heart from you ..."

"What's that in the background?" asked Jim Ed. "Are you back to watching some TV show while we're discussing business?"

Randall imagined Jim Ed's bulldog jowls shaking on the other end. "I am a private person," he said. "I really don't like having a lot of fuss made over me, and I especially would not appreciate what happened with my grandson being dredged up all over again."

He heard Jim Ed huff. "Randall, you listen and listen good." Real menacing-like. "You need to rethink this and come to some different conclusion, because otherwise you know what you're making me do? You're *making* me put you between a rock and a hard place. We've got people on call, people you don't want to meet, who will come to you if I ask them and—"

"Jim Ed, I don't think that'll be necessary. Look, Randall, let's be reasonable, reasonable and honest. A minute ago you asked if we were wanting to take advantage of you. The answer is yes. You are a commodity now, like something bought and sold. And you with a store, you understand that completely. And in that sense of the word, commodity, we want to sell you but it's important you're on board with this. I mean, you wouldn't make a very good spokesperson if the resentment was coming through in your expression or your dialogue. It's not like we're asking you to do this for me or for Jim Ed—"

"Although you do owe me a couple favors," snarled Jim Ed.

"As I say, you're not doing this for us but for the entire organization, an outfit that has stood proud for damn near a hundred and fifty years. Everything we believe in is resting on your shoulders. You are poised to be our ambassador, you hold the key, man! So, please, *please* look at the big picture."

Silence. Randall could feel Jim Ed's hands coming through the telephone wires and trying to throttle him.

"Well?" came the demand.

He'd given his answer twice, what good would it do to repeat it? He turned the volume up even more, the song apparently wrapping up, Dolly, just a kid then, singing, looking at Porter like he held the moon. "You and me we are the right combination, for love we're all we need, it's just you and me, we make the right combination, straight from the heart, love is the key."

No Big Thing

THAT EVENING as they were laying in bed about to turn in, Randall asked Eveline if she knew where his robe was. She knew which robe he was talking about. "It's in the closet," she told him, "where it's always been."

"May I see it?"

She sat up in her flannel nightie, hair undone now, falling about her shoulders. She looked at him but not in a puzzled way, for it was not an odd request. "Sure," she said, getting up and going to the walk-in closet across from their four-post bed. She rummaged around for a brief spell and came out with it—a long, immaculate white robe with purple piping on the sleeves and above the lower hem. On the upper left front a symbol, a red circle with the Klan's well-known "blood drop cross." It was on a hanger, shrouded in a clear plastic bag, placed by some dry cleaner underling long ago. She held it up high for a good look-see.

"Is my sash there, too?"

"Sure is." She brought it out, the thing looking just like a Girl Scout sash but with different insignias.

"How long's it been?" he asked.

"Since you've worn it?"

"Yeah, seems like a long time."

"Well, there's a tag here, but I'll need my glasses." She padded over to the nightstand, got her cheaters, and studied the yellowed tag. "It says April six, nineteen seventy-seven. Wow, talk about time flying. That was way before we were married. Do you want me to lay it out? Are you going to wear it before long? I know you had that call today."

He looked at her and smiled favorably, knowing he was lucky to have such a woman. "No, you can put it back, I just wanted to see if it was still there."

No Big Thing

Postscript

TRISH FORTNER closed her shop in Beaumont and moved in with her father and stepmom. She helped Eveline care for Randall in his dotage and took an interest in his museum. Filling in at the Grain Elevator & Mercantile, she found the work enjoyable. One day while working the counter she met a shy farmer of modest means, Jim Boynton, and they formed a relationship based on a mutual like for Abbott and Costello movies.

BIRCH FORTNER nurtured his feelings for LEAH SAMPSON, paying visits to Duke University and to Leah's home in Portland, Maine. They grew very close, happy and content in each others' company. After graduation, she set up a psychiatric practice in Portland and he moved there to "cast his fate." The cast proved fortuitous when he got on with the *Portland Press Herald*, first as a free-lancer, then as a staff reporter and later, much later, as a personal opinion columnist with a flair for folksy humor. Birch and Leah married in Portland's Etz Chaim Synagogue on December 31, 2000, the last day of the millennium, because they saw beauty and hope in the words of T. S. Eliot: "And to make an end is to make a beginning. The end is where we start from." Each year, on Thanksgiving, they take their places at the family table in Pine Grove.

CASSIE TELLER stayed in San Francisco, having met and subsequently shacked up with Scooter Hart, nephew of Grateful Dead drummer Mickey Hart, at the Jerry Garcia Celebration of Life and Death. When not working as roadies with the various band incarnations of the post-Garcia Dead, they run the Grateful Gear Emporium on Haight Street. They have a daughter, Sunshine Daydream.

Fate smiled on DALTON HANKINS when he was able to obtain the rights to reprint *Voice of Our Ancestors*, a seminal yet obscure tract penned by Wulf Sorensen and first published in 1933. Sorensen details how fables and fairy tales have been used to perpetuate old Nordic-Aryan wisdom and to mask controversial ideas. As a guest on a radio talk show, Dalton brought up *Snow White*, illuminating the allegory of the Wicked Queen who came over the mountains to kill Snow White, and those mountains were the Alps—the queen herself an emissary from Rome, the deadly enemy of everything Nordic. Christianity sought to convert the proud pagan Norsemen, intending to enslave them spiritually. But this disparaging talk of Christianity that Dalton was promulgating brought him into disfavor with REV. PINKARD, who strongly believed that pagans should be converted as long as it wasn't into Catholicism. As sales of *Voice* climbed so did other titles in Dalton's inventory such as *Where's Oswaldo? The Real Truth Behind the Kennedy Assassination* and *White Man in America,* and he was kept busy mailing orders all over the globe.

While rummaging in the junk pile outside his trailer looking for a section of tubing, BILLY GOLDIE stepped on a timber rattler and was bitten on the calf. Billy was alone, no way to call 911. Trying to drive out, he swooned and hit a tree. He sat in his van for two days, in and out of consciousness, hallucinating, his leg so swollen and painful that he tried to amputate it with an entrenching tool. Finally he crawled to the road and reached medical help, but the experience was an epiphany for him. The new Billy tried hard to get clean, and, getting no support whatsoever, he joined a 12-step program. Faithful in attendance, he reached the 11th step and backslid. Upon learning that the Merchant Marine did not require a drug test, he signed on and said goodbye to Jefferson County.

JAMIE WAINSCOTT was already an able hand at cutting out calves on the Bar None Ranch, and when he learned a fortune could be made from it he joined the National Cutting Horse Association, bought a one-year-old Quarter Horse—Dunbar—and worked with him every day, training for the Champion Futurity in Ft. Worth. With his family watching, Jamie made it to the fourth round of the NCHA Open World Finals. The NCHA did not skimp on prize money; Jamie and Dunbar walked away with $103,450. "He's a good

No Big Thing

hard-knockin' stallion," a proud Cy Wainscott told the cub reporter from the *Star-Telegram*, "he's got a lot of try, a lot of grit, and good style." The young reporter blushed and asked if he was talking about Jamie or the horse.

JIM ED BURNETT eventually gave up on his plan to promote Randall Fortner as a folk hero. Years later, en route to the annual Nathan Bedford Forrest Celebration March in Pulaski, Tennessee, Jim Ed was run off the road by rowdy teenagers incensed at seeing the big magnetic Confederate flag on the side of his Cadillac.

Catapulting to prominence on the heels of the KKK sign debacle, TOM CONSOLINO eventually left the ACLU and put out his own shingle as a criminal defense lawyer. He is the 2008 recipient of the Charles Shaw Trial Advocacy Award. The prize is conferred by the Missouri Association of Criminal Defense Lawyers honoring those who "exhibit outstanding trial skills and a passion for trying cases involving the innocent accused."

TYRA SINGLETARY got her masters in Sociology and PhD in Public Policy. Through connections at Duke, she landed a position as an aide to Richard Cantwell, U.S. Senator from North Carolina. After Cantwell's ouster for perjury and defamation in the notorious Backscratch Scandal, Tyra found herself out of a job. On the verge of losing her bachelorette apartment, she solicited help from Janis Dierker, Democratic Caucus Vice-Chair, who had once suggested that Tyra would look great in a leather bustiere. They are now a vaunted power couple on the Capitol social scene. Tyra's truncated memoir, "Redneck Rendezvous: My Harrowing Encounter with Rural Racists," appeared in the August, 1999 issue of *Ebony*.

ACKNOWLEDGEMENTS

Thanks to Mary Stage, Mike Myers, Pete Bastian, and Wes Fordyce for their valuable reading of the manuscript and helpful suggestions. Special thanks to Matt Martin for his knowledge of meth production. Matt is in the business of busting up meth labs and forcing cooks to retire. I also wish to acknowledge a couple editors who helped shape my writing back in the days when newspapers and tabloids were eagerly read for their scintillating content and used as bird cage liner afterward: Suzanne Goell and Safir Ahmed.

Brief excerpts were taken from the following:

A Trip to Cairo, Illinois by Sherman Cahal; "The Herrin Mine Massacre" from The Marion Illinois History Preservation Society; "Copperhead Road" lyrics, Steve Earle; "Everyday People" lyrics, Sylvester Stewart.

The Battle of Fort Davidson also known as The Battle of Pilot Knob was an actual event that took place on September 26-27, 1864. Randall Fortner's description of that battle was taken from battleofpilotknob.org, the website of the Friends of Fort Davidson, in addition to the author's first hand look at the battlefield at Fort Davidson State Historic Site in Pilot Knob, Missouri.

No Big Thing

Also By Wm. Stage

Creatures On Display

Saint Louis, 1981. Epidemiologist Shaun Malloy is overworked and under-appreciated. Chasing STD cases day in and day out, Malloy and his fellow investigators in the clinic are not prepared when a fatal wasting disease appears that seems to hone in on the city's gay community. As they strive to understand this new threat, matters are made worse by Trey Vonderhaar, a talented entrepreneur who runs a lucrative private men's club that caters to the appetites of a privileged class. Despite warnings from health officials, Vonderhaar is determined to benefit from his enterprise without regard to the dangers the luxury sex hotel presents. Perhaps too dedicated to his job, Malloy is just as intent on shutting down Vonderhaar, and, along with best friend and bondsman Teri Kincaid, isn't above resorting to extreme measures to do it.

"*Creatures On Display* is not for the faint of heart; it is quick-moving, irreverent, often explicit in the situations and attitudes it describes. But it also displays the author's ability to combine history and memory, bold acts and flawed heroes, the devilish and the noble." — Aarik Danielsen, *The Columbia* [MO] *Tribune*

"Stage's novels excel at capturing the grit and weirdness of life on the streets of St. Louis … [*Creatures*] envisions a fascinating historical moment as the tab came due for the Dionysian revels of the 60s and 70s … a fun time-travel back to St. Louis in its more feral days."
— Stef Russell, *St. Louis Magazine*

"The story reads as a crime novel without the dead bodies, gun battles, barroom brawls or frequent fisticuffs. But none of these elements seem to be required for a thought-provoking novel that is unique in both subject and insight."
— Stuart Shiffman, *The Illinois Times*

Fiction / Literature / ISBN 978-0-692-87027-3

Fool For Life

Wm. Stage Gets Paid to be a Nuisance, and he is good at it. A process server in St. Louis, bearing bad news to strangers—no wonder people shun him. Apart from this peculiar work, he has his own secret mission: To find his unknown biological family and have cocktails with them. His neurotic mother aids in the search, hoping to bolster her theory that the child she and her husband adopted has indeed become a sociopath. Meanwhile, Stage desperately seeks a woman with a "friendly womb". Why is he trying to reproduce like some rutting animal? It takes a series of painful and awakening life-lessons for him to find out.

Troubles abound yet Stage takes it all in stride, stumbling through life like a hod carrier at a tea party. Whether trying to weasel out of a shoplifting charge, chasing after troublesome factory workers, or being held prisoner at Lambert International Airport, he manages to land buttered-side up. But where will it take him?

"Stage weaves a journey filled with hilarious situations, tightly written with sharp one-liners."
— Jim Orso, *The St. Louis Beacon*

"Stage's vignettes and life stories are all over the map, some heartbreaking, some satirically funny, but all of them telling of the human condition. And humor, some of it dark, pervades the book."
— Lynn Israel, *The Columbia* [MO] *Daily Tribune*

"... a poignant and illuminating work that walks a fine balance between side-splitting humour and philosophical seriousness."
— John Gillis, *The Inverness* [Nova Scotia] *Oran*

Memoir / Literature / ISBN 978-0-962291247-4

No Big Thing

Not Waving Drowning [Stories]

A PANHANDLER HAS A PLUM SITUATION in the city, until she takes in a stray dog. A process server is caught relieving himself in an alley, a seemingly mundane event that sets off a cascade of ever-worsening misfortunes. During their getaway, two bank robbers make a wrong turn and accidentally end up in St. Louis' Hibernian Parade—a serious problem since Black Irish are not welcome. These are some of the hapless characters in *Not Waving, Drowning*, Wm. Stage's new work containing eight short stories, all set in the St. Louis area. Drawn from people he has either known or observed, the characters in these stories ring true, evoking drollery, pathos, and wonder.

"For what it's worth, reviewing serious literature from 'Midwestern' writers always seems to be an afterthought versus the treatment given to newest, hottest writer emerging from New York with her trendy version of life in the Big City, a story that frankly makes you want to gag. Stage's stories are about real people who face up to life like the rest of us.

No bullshit, no pretense, just the guts of what makes life work for the fringe players in this old river town."
— Steve Means, *St. Louis Journalism Review*

"Stage has developed a prose style that is quite his own, and really can carry a story convincingly."
— Chris King, *St. Louis Magazine*

Fiction / Literature / ISBN 978-0-9629124-9-8